LADY AND THE DON

A Novel

Book Two: SAGA OF A LADY Series

Books by Sherri Leigh James

LADY AND THE DON
SAGA OF A LADY

GIRL WITH A PAST

LADY AND THE DON

A Novel

Book Two: SAGA OF A LADY Series

Sherri Leigh James

BLACK HAWK PRESS

April 2018 Trade Paperback Edition
Black Hawk Press, Inc.
P.O. Box 57737
Sherman Oaks, CA 91413

Cover design by David Oh

Library of Congress Control Number:2018940584
Trade Paperback Edition ISBN: 9780999858233
eBook Edition ISBN: 9780999858219

www.SherriLeighJames.com

DEDICATION

*To the indigenous peoples of California, who lived
peacefully and lightly on the land
preserving its natural beauty for nearly fifteen thousand
years before the Europeans arrived.*

"The miners came in forty-nine,
The whores in fifty-one;
And when they got together
They produced the native son."

~19th Century San Francisco Song

PART ONE
Yosemite Valley
December 1848

Chapter 1

Snug in our featherbed, I struggled to move my body, heavy with child, closer to my snoring husband. His handsome face and dark hair were half hidden by a pile of furs. I squirmed to cuddle against him and smiled at how fortunate I was that my earlier indiscretion had less disastrous results than I deserved. Certain that I had been played for a fool, that Carlo's proclamations of love were meant only to seduce me, I had left him behind in Panama City. Then I rode away from my stepmother's Rancho del Mar determined not to shame my family with my unwed pregnancy. Now rather than facing motherhood on my own, I was cared for by a loving husband and several dear friends.

I had only one complaint. My husband refused to make love to me. Pressing against him like a spoon, I felt his manhood against my bottom. But I knew he would refuse me.

Memories would have to do. I relived the last time my husband made love to me. I smiled recalling he was not yet my husband then.

*   *   *

My hips lifted, twisted, my body begging for attention. Carlo trailed his tongue down my body and ever so gently drove me to a frenzy of pleasure. My body shuddered with pleasure.

But Carlo persisted even once the convulsions passed. Even more gently, softly his tongue and fingers brought waves of blissful sensations opening like petals of a blossom.

I pulled his head to mine, found his mouth with my tongue, "I want you inside me now."

He chuckled against my mouth. "Now?" he said.

"Please, yes please."

He slipped his manhood into me but didn't move.

"Are you afraid to hurt me?" I whispered.

His lips were back against my throat. "I will not hurt you." His hands grabbed my waist, rolled his body pulling my body with him so I sat astride him. He lifted me up and down. Soon my body moved of its own accord. Grinding against his hips, feeling his hips move against mine.

"Look at me," Carlo whispered. The love in his eyes, the joy in his face, oh how I love this man.

*   *   *

I groaned at the memory of that moment. How long would memories of love making have to be all I had? Now that we were married, had my husband lost interest?

With the baby close to coming, Carlo refused to do more than tenderly kiss my mouth and belly.

I felt him stretch as he awoke.

"My darling, we have a lifetime to make love," Carlo wrapped his arms around my non-existent waist and snuggled against my back. "But soon our child will be in our arms. I do not want to harm him, or rush his debut."

I sighed, relinquishing my dreams of lovemaking.

Debut. Even if a girl, this California born child would not need to be a debutante. I remembered the nightmare of my New York debut.

When I made that debut was when I missed having a mother the most. I knew I looked silly in the white dress. At sixteen, I was pale and skinny. I had no breasts. The fashions of the day emphasized cleavage and feminine curves, none of which I yet had.

I looked like a colorless white stick in my ruffled dress. I had no idea how to apply cosmetics, nor did my old maid aunt. I was sure my mother would have had the dressmaker style a dress that flattered me, and although the white dress was unavoidable, she would have applied rouge to my cheeks or found sapphire jewels that brought out the blue of my eyes.

My English debut was quite the contrary. Fortunately, when my brother, my aunt, and I arrived in London at the home of my English grandparents, my grandmother rushed dressmakers into fashioning a dress that magically transformed my thin body into slender elegance. The creamy white silk brought out the gold in my complexion and hair. The sapphires in the inherited tiara and necklace matched my eyes. The dress gave me new confidence as I made my curtsies to Queen Victoria and her prince.

The newly found confidence served me well during the adventures that lay ahead. Discovering that a proper wardrobe made me more comfortable in even the strangest new circumstances, had carried me through traveling to California; meeting the man of my dreams only to, perhaps mistakenly, conclude that he was a philanderer; leaving the shelter of my stepmother's rancho upon discovering I was with child, becoming allies with a native woman named Lopa, finding the means to care for myself and two young girls we had rescued from kidnappers; and finally marrying the father of my child in a cave high in the Sierras.

As to whether or not my new husband was a philanderer, well, I was hardly in a position to worry about that now. In fact, I was doing my best not to worry about anything. But I was anxious at the prospect of childbirth. I knew little about birthing. And even less about babies. Fortunately, Lopa seemed to know about everything. She had seen me through many difficulties. Surely, she would help me be a good mother.

I did my best not to dwell on the fact that my birth had killed my mother.

Chapter 2

Carlo and I enjoyed the winter holiday snug in our snow-covered log cabin in the Yosemite Valley. On Christmas eve, the rescued girls, Sara and Susanna had stood on our porch to serenade us with Christmas carols, their sweet voices accompanied by howls from their puppy Smokey. We invited them in for steaming hot chocolate that we sipped in front of the fire while Carlo told us stories about Spanish, French and California adventurers and heroes.

The next afternoon we joined a congregation gathered, in the same enormous cavern in which we had married, to celebrate the birth of baby Jesus. Long benches flanked tables lit by torches and candles nestled in evergreen boughs. Families dressed in an extraordinary mix of costumes made from furs, tanned animal skins, muslins, silks, and wool sat on the benches.

Chief Teniyakena stood at the head of the cave and raised a goblet to open the feast. In a mix of his native language, Spanish, and English, he proposed a toast to all who were present and to all friends and family who were missing from this gathering.

The Spanish missionaries had converted many of the native Californians to Catholicism, but that conversion did not preclude the celebration of their earlier winter holidays in conjunction with the Christian. These gentle people, in many ways more civilized than the Europeans who had attempted to enslave them, marked the passage of the shortest day of the year and the daily lengthening of time lit by the sun much like pre-Christians had done for centuries. Both holidays celebrated hope—one the hope that the bounty of nature would return, the other that life would continue beyond death.

Our common hope was that our loved ones outside the valley were safe from the dangers brought by gold seekers to what had once been a peaceful countryside. We assumed we were safely snowbound inside the magnificent valley.

Chapter 3

WESTERN ENTRANCE TO YOSEMITE VALLEY
JANUARY 1849

MAYBE NOW I KNEW A WAY TO GET INTO THE VALLEY VILLAGE, BUT NOT HOW TO MAKE MY ESCAPE ONCE I'D ACCOMPLISHED MY TASK. THOSE FOUR BITCHES HAD TO BE TAKEN CARE OF, AS DID THE MEN WHO HAD SNATCHED THEM FROM UNDER MY NOSE. FROM THE RUMORS, IT SEEMED I WOULD BE UP AGAINST A FEW HUNDRED INJUNS. STEALTH WOULD BE IMPORTANT.

THE DEGENERATE SAID HE KNEW THE WAY IN. AS I STRUGGLED TO LIFT THE SNOWSHOES, I HOPED IT WAS TRUE AND WE WEREN'T JUST WANDERING IN THIS FROZEN WILDERNESS FOR NAUGHT.

I HATED THE WAY THE SNOW THAT CLUNG TO MY HAIR AND MY MOUSTACHE TURNED TO ICE. DESPITE THE INTENSE COLD, THE EFFORT EXPENDED TO MOVE THROUGH SNOWDRIFTS

CAUSED SWEAT TO RUN DOWN MY SIDES, STAINING MY CLOTHING. WELL-TAILORED GARMENTS WERE SO DIFFICULT TO COME BY IN THIS BACKWOODS, ROUGH COUNTRY.

THE THOUGHT OF FOUR MORE TRESSES, TWO BLONDE, ONE GOLDEN, AND ONE BLACK TO ADD TO MY COLLECTION KEPT ME FIGHTING THE BLOWING SNOW AND ICY COLD.

Chapter 4

I still couldn't understand most of the native words, but I knew something bad had happened and I understood the word for tracks. Snowshoe tracks. Americanos.

"What?" I asked Carlo as I watched him struggle to add layers of outdoor clothing.

"Just something to check on. It is probably nothing. I will be back shortly."

I paced the short distance of our two rooms.

His anxiety to get into those clothes and out of the cabin was not a sign of "nothing." I pulled one of the four rocking chairs up to the fire, took several deep breaths.

A twinge at the bottom of my belly soon had me pacing again. Several minutes went by then another dull ache, this one more intense than the last. Where was everyone? Could this be the baby arriving?

For several days Lopa had been with me every second that Carlo wasn't. She watched me cleaning the two already pristine rooms, arranging baby clothes, rearranging furs on the bed and in the cradle, and nodded in her knowing fashion with a soft smile on her square face.

I asked her what she was smiling about.

"Baby come," Lopa said.

"How do you know that?" I demanded.

She grinned. "Mama make nest."

"Humph," I answered as I tried to scrub a spot off the floor that turned out to be a knot in the wood.

As I had come to expect, wise Lopa was right once again. But where the hell was she now? Where the hell were they all? How many of them did it take to check out some tracks?

A sharper ache that lasted twice as long as the last hit me. I paced and swore, cussed out every bloody one of my friends that had deserted me in my moment of need. For hours it seemed, although in a panic, I didn't know how long it had really been. Several more pains followed by blissful relief came in waves. I couldn't decide whether to sit, to lie down, or pace, but walking seemed to help.

*　　*　　*

Finally, Lopa poked her head around the door from the porch. She saw me pacing and grimacing. She took a bucket to the river, filled the kettle over the fire and then stood behind me and kneaded the small of my back.

"What is happening?" I asked.

"Baby come."

"No, with the tracks, I mean. Did Americanos come into the valley?"

"Olemacote shot in head."

"Is he okay? Will he live?" Olemacote had stood

sentinel on the highest rock formation at the western entrance of the valley.

She shook her head. "Maybe he be white woman."

"What do you mean? What white woman?"

She nodded at my belly. "Olemacote, new body."

"How do you know this baby is a girl?" I asked.

She shrugged as though she didn't know how to explain with her limited English vocabulary. But she knew.

*   *   *

It was a girl.

I held my daughter to my breast, snuggled in our bed, stared at how beautiful and perfect she was, promised her the best I could do as a parent. "I'll do everything I can, to see you have a happy childhood, the best education possible, and never feel the sting of prejudice against any of your ancestry. Most of all, I promise to surround you with love."

I looked up and saw Carlo standing by the bed.

Beaming, proud, he said, "You are the two most beautiful women in the world. May I hold her?"

He placed the tiny creature in the crook of his arm, smiled down at her. "She is lovely, so very lovely." He smoothed her auburn hair, showed her to Lopa, "She has my French grandmother's auburn hair color and those eyes will soon be green. Is she not the prettiest baby you have ever seen?"

Lopa, who had delivered her, cut the cord, and bathed

13

her, already knew she was the best baby ever.

It wasn't until the next day that I thought to ask what had happened to Olemacote.

Chapter 5

"He was shot in the head," Carlo answered. "White Owl shot back at two men, but he went to aid Olemacote and did not chase them when they turned around."

"I don't understand why there were different tracks. Chief Teniyakena's warriors wear snowshoes." I rocked my chair gently while I nursed the baby. One of the joys of birthing a baby in such a remote location was that I could ignore wet nurse conventions.

He pulled his chair closer to us. "Awani's wear bear paw shaped snowshoes. These tracks showed beaver tails, the kind Americans and Eastern or Midwest natives use."

"Eastern natives—what do you mean?"

"Legend has it that early aborigines crossed over what we now call the Bering Straits using shoes made of wood and animal skins. Those who settled in different parts of the Americas adjusted the style of their shoes to suit the snow and conditions where they lived. Awani's shoes are small, oval shaped, very tightly woven deer hide strips attached to curved pine branches."

I remembered seeing the shoes he described. Two pair

of them often resided on our covered porch. "What does this mean?"

"Americans have discovered how we come and go from the valley." He took the satisfied baby from me, put her to his shoulder, patted and rubbed her back until she burped.

"Are we in danger?"

"Teniyakena increased the number of sentries. And the snow deepens each day. Soon they would have to dig their way in through the pass."

"For how long will we be safe?"

"In the spring, I will take you and the girls to Rancho del Mar, or to my rancho." He took our daughter, Emma Rose, named for his American grandmother, off his shoulder and rocked her in the crook of his arm. "We will see then which place seems safest."

"When is spring?"

"Maybe April."

"And what of the tribes?"

"They will move farther into the mountains, maybe north to the Hetch Hetchy canyon."

"Couldn't they come with us?"

"I do not think I could protect them." His eyes looked sad until he looked down at the small bundle in his arm. He smiled and cooed at Emma Rose. "My darlings, some very bad men have arrived in the last few months . . . the idea of easy riches has drawn some of the worst to California. And these criminals are attempting to take over. They are in particular harassing Californios and native tribes, but also causing trouble in the cities. San Francisco has formed a vigilante group in an effort to deal with them."

"Won't the vigilantes be able to handle it?"

"If they hit the right men, but those groups often get it wrong. Especially when they are emotionally reacting to an incident. And even worse, rumor has it that criminals have infiltrated the vigilantes, twisting its activities to suit their nefarious ends."

"Does that mean that you will get involved as this Spanish fox?" I asked.

The thought of my husband returning to his criminal activities was frightening. Of course, he did not consider what he did as criminal although many did. He saw himself, and the men of his family who had held the office of Spanish Fox before him, as protectors of those who could not protect themselves.

Emma Rose whimpered, and then cried.

"Most likely so." He jostled the baby and walked to the door, opened it and showed her the view. "This beautiful valley is yours Rosa. Yours to protect."

Watching them, I understood that my husband had been charged with protecting California, the Spanish Californios, the indigenous people of California, and any-one who could not protect himself. Carlo and his uncle, don Diego, worked together now, but in time the responsibility would pass entirely to Carlo. And from my husband to our children.

Chapter 6

GOLD COUNTRY, TUOLUMNE COUNTY

THE DEGENERATE WOULDN'T SHUTUP. KEPT SAYING STUFF LIKE ""DAMN INJUN. HE SHOT AT ME, NEARLY GOT ME TOO, THAT SHOT WENT WHIZZING RIGHT BY MY HEAD, BUT GOT THAT OTHER ONE, BAMMO, RIGHT IN THE HEAD. GOOD SHOOTING. HUH? TOO BAD WE COULDN'T GET TO HIM SO AS YOU COULD MARK HIM THE WAY YOU DO WITH THAT KNIFE OF YOURS. WICKED KNIFE." THEN HE CACKLED LIKE AN OLD CRONE.

I WISHED THE PERVERT WOULD STOP HIS BLATHERING. JUST A MATTER OF TIME BEFORE HE SAID THE WRONG THING TO THE WRONG PERSON. PROBABLY HAVE TO KILL HIM SOON.

ALL THE WORK TO GET INTO THE NECK OF THAT VALLEY ONLY TO RUN INTO SENTRIES. WE'D HAVE TO FIGURE OUT ANOTHER WAY WHILE THEY WERE STILL TRAPPED IN THAT VALLEY.

I'D ORGANIZE A GROUP OF MEN. TELL 'EM

THEY NEEDED TO RESCUE THREE WHITE WOMEN KIDNAPPED BY THE INDIANS. MAYBE THAT'D WORK. I'D START SOWING THE SEED ABOUT THE WOMEN THAT NIGHT. MAKE IT THE SUBJECT OF INTEREST IN THE SALOON SUBTLY. I'LL SAY SAM TOLD ME THEN I WOULDN'T BE KNOWN AS THE SOURCE OF THE RUMOR.

Chapter 7

Our baby grew at an astounding pace. It took the sewing and knitting efforts of four women to keep her in clothes. We spent our days in front of the fire with our needlework and my breastfeeding.

I grew restless and anxious to go past our porch. I strapped on the snowshoes, the bear paws, and promptly fell off the porch trying to walk.

I pulled myself back up with the aid of a post and made my way along the river to the pool at the bottom of the half-frozen falls. The sun lit up jagged ice sculptures formed by the falling water. I looked up at the face on the stone and wondered anew at the magic of this valley. The safe haven it had provided had nearly run its course. No new snow had fallen in days.

Carlo prepared to leave for my stepmother's Rancho del Mar and his own rancho to scout out a new place for his women to be safe. "I think with your father at del Mar. Americans will be less likely to mess with well-respected fellow Americans, and the father of an English lord," he had told me, but he wanted to see how prepared Father was for dealing with any trouble that would come his way.

I knew Carlo felt some guilt for abandoning his duties to spend the winter months with us. I hoped that conditions outside our peaceful valley did not make him feel worse.

I heard the soft shuffle of snowshoes behind me and turned to see Carlo making his way to me.

"The neck of the valley is passable with shoes. I see you're doing pretty well on those shoes. I'm tempted to take you girls with me. I will do a quick scout and return for you. We will not wait for the snow to melt to leave here."

"How soon would we leave?" I gazed at the waterfall, the snow-covered cedars, pines and redwoods, looked back at our snug cabin caught in a shaft of sunlight.

"A week, maybe less."

"It's been so good here. I hate to leave." I took his arm, held it to me.

"It will be good everywhere." Carlo pulled me into his arms. "As long as we're together."

"Once we leave here there will be the whole world to deal with. It won't be the same." I wondered how my father and his new family would respond to my new family, my new marriage.

"I will make it good," Carlo promised.

His tender kisses soon turned passionate. He carried me to our bed closing the door behind us.

He had learned my body well over the last weeks soon knowing exactly how to trigger the spasms of pleasure, how to turn me into a wanton lover, begging for him to enter and press against my sex.

Our passions spent, I held him close wanting the feeling to last.

He left the next morning.

Chapter 8

I took Smokey Junior, commonly known as Junior, out on my next snowshoe outing. The dog had nearly grown into his big feet but still had few manners and seldom obeyed. With puppy energy, he leapt and bounded through mounds of melting snow ignoring my command to come.

Winter was ending along with the hibernation of the other residents of the valley. Perhaps Junior startled the grizzly, awaking from his winter nap, or interrupted it. I watched in horror some twenty feet from where the enraged bear gave the pup a quick swipe with his paw, like a man swatting a fly. The pup flew against a tree, landed with a thud at the base of the trunk.

I started towards the pup when Lopa appeared next to a nearby tree and spoke calmly, quietly. "No move."

"But, the pup—."

"Dog dead," Lopa said.

The enormous, monstrous animal lumbered deeper into the valley disappearing behind a grove of evergreen trees.

I turned to Lopa.

"Mucho bears in Yo-Ha-Mite," she said as though we

were discussing insects.

I hated telling Susanna and Sara that still another of their dogs had perished, but their stoicism surprised me.

"Thank goodness, you weren't attacked." Susanna wiped away a tear and hugged me.

"Once we saw a man that had been mauled by a giant bear, took his head clear off, I thought at first the bear had eaten it, but turned out he just hit it, scared me to death I tell ya, I hate those things, can't wait to get out of here before they all wake up, in the summer this valley is full of bears . . ." Sara chattered on and on. I remembered she had not spoken a word for months after we had rescued her from the kidnappers who had abused her as a child. For weeks now she had been making up for her earlier silence.

After a sharp rap on the cabin door, Chief Teniyakena entered with a black pup in his arms. He handed the pup to Sara and cautioned me about going any distance from the cabin without an escort.

The pup was dubbed Smokey the third, and soon became known as Three.

Carlo returned five days later.

Chapter 9

Carlo kissed Emma Rose's forehead, pulled me to share his embrace.

"I took your father aside and explained everything to him."

"Everything?" I asked.

"It turns out he already knew much of what I told him, but he patiently allowed me to tell him recent occurrences. I told him he had a beautiful granddaughter." Carlo pulled me closer, kissed my lips before he continued. "I was honest with him when I asked his permission to marry you. He knew who I was, about my family's complicated history and my future responsibilities. But I reminded him. He was so pleased about the baby and anxious to have you both at Rancho del Mar, I don't think he paid much attention to what I said."

I reached my hands to his face, smiled and was rewarded with the sight of the dimples his grin produced. I would miss those dimples when his winter beard grew thicker again.

"Your father has hired Pinkertons and Rancho del Mar

is well prepared for any problems." He looked both sad and anxious. "And there have been problems. Including signs of more attempts to get into this valley. Between that and the bears, I want to get you out of here."

I kissed the worry lines on his face, took the babe from his arms, and handed her to Lopa. I took his hand and led him to our bedroom.

I unfastened his jacket, his shirt, eased his clothing from his body while enjoying the grin on his face.

I took his manhood in my hands while I sucked his tongue into my mouth until I heard his groan of desire. I startled him by replacing my hand with my mouth moving my hand to cup his testicles.

Carlo opened my blouse, reached for my breast, rubbed my nipple with his thumb.

He groaned, pulled me onto the bed, and rubbed his thumb along my sex. His fingers, now wet with my desire roamed freely, rubbing and caressing, causing me to ache for him to enter me.

"You want me?" He grinned.

"Yes," I growled.

Chapter 10

Carlo's beloved California had been overrun with mad men; men motivated by greed, or lust for power, or pure, beyond comprehension, madness.

Once Spain and then Mexico had relinquished possession of California, violence had gone from being nearly non-existent among the easy-going Californios and the native tribes, to being rampant with much of it directed towards those very same innocents.

Vigilante groups formed in an effort to fight back, but the Americans had a tendency to hit the wrong target in their innate mistrust of those different than themselves. The Chinese, Spanish Californios, and natives were most often mistreated in the name of justice.

Carlo felt every bit as guilty as I was afraid he might, and he was anxious to get us women settled at Rancho del Mar so that he could take up the duties of his Spanish Fox office. We packed only irreplaceable, sentimental items knowing everything would be more plentiful once we left the valley. And Carlo assured me that we would return.

In my heart I doubted that would happen soon and I begged to take Emma Rose's cradle and my rocking chair.

Carlo promised such items would be brought to us when the snow melted, but in the meantime, we must leave on snowshoes and with only what we could carry on our backs.

I had the baby in her woven cradle basket carrier, no light burden as she was already over twelve pounds and squirmed to get down even when held against her mother's breast. Sara, Susanna, and Lopa carried our jewelry, some food, and we all wore numerous layers of clothing.

Chief Teniyakena, Carlo, don Diego, and White Owl would escort us to Rancho del Mar. From there the natives would return to the valley and Carlo and his uncle would travel south to don Diego's lands.

The morning we left saw the first snowfall we'd had in two weeks.

I wrapped my face using my scarf as a brim to protect my eyes, the same scarf sat lightly over the baby's face allowing a pocket for her to breathe. I stepped off the porch of our snug home onto a shallow layer of fresh snow covering mud turned to ice.

I stumbled, caught myself on a tree, and Lopa rushed to my side.

"Lopa carry baby," she said.

"No, I'll be alright." The baby was my responsibility even if Lopa did feel a special connection to her.

Lopa stayed close at my side occasionally grabbing my left arm as we climbed out of the valley. Carlo and Chief Teniyakena led the way. We passed four sentries who assured us they had seen no sign of trouble.

I was breathless by the time we reached the top of the neck. We took a five-minute break.

"Darling, I would carry the babe, but I think at the front of our little march I am the most likely to see trouble. Let Lopa help you with her," Carlo said.

"I'm fine." I trusted Lopa completely, but I wanted to know each second that Emma Rose was doing well.

"It will be easier going now. It is downhill for the most part from here, and we do not have far to go to get below the snow line and to where the horses are corralled," Carlo said. "I had planned to travel through the night once we reached the horses, but this snow will be rain in the valley. Make for tough going. We will camp at the corral if it is raining."

With every step, my feet grew heavier, the snow got sticker, the air colder. Sweat ran down my sides, but my chest ached from breathing the cold. Each time I slid another step I wondered how many more I could manage.

"Lopa," was all I needed to say and she lifted the baby basket from my chest and slung it onto hers.

Given that I felt as though I had been sloshing through snow for days, it was disorienting for it to be still daylight when we reached the snow line. My feet freed from the snowshoes felt weightless. My energy returned until we got a little further down the hill and now instead of snow, we fought mud.

The men huddled with the horses for the wet night in a part of the corral covered by a flat roof. The caretaker's hut barely held us four women. Emma Rose, usually a quiet happy baby, cried much of the night. I held her to my breast and then Lopa jostled her while I caught some sleep.

It was an uncomfortable night, but the next day dawned clear. We got an early start and now that we would be on horseback, we agreed to push forward even into the night to make the rancho.

We left the shelter of the foothills and the oaks, headed across the plain of the central valley, through the tall grass and toward the gentler coast range. I was exhilarated to be out in the open, moving through enormous space after a winter of being enclosed in the snug cabin and the valley surrounded by tall cliffs. I loved the wind in my hair and the feel of the horse's muscles galloping whenever the terrain allowed.

Late in the day, Chief Teniyakena halted our little caravan, pointed to a dust cloud to the north of us indicating riders speeding toward us.

"Head for that clump of trees." Carlo shouted and waved at a circle of tall sycamores.

Trees lined both banks of a creek swollen with winter rains. We made their shelter while the dust cloud was still far away.

Carlo beckoned to a spot behind a large outcrop of rock; we four women crouched beneath it. The men tied the horses to a tree twenty-feet away from our position and encircled the outcrop.

I put Emma Rose to my breast. Susanna softly sang a soothing lullaby to quiet the baby and her sister Sara.

When the riders grew closer, we could make out ten

men on horseback, dragging three men tied to ropes behind them. The victims stumbled and tried to stay upright. One had failed to do so and appeared to be unconscious.

"Stay here." Carlo handed me a revolver and Chief Teniyakena gave Lopa a second large knife. The four men mounted, galloped after the riders.

From our hiding place I saw Carlo's sword cut loose the ropes used to drag the bodies. Don Diego and Carlo held their guns on the riders while White Owl and Chief Teniyakena saw to the victims.

"Keep your hands where we can see them," Diego warned.

I recognized two of the mounted men. One was the sandy-haired gambler from the *SS Crescent City*; the other was one of the men who had kidnapped the sisters.

"Girls, stay down." I whispered. I didn't want them to be seen, or for them to see that man. Either way, it meant trouble.

Carlo, when in his Charles Anthony persona and clothing, looked and sounded like an Englishman. But in his fandango hat, and riding chaps, mounted on the saddle with silver embellishments, he looked every bit the bearded Spanish Don. The resentment of the ten men being held at gunpoint by two Californios and two natives was palpable even at a distance.

I hoped the full beard Carlo had recently grown would keep the gambler from recognizing him. I couldn't hear what the gambler was saying, but remembering his arrogant bigotry, I could imagine his commentary. I saw Carlo motion for the gambler to get off his horse. The man refused to give up his mount. Silently, Carlo used the point of his sword to nudge him into action.

I couldn't see how this was going to be anything but bad. Ten to four were not good odds. I was tempted to go to their aid, but before I could move, Lopa grabbed my arm, "Stay." She handed over the baby basket.

She walked in a crouch to where our horses were tied, jumped on hers and raced off with another two horses in tow. She threw the unconscious man over one horse, aided the other two onto a horse while don Diego and White Owl collected weapons from the now dismounted ten men and Chief Teniyakena drove off all but two of their horses.

Carlo brandished his sword, drew a Z for the first letter of the Spanish word for fox in the earth and on the shirt of one man who initially refused to dismount. Lopa headed west toward the coast range. I gathered the girls, and we rode two on a horse following Lopa.

The men did the same bringing with them the two horses. Carlo caught up with us. Like a trick rodeo rider, he snatched Sara from behind her sister without slowing. We didn't stop until we reached the shelter of the coastal range and the arroyo canyon Lopa and I had used nearly a year earlier.

Under the canopy of a coast oak, Lopa and White Owl tended to the wounds of the three men: two of them Californios, one Chinaman. The unconscious Chinese died without coming around. The other two explained they had stopped to talk to the Chinaman when the so-called posse lassoed them. They had no idea what they were supposed to have done to deserve such treatment.

"We cannot stay here." Carlo said. "Even without them having horses. I want to put more distance between us and them."

He assisted the wounded onto the two stolen horses and we rode into the canyon on the trail that showed signs of having seen more traffic than when Lopa and I had last used it; sufficient traffic to have beaten a path that we could follow even by moonlight.

Dawn found us near the El Camino Real. We dragged, nearly asleep in our saddles, into Rancho del Mar by late afternoon.

"Clarissa, my darling girl." My father was beside himself with excitement, hugging me, holding and cooing at his granddaughter, grinning from ear to ear. "Oh, how I've missed you, and look at the beautiful gift you have brought to me."

My father's wife, doña Maria Elena immediately set to planning a fiesta barbecue for the next day. Gauchos were sent to select and slaughter beef, natives ordered to prepare beans and tortillas, girls to set tables and cover them with flowers. Barrels of wine and brandy were rolled to the courtyard.

"Doña Maria Elena, look at these exhausted people, we must give them a full day of rest." My father looked up from his granddaughter to order. "Make your preparations quietly and your invitations for two days from now."

Doña Maria Elena nodded, "Yes, my darling."

Doña Maria Elena's youngest daughter, Claudia and my father took over babysitting while we fell into our beds and slept for fourteen hours.

PART TWO
Rancho del Mar
1849

Chapter 11

I awoke to the sounds of party preparations and my husband's snores, a reassuring sound, which over the last weeks had become a lullaby of sweet security letting me know he was asleep at my side. I turned my head to study his face. Eyes closed in slumber showed off his long, thick, eyelashes, dark hair curled around his ears and forehead, golden tanned skin set off a dark moustache over a tender mouth.

Green eyes opened and met my stare. "Well, well, what have we here?" His arms pulled me close, he spoke into my hair, "Your father certainly is enamored of our daughter. Shall we see if we can give him a grandson next?" His hands ran down my back, pulled my hips closer, and teased my pelvic mound. His lips nibbled my neck and sucked my mouth in a tender kiss.

I ran my fingers through his hair, down his back, down his buttocks, pulled him inside.

No hurry, no pressing matters, no babe to care for. Perhaps he was correct when he said we would be good anywhere. Lazy mornings, languid lovemaking, I could get used to this.

Chapter 12

SAN JOAQUIN VALLEY
APRIL 1849

I COULD SCARCELY BELIEVE MY EYES. TWO CALIFORNIOS, TWO INJUNS. WHERE DID THEY GET THE NERVE? CUTTING LOOSE THESE THREE WE WERE TEACHING A LESSON TO.

THEN TO TOP IT ALL, THE FOUR WOMEN I'D HUNTED FOR FOUR MONTHS RODE AWAY WITH THE OUTLAWS. IT HAD TO BE THEM. I'D RECOGNIZE THAT GOLDEN HAIR, THE TWO BLONDES, AND THE HEATHEN BITCH ANYWHERE. THE GOOD NEWS, THEY WEREN'T IN THAT DAMN FROZEN VALLEY, I DIDN'T HAVE TO WASTE ANYMORE TIME OR EFFORT TRYING TO GET IN TO THAT GOD FORSAKEN PLACE.

IT WAS A LONG TREK TO THE CLOSEST SHERIFF, BUT I'D MAKE IT AND THEN I'D FIND THEM. THEY LOOKED TO BE HEADED FOR THE COAST. TO ONE OF THOSE RANCHOS. HORSE THIEVES WERE

PUNISHED BY HANGING. I'D GET THE SHERIFF TO TAKE CARE OF THE MEN. THE WOMEN WERE MINE.

Chapter 13

Hot cocoa, hot biscuits and strawberry jam, eggs, oranges, roasted potatoes, real coffee, black tea . . . all everyday breakfast items for wealthy Californios, but luxuries for those who had been living in the snow-covered Yosemite Valley.

An afternoon of socializing and showing off our beautiful green eyed, auburn haired daughter, preceded eating barbecue, and an evening of dancing. I never dreamed when I left the rancho a year ago that I would return with such joy and an intensified love of California.

The only negative aspect of the occasion was a conversation the Don of the land grant just east of ours had with Father. "A sheriff with a posse stopped at my rancho just as we were readying to leave this afternoon. They were looking for horse thieves."

Don Juan Vasquez stepped into the conversation. "They came by, searched my place also."

I saw Carlo and don Diego exchange a look, then Carlo left the patio headed toward the corral where I saw him speak with Chief Teniyakena. Moments later the Chief and

White Owl took off leading the two horses we had "borrowed" from the bad guys.

"Will they be safe?" I asked Carlo when he returned.

"They will be fine. They need to get back to the valley before it is accessible. They'll leave the horses on the creek near where we picked 'em up."

The next afternoon the sheriff and his posse kicked up a dust cloud as they rode through the gates and up to the main adobe of Rancho del Mar. I took Sara and Susanna into my rooms. We listened from behind the shuttered window.

Carlo, now clean shaven, and my father, both having had time to change into their most American gentlemen attire and flanked by a half dozen similarly attired Pinkertons, greeted the men at the front entrance gates of the hacienda.

"How may I help you gentleman?" my father asked.

"I'm Sheriff Bill Palace out of Sacramento," I heard a gravelly voice say.

"Pleasure to make your acquaintance, sir. I'm Edward Wells; this is my son-in-law, Charles Anthony. Pretty far from home aren't you?"

"Lookin' for some horse thieves."

"You won't find 'em here," my father said.

"No, don't imagine we would."

"May I offer you some refreshment? At least some cool water?" As Father spoke native help poured lemon water and handed cups to the men.

"Kinda ya, sir."

Despite the sheriff's assurances that they did not expect to find horse thieves at Rancho del Mar, from my shuttered window, I saw them circle the corral before leaving. I also saw among the posse the dandy, who—I was pretty sure—shot me, and one of the girl's captors. I wondered if he had also shot Sam, my friend and protector while we were in the Gold country.

Was that sandy-haired man the gambler? I had yet to mention any of them to Carlo.

I ran to the courtyard entrance and took my husband's arm. "Carlo, the gambler from the *SS Crescent City* was with that posse. And he was with the group that dragged those three men. Who is he?"

Carlo shrugged.

"No! Don't do that. I can tell that you and he have some history. What is his name?"

"His name is Augustus Pennyworth," Carlo said as he removed my hand from his arm and continued walking through the courtyard.

I pulled on his arm, dragging him into our rooms.

"Please don't keep whatever this is from me."

Carlo turned to face me, wrapped his arms around my waist and pulled me to him. His mouth sought mine, but now I pulled away.

"Did you meet him on the steamship where we met?" I asked.

"Yes. Well, not exactly." His fingers turned my face to his.

"That wasn't the first time you met?"

"No."

My heart began to race with panic. "Did he recognize you when you rescued those men?"

"I doubt it, you may have noticed I did not speak to those ten men. My voice would possibly have given me away." Carlo quieted my questions with kisses and fondling. "I promise to do my very best to keep you and my family safe. I will not endanger you or my family with carelessness."

His hands traveling the length of my body distracted me from asking further questions.

Chapter 14

Days melted into weeks, weeks into months. The mild weather influenced by our proximity to the ocean gave only subtle hints of seasons. The spring marked by wildflowers and fruit trees in bloom, the summer by more fog than usual, the fall by the green grass turning to gold. The undulating coastal range covered in the velvet of golden grass was as sensual as any nude in Raphael's paintings.

Emma Rose's transformation from infant to crawling baby reminded us that time was passing. Soon her coos began to sound like words. It was not surprising that her first distinguishable word was Papa, the way she addressed both Carlo and my father. She waved her tiny hands with excitement any time either of them were near her.

Carlo and don Diego were frequently absent for days at a time but always returned on schedule thus alleviating any excessive worry. Neither of them explained these absences other than to occasionally mention the ranchos they owned. Don Diego's land was far south of Rancho del Mar, Carlo's just north.

The only thing that marred our idyllic existence was

my concern about my friend Sam, not knowing if he had survived the incident that burned our shack in Clementine. I owed Sam for the kindness and assistance he had shown us while Lopa and I were on our own in the gold country. Surely my husband and my father would wish to thank the man too.

I watched Carlo and Father dismounting from a morning ride to check on the estate.

When my father and husband entered the house, I asked, "I sure would like to know if Sam's safe."

"I'd certainly like to thank the man who helped you out my dear. Perhaps Charles and I should take a ride over to Clementine one day soon," Father said.

Carlo nodded his agreement. "After the holidays."

"I'll come with you," I said.

"I'd rather you not," Father said. The men were in agreement on that point.

I would have to persuade them. I tried out various schemes in my imagination, but none of them seemed convincing even to me.

Chapter 15

CALIFORNIA COAST
1849

I'D THOUGHT FOR SURE WE WOULD'VE FOUND THEM INJUNS AND SPANIARDS BY NOW. THREE WEEKS RIDING FROM RANCHO TO RANCHO, HUGE DAMN PLACES, AND NO SIGN OF THE HORSES, OR THE BITCHES. TIME TO HEAD BACK TO CLEMENTINE.

Chapter 16
Winter Holidays
1849

November was a busy month with lots of work for everyone on the rancho. Cattle were slaughtered. Hides and tallow were prepared and sold to Yankee traders. Extra hired men, lured from gold seeking, had to be to be fed, housed and supervised.

But Father knew the horrors of what had occurred to Sara, Susanna, Lopa, and myself that caused us to miss our carefully prepared Thanksgiving last year. He arranged for a lavish American style Thanksgiving celebration to make up for the one that had been destroyed by violence in Clementine. A long table, pumpkins, potatoes, corn, pies and the centerpiece of the day—an actual turkey. Where ever had Father found that bird?

Once the last hides headed overseas had been loaded on board ship in Monterey, the preparations for Christmas began. Cooking and baking, woodworking of ornaments, tuning of musical instruments, making piñatas and costumes, harvesting evergreens and trees, constructing garlands and wreaths—everyone had a job as we planned to celebrate all of our traditions. English, American, French, Spanish, and Californio traditions would be mixed into one long holiday period beginning December 16th and continuing through January 6th.

Those who were to play parts in the performance of Los Pastores rehearsed every night. I was curious as to what the play was about but I was shooed out of the room in which they practiced.

"Why won't you tell me the story?" I asked my stepsister, Claudia, after Carlo had refused to divulge the plot.

"You will enjoy it more." She laughed. "You'll see soon enough. I need to please borrow the cradle Emma Rose has out-grown to use for the Nacimientos."

"The what?" I asked.

"You know, for the baby Jesus."

"Oh, a crèche. Certainly, I'll get it for you." I found the cradle we had stored away in hopes of further need and carried it to the courtyard porch where Claudia and Juanita had placed the wooden statutes of Mary, Joseph, Angels, and Shepherds. Claudia placed the Baby Jesus in the cradle and arranged straw around the base.

"Shall I bring the three kings over here?" I motioned to where they stood near the entrance to the courtyard.

"No gracias," Claudia smiled at me. "Each day until January six we move them closer to our Bethlehem, to here where the Baby Jesus sleeps. When they finally arrive at our nativity, it is time to share gifts."

"We don't share gifts on Christmas?"

Claudia and Juanita frowned at me. "We give food and clothing to the priests and natives on Christmas." Claudia said.

"Oh, we do that on boxing day, December 26. I guess this year we'll do it on Christmas."

Claudia nodded her agreement.

"What about Father Christmas?" I asked.

Blank looks from both of them.

"You know, Papa Noel? Saint Nicholas? Santa Claus?"

Claudia shook her head.

"Well, this year, Papa Noel is going to be filling stockings for the children, for Emma Rose and any other children that may be around." I wondered where I would get materials to have Christmas stockings made when I realized that at least a couple of my gowns that were too warm for the climate, especially the pine green wool, would make lovely stockings. "How many children will be here Christmas eve?"

Claudia frowned, shook her head.

"Nochebuena?"

"Sí, church, we go to the mission."

I went in search of my gown, and doña Maria Elena. She would be able to tell me how many children would be staying at the hacienda on Christmas Eve.

I found doña Maria Elena sitting with Father on a bench outside the family chapel. He had his arm resting on the back of the bench behind her shoulders. They were laughing and smiling into each other's eyes. Looking at doña Marie Elena, her face raised to gaze lovingly at Father, I saw what a beautiful woman she was. Father's return had brought new life to her. And I had never seen my father so content as he was with doña Maria Elena.

My eyes filled with tears of joy. His long years as a widower were finally over.

I decided not to disturb them, but Father caught sight of me. "Clarissa, my dear, please join us. We are making Christmas plans."

I explained my Christmas stocking plan asking doña Maria Elena for the number of children which led to Father explaining Father Christmas, Papa Noel and several other of our traditions to his wife.

We agreed that our Boxing Day could be moved to Christmas Day, that we would observe California tradition of traveling to the mission to attend mass on Christmas Eve followed by a fiesta. And then the performance of Los Pastores on Christmas Day after we finished the children's stockings and brunch and before Christmas dinner. Adults would exchange gifts on January 6th, but the presents could be placed under the Christmas tree any time before that day.

"Carlo is at his rancho?" Doña Maria Elena asked.

"Yes, he has a lot of organizing to do to prepare for us to live there." I said. "Doña Maria Elena, I am so grateful for your generous hospitality while he brings his hacienda up to his standards."

"My dear Clarissa, this is your home. I know your father is pleased to spend the time with you and your family after the years of separation and I also enjoy having you and your sweet child and your brilliant husband as part of our household. Please also remember this is your father's rancho."

"My dear, this property will belong to your children." Father quickly said, "It is only registered as my property to safeguard possession for your family. My children have no need for it. William has his English properties, as well as estates in Wales and Scotland. As for Clarissa, her husband has refused to accept the dowry I offered so I have placed the funds thus earmarked for her personal use. I am merely temporary custodian of the estate for you."

"As you please." Doña Maria Elena kissed Father full on his lips in an unusual public display of affection.

The sound of horses racing through the gates of the rancho interrupted any further discussion. Father stood, walked to see who arrived in such a hurry. I followed him, hoping to see my husband.

Don Diego, Carlo, and White Owl pulled their mounts to sudden stops, jumped to the ground. Don Diego and Carlo, dressed entirely in black, were mounted on black stallions that I had never seen before. White Owl uncharacteristically looked ready for battle including war paint.

Carlo shouted, "don Eduardo, we are being chased."

"Quickly, hide," Father motioned them to the stables, closed the stall doors, and ambled to the heavy wooden gates to greet the pursuers.

"Gentlemen, how may I help you?" Father addressed

the six riders who stopped just short of the entrance.

"We are chasing bandits."

"Bandits? That's terrible. What did they steal?"

"Chink workmen," blurted one of the men.

"Chinese. We was taking them to work the mine," said another.

"Sir, I assure you there are no Chinese workmen here," Father said.

Carlo, now dressed in American cowboy attire with a grey jacket and white shirt, strolled to Father's side. "Edward, what seems to be the matter here?"

"These gentlemen seemed to have lost some Chinamen." Father replied.

"How the blazes does one misplace Chinamen?" Carlo said.

"They was stolen by a gang of Mexican outlaws and Injuns," said one of the riders.

"I haven't seen anyone like that around here. Have you Edward?" Carlo turned to Father.

"Definitely not, but now that you are here gentlemen, allow me to play host. Won't you join us for uh, lemonade, and perhaps a little whiskey?" Father smiled.

"Perhaps a friendly card game? We have so little male company here." Carlo looked to where doña Maria Elena and I sat on the bench outside the chapel.

Two of the men grinned and started to dismount, but the man who seemed to be in charge said. "Nah, we gotta find 'em."

"At least accept some cool water," Carlo said.

"Yes." Father motioned to Juanita. "Please get some water for these men." Father addressed the mounted men. "Would you care to water your horses?"

Juanita, Sara and Susanna brought water for the men. The two blonde girls were maturing into attractive young ladies and managed to distract the men from their mission. Carlo and Father also continued to chat with the men.

When the men finally rode away, I asked Carlo, "I take it you wanted to keep them here as long as possible?"

Carlo shrugged, "Just being hospitable."

I grabbed his arm, took him toward our rooms. "What have you done with the Chinamen?"

"Couple of my men escorted them back to Yerba Buena . . . San Francisco where they can get lost in Chinatown."

I grinned, put my arms around his neck. "I'm glad to see you."

He pulled my body tight against his. "Glad to see you, let me show you how glad." He swept me into his arms and carried me through our bedroom door. He tossed me onto the bed and while I giggled, he unwrapped the sash from my waist, pulled my blouse over my head, and kissed my breasts.

I reached to unbutton his shirt, ran my hands over his chest.

Carlo raised his face to mine, brushed his lips against mine, and then captured my mouth with his. His tongue probing my mouth sent sensations the length of my body culminating in an ache between my legs.

I pushed him away long enough to disrobe while he shed his clothes as well.

"Oh, my beautiful wife," he murmured against my neck, his hands roaming my body, finding the ache, his fingers building the ache to blossoming explosions.

My hands found his manhood, slipped him into me. I smiled into his eyes as we moved in gentle thrusts that gradually grew faster, deeper, stronger until we lay exhausted in each other's arms.

"Will they be safe in Chinatown?" I whispered.

"Perhaps, perhaps not, but those men will not be able to tell the four we freed from any others." Carlo rolled us over so that we lay side by side. "We will need to find the mine, they apparently have others enslaved there."

With that statement, I knew my husband would be absent for days once again.

Chapter 17
Mission Carmel
Christmas Eve

Dressed in our finest velvets and silk ruffled blouses, the entire household rode to attend evening mass. Emma Rose rode on her father's lap, giggling with excitement. The padres told the story of the Christ child as we gazed at scenes from the Bible painted on the mission walls.

After the service the attendees gathered on the steps of the mission and greeted one another. "Feliz Nochebuena," I heard from all.

Wood statues of Mary and Joseph were carried from the mission and we formed a procession behind them walking among the homes nearby the mission. At each home we asked permission to enter in song. I hummed along once I heard the tune, but I couldn't follow all the Spanish words except for the last phrases, "Gloria a Dios en las alturas, y paz al hombre en la tierra." Meaning, "Glory to God in the highest, and on earth peace to men of good will".

When we were denied entrance, we wished the

residents, "Feliz Navidad" or "Happy Christmas." Then they joined our procession.

At the last stop we asked for a place to rest. The man of the house denied us shelter, but when, in song the identity of Mary and Joseph was explained, he opened his door and beckoned us in. The procession then turned into a scene of hugging and kisses among all the participants.

Guitars and mandolins played music on the patio where young couples danced fandango accompanied by enthusiastic clapping by their elders. On the veranda, Emma Rose loved the hot chocolate served to the children, I sipped coffee laced with brandy and Carlo joined the men in shots of aguardiente, a fiery liquid made from the juice of pressed sugar cane.

Once all guests had enjoyed refreshments, a piñata made with paper and wood shaped in the form of a star was lowered from the ceiling of the sala. Emma Rose being the youngest child was given a stick with which to hit the star. In her father's arms, she swung at it, managed to hit it a few times but the only result was to cause it to swing back and forth. She burst into giggles.

The next child, a young boy was blindfolded before he gave the piñata a good wallop which burst a hole through which sweets fell to the floor. I held my breath when all of the children including Emma Rose dashed to pick up the candies and cookies with the blindfolded boy still swinging the stick.

Carlo stepped in, holding the boy and the stick until the last child had cleared the area. "You did well young man.

Let's give someone else a turn shall we?" he said patting the boy's shoulder.

The boy pulled off his blindfold and smiled when he saw the hole he'd made in the star.

A larger boy swung the stick with such force that the paper and wood flew apart and a torrent of sweets and small toys scattered around the room. Emma Rose screamed with delight as she scrambled on hands and knees to get her share of goodies.

After Emma Rose had consumed most of her sweets, she stuffed the top and small ball into pockets. When she began to cry because the top did not easily fit in her pocket, I signaled Carlo that we should take her home.

Our household and several other families galloped to the hacienda where Lopa took sleeping Emma Rose from Carlo's arms and we adjourned to the patio where dark coffee, tortillas and tamales de pollo awaited us.

Well fed, I asked Carlo to assist me in filling the half dozen stockings we had made for the children. We had stuffed wrapped candies, small decks of cards, tops, and building blocks into all six. Lopa handed me a small rag doll with auburn yarn hair she had made. I tucked it into the top of the stocking embroidered with Emma Rose's name.

Lopa returned to watching Emma Rose sleep while Carlo and I joined the dancers in the courtyard where we enjoyed the music and the sexually suggestive Jarabe, Mexican Hat Dance, as well as other dances until the first light of dawn. Our guests then retired to the hammocks strung under all of the courtyard eaves.

And Carlo and I enacted our own version of the Jarabe in the privacy of our bedroom.

Chapter 18

Christmas day activities did not begin until noon as most of the adults had stayed up until dawn. Emma Rose tried to awake us in what seemed like minutes after we'd fallen asleep. She'd seen stockings hung on the mantel, been told what they were, and was beside herself with excitement.

Baby yelps of "Pa Pa, Ma Ma" while jumping on us finally prompted Carlo to fetch her stocking from the sala. Emma Rose sat between us on our bed and happily dug through her sweets and small toys. She hugged the small rag doll to her neck and covered it with kisses in imitation of how she was treated by the adults in her life.

A beautiful, blue-sky California day greeted us as our little family emerged from the dark bedroom into the atrium patio. Coffee in hand, I ducked into the shade of the grapevine-draped trellis and watched my giggling daughter lovingly cover her father's face with baby kisses.

A buffet of eggs, sausage, fried tomatoes and potatoes, beans and biscuits filled a table warmed by the sun. Sleepy houseguests whispered, in deference to those who had over indulged the night before, as they piled their plates with enough greasy food to counter act their queasy stomachs.

The benches next to the long, planked table in the center of the courtyard were soon filled.

The children were the only ones speaking in normal voice tones until Claudia addressed the gathering. "Actors please report to the sala with your costumes in your arms as soon as you finish eating."

Claudia had refused to divulge any more details about the "Los Pastores" play, but I was able to glean a certain amount of information from asking others. "Los Pastores" was another mix of the pagan and Christian customs. Pre-Christian Mexicans had addressed their gods with musical plays that included song and dance. The Spanish priests used the custom to tell the story of Christmas, but the story, influenced by the irreverent Mexican culture that enjoyed playful jokes, had evolved.

Thirteen actors played the principals in the Christmas story: King Herod, Joseph, Mary, Baby Jesus, the three Kings, the Devil, Archangel, and the three shepherds. In the Rancho del Mar version of the story, the shepherds following the star of Bethlehem to find the Christ Child were the main actors. The Devil does everything possible to prevent them from completing their journey. The slapstick shepherds dance and clown around each obstacle. The most scatterbrained of the three shepherds attempts to explain what is happening to the audience eliciting bursts of laughter. When the Archangel Michael intervenes to defend the shepherds, the three leap for joy in a dance display rivaling any ballet performance.

Stomachs sore from laughing, the audience and per-formers returned to the courtyard patio for another long evening of feasting.

Chapter 19

Three days later was Día de los Santos Inocentes. The Saint Innocents' Day was explained to me repetitively but it required watching it in action to understand how it worked. The day was meant to honor the infants killed at the order of King Herod in an effort to eliminate the Baby Jesus. But in fact, it could have been called Prankster Day.

The teasing, joking, and playing of tricks seemed at first to me to be a strange, dark manner in which to commemorate the massacre of innocent children. But, if I understood correctly how the celebration had evolved, it was based on the trick played on Herod because he thought that by killing every male child under two years old in Bethlehem, he had rid himself of a rival. In fact, Mary and Joseph had fooled him by moving the Christ child to Egypt.

Everyone seemed to be having so much fun I thought it inappropriate but Claudia and Esteban explained that as the infants killed had immediately risen to heaven and been granted sainthood, it was a happy day.

I watched my child and doubted that the mothers of those infants had rejoiced the day their children were killed.

The day started over late breakfast during which doña Maria Elena announced she was expecting a baby. I had understood she was perhaps past childbearing age, but also thought that she and Father would be thrilled with this miracle.

"How wonderful!" I said with a happy smile.

I was startled by the laughter that greeted my reaction to her announcement. And Father was not smiling with pride, he was chuckling.

"Inocente! Innocent!" everyone at the table shouted at me.

"What in the world?" I responded which evoked all present to recite a long phrase in Spanish that Carlo explained meant, "You innocent little dove, you let yourself be fooled." He also explained that if I allowed anyone to borrow anything from me that day I would have to pay to redeem it.

"What do you mean, redeem it?" I asked.

"You will have to pay with either coin or favors to get it back," Carlo said.

"Pay?" I asked.

"Allow me to demonstrate. May I borrow your pearls?" he asked.

I unclasped my necklace and handed it to my husband. He wound the pearls around his wrist forming a bracelet as he snickered. "Inocente. Innocent my little dove. I will collect my favors in private."

I blushed, embarrassed in front of all the family who sat at the table.

The pranks continued throughout the day. The visiting Padre had his rosary "borrowed" by one of the children pretending to desire instruction. Padre offered a coin when he realized his error.

Esteban loaned his spurs to Father, perhaps not expecting a gringo to participate in pranks. Father had trouble saying the word "inocente" as he was laughing too hard to speak.

Thus, when we gathered at the extended table in the courtyard for the long evening meal that was to occur every night of the holidays, and White Owl entered the courtyard yelling "fire," everyone but Father and Carlo assumed he was pranking. They both understood that White Owl did not take part in such foolery.

Lopa also knew better than to think White Owl would prank. She grabbed Emma Rose from Carlo's lap and carried her to a room that could be shut off from any danger from flames and smoke. She demanded that Sara and Susanna accompany her.

But it was not a brush fire. The wood interior of the stables was burning.

White Owl needed assistance rescuing the valuable mounts housed in the stalls. He had opened all the gates and doors opening to the corral but many of the animals were too cowed by the flames to leave their stalls.

This was a serious matter to all of the men. Common horses were very plentiful, and freely given to anyone needing a mount. But fast and beautiful horses were never more prized in any country than in California, and each man had his favorites. A mustang of a peculiar light cream-color, with silver-white mane and tail, or dappled-gray or chestnut were much admired colors. Such animals, of speed and fine bottom, sold for more than horses of any other color. Prized horses lived in the stables of Rancho del Mar.

When Father and Carlo jumped from the table and ran for the stables, every man in the room followed. Claudia and doña Maria giggled at the good prank White Owl had played, but I too doubted he was joking. I ran to see if my favorite dappled-gray was safe.

When I stepped outside the courtyard onto the veranda I saw six riders had entered the entrance gates but stopped just inside. I recognized two of the men and guessed that they were the same men who had recently chased don Diego, Carlo, and White Owl onto the rancho. And one of the riders was Augustus Pennyworth.

Were they waiting to see if two shiny black stallions emerged from the stables? Or were these the men hunting for Sara and Susanna?

I did not wait to see what they were up to, but ran to my room to the high shelf were I kept my rifle. I grabbed it and ran back to the veranda.

Doña Maria Elena, having seen me run by with my rifle, followed my example and retrieved her rifle from above the fireplace.

The two of us stood in plain sight of the six men, flourishing our firearms. In our snowy-white dresses, which Spanish ladies of the upper classes of California wore during the day, we were hard to miss being seen, although I doubted that we looked threatening enough to keep them away.

But they wouldn't see black stallions. Those horses were kept at don Diego's rancho or were hidden in the mountains. And Lopa had taken the two blonde young girls into the safe room. I prayed they stayed there.

Glancing over my shoulder, I could see that all of the horses including my favorite were now in the corral and were being moved two at a time to a paddock away from the burning stables.

Bridles and ornate saddles were carried from the building.

Flames were beaten with blankets. Smoldering embers were doused with buckets of water.

Father, Carlo, don Diego, Esteban and several male guests emerged from the stable covered in soot, but doña Maria Elena and I did not hesitate to hug them.

I kept my eyes on the six men even as I pulled Carlo close. "Do you see them?"

"Yes, we saw them," Carlo answered.

"Did they do this?"

He shrugged, but said, "Seems likely, does it not?"

He rubbed my arms streaking black down my white dress. "You're trembling. Don't be afraid my darling. Six men do not pose a threat. They won't come any farther onto the property. Especially now that they've seen how many men are here today." He whispered against my neck. "They are probably unaware that Californians gather with their families for weeks around the Christmas holidays."

"So, what happens after January sixth?" I asked. His answering shrug was not reassuring.

Chapter 20

Nothing untoward happened shortly after January six. But after the excitement of the holidays, I felt bored with our daily routine that required so little of me. Riding on the dunes was still breath taking, but I couldn't do that all day.

I loved playing with my daughter who was learning to talk and charmed us all with her sweet voice. She was not concerned with walking as she moved much faster scooting along in a fast crawl, but Lopa followed her everywhere moving danger out of her path. Lopa seemed to accurately gauge where she was headed. I hovered over her when Lopa was not on duty, but Emma Rose often fooled me by sharply changing direction.

Emma Rose still napped long hours of the day, leaving me with little to occupy myself.

Evenings were filled with leisurely meals and card games.

Carlo was gone much of the time readying his rancho for his family. I begged to accompany him, but he insisted that he wanted to surprise me with his arrangements. He assured me I would be happy with the accommodations once the restoration of the hacienda was complete.

The hacienda had sat vacant while he traveled and studied abroad. The cattle had been cared for but the natives who oversaw the rancho had no desire to live in the main house and it had fallen into a neglected state. As the hacienda had been but a second home to his deceased parents it had never been of sufficient size or quality to house his current family in the style he wanted to keep them.

Or so he said. But I suspected that his absences could also be explained by his desire to keep his justice-defending-activities separate from his family. I wondered how he intended to do that once we were living at his rancho, but I hesitated to ask him for fear he would decide to lie to me.

I asked Lopa who shrugged me off initially, but I pestered her until she offered tidbits of information.

"They fix caves."

"The what?"

"Caves on rancho, near casa."

The next time Carlo made an appearance at Rancho del Mar, I dragged him to our rooms. "What is this about caves?"

Carlo studied my face for several moments as though deciding what he could get away with, how little he could tell me that would satisfy my curiosity.

"Caves?" he asked.

"Yes, caves, Lopa said you are fixing up caves?" I glared at him. I hated that he excluded me from part of his life.

Carlo sighed, but did not speak.

"I thought you said your rancho is near the San Juan Bautista mission. Are there caves there also?"

Carlo sighed again, reached out to pull me into his arms. I resisted.

He leaned into my face, brushed his lips against mine.

"You are not going to distract me," I said. "I want to know."

He nibbled the back of my neck knowing I found that seductive.

"That's not going to work." I squirmed out of his grasp, walked across the room. "Don't you trust me?" I pouted.

"Oh, my darling. I'm sorry. Of course, I trust you, but I want to keep you safe."

"How does keeping secrets from me keep me safe?" I looked at the floor. His lopsided smile was not going to melt my resolve.

"Come here and I will tell you all."

I didn't move toward him, but I did look up. I saw in his eyes that I had him concerned. "Promise to tell me all?"

"Yes, I promise to answer all your questions."

I walked to where he sat but kept an arm's length away.

"My rancho, our rancho is near the Mission de San Juan Bautista but not right on top of it. The grant to my great grandfather included an area of rolling hills, a fertile valley through which a wide river flows, and the Gabilan

Mountains, which contain the remains of an ancient volcanic field. There are numerous caves within that field."

"And they are a secret?" I asked.

"The caves have been used by natives for over ten thousand years. But only a few Californios, mostly my relatives know of their existence," Carlo said.

"And what are you doing to fix them?"

"Fixing is not the correct word." He smiled. "Some of the caves are inhabited by millions of bats. Others are susceptible to flash floods," Carlo explained. "White Owl, don Diego and I are exploring to find the best location to hide the horses and the other things that we use when we are . . ." His voice trailed off as he hesitated to actually state what they were up to.

I understood. "Thank you." I moved closer, put my arms around his neck. This time I did not resist his kisses.

In fact, I welcomed his tongue to my mouth, sucking with all the pent up passion his touch awakened in me.

His fingers traveled down the front of my white blouse, fumbled with tiny buttons to free my breasts. He rubbed a nipple between his thumb and forefinger while his other arm pulled me closer to his hips.

I entwined my fingers in the black waves of hair on the back of his neck and pushed our mouths even closer. My other hand slipped between our hips and found his breeches swollen with hard desire.

I pulled away intending to rid us of the garments that kept us apart.

"No hurry my darling," Carlo whispered against my

neck as he pulled me closer. His teeth gently nibbled at the back of my neck sending waves of sensation through my body down to my sex. His hand slid beneath my full white skirts and into my pantaloons as he turned me around so that my bottom fit against his hard member.

His nibbles turned to bites at the nape of my neck. His fingers pushed against me.

My body reacted like a cat in heat arching my back to press against his hardness.

His fingers now wet with my desire rubbed and caressed between my legs sliding between my bottom cheeks. His fingers lingered in that forbidden place.

I thought to resist, but my body fought my reluctance by continuing to arch against his hard member.

Carlo yanked away my pantaloons, threw my skirt over my shoulders and pressed me against the bed. He entered me from behind while his fingers continued to caress with both hands one to each side of his organ.

Overwhelmed with sensations, I entered another world where all I knew was ecstasy. I was still in such a trance when Carlo undressed me and laid me on the bed.

Chapter 21

After a great deal of whining and huffing around, I finally convinced my husband and Father I should accompany them to Clementine. I had argued, I was much safer traveling with them than I was when I made the journey with Lopa. Sam was my friend. Neither of them even knew whom to look for, nor was there any reason for Sam to trust them.

My husband and Father opted to dress in their American attire, no silver, no swords. Remembering the attitudes towards Californios in gold country, I was relieved that we did not need to discuss the matter.

Lopa elected to stay behind with Emma Rose.

We traveled with two manservants and a pack mule that carried a tent for me. I had forgotten how much I enjoyed camping under the stars and the three-day journey to Clementine was pleasant, but we arrived to find Clementine much changed. The nearby settlements of Sonora and Columbia had grown while Clementine shrank. All we found were a few shabby, deserted shacks and two ragged men; skeletal madmen who were unable to answer any of our questions with reason.

My heart ached at the sight of the burned-out ruins of what had been our home for a few months.

We rode on to Sonora, which had become a bustling center, and found rooms in a reasonably acceptable hotel. From the balcony I watched horses, wagons and even some carriage traffic in the main street.

We had asked every person we met about Sam but no one seemed to know him at all. I was yet to see anyone I recognized. The population changed surprisingly fast in these foothill communities.

Carlo and Father were united in their refusal to allow me to accompany them to the two saloons. I argued that I had spent some considerable time in a much less sophisticated saloon than those that had been established in Sonora. But they were having none of it and even went so far as to go one at a time to check the saloons so that I would never be unescorted. I bristled at their lack of trust.

"Father, will you please allow me to go to the general store while you and Carlo go to the places you feel inappropriate for me? Certainly, that would be a more efficient use of our time."

Father chuckled, took my elbow, "Where would you like to go my dear?"

We walked along the wood planked walkway stopping in at the shops and tearooms and rooming houses.

I stopped in to say hello to the dressmaker who had made tea dance gowns for Susanna, Sara and me in the days when my solution to destitution had been offering miners companionship of true ladies rather than that of soiled doves. But she had left town.

"She sold this place to me," said the tailor. "Pretty sure she headed for San Francisco."

As we walked I remembered with pride that I had managed to care for myself, admittedly with Lopa's assistance, and the two girls even though it was just a few months.

There were still very few women to be seen. The so-called ladies of the night of course seldom ventured out during the day.

Father escorted me through the merchants while Carlo checked the saloons.

One shop seemed to sell pretty much anything the proprietor could lay his hands on, food stuffs, mining equipment, canvas overalls, a few pieces of china, chairs, a book or two. There, finally I saw a familiar face, one of the women who had worked with Nellie in the saloon.

"Matilda?" I thought it must be her. "Is that you? Nellie's friend."

Matilda stared at me literally as though she saw a ghost. "You're alive?" she stammered. "Is Nellie? Has she been with you?"

I shook my head. "When did you see her last?"

"She set out to walk to your place, to one of your tea dances. When she didn't return, well, I hoped she had decided to throw in with you lot. Then a couple weeks later, I heard that your cabin had burned down, that you all had disappeared. Attacked and captured by injuns is what I heard. Never knew if you . . . well, I thought—."

"Matilda, did you see Sam after that?"

She shook her head. "Didn't he go with you?"

"No." I sighed. "Are you alright?"

"I must go," Matilda said glancing around the store. She turned to me. "What about those young girls? Did they . . .?"

"Sara and Susanna are fine."

She flashed me a sad smile, turned and hurried out the door.

I thought I caught a glimpse of the gambler, Augustus Pennyworth, heading into a saloon across the street.

"Father, quickly, see that sandy-haired man." I pointed to the saloon. "In the pale blue coat, tight britches, he might know about Sam, but he's trouble, part of the posse that dragged the men, the ones Carlo rescued. Do you think he might recognize Carlo from that incident?"

"Carlo's in there. Dammit girl, you stay right here." He rushed out the door, crossed the muddy street, and entered the saloon.

I walked out the door, went down the wooden walkway two more storefronts, lifted my skirts and crossed the mud. Once on the other side I crept along to a window of the saloon. Something told me that seeing me in connection with Carlo and Father would bring trouble. I took care to stay hidden but I had to know what was happening in there.

I could see Carlo's back, I saw Father next to him at the bar. They had engaged the barman in conversation.

Father glanced around, found the pale blue coat. The gambler sat at a table, his hands shuffled cards, while his eyes watched Carlo and Father. Did he know who they were? Father kept his back to Carlo, watched the gambler.

The barman shook his head, called out to a customer who sauntered over to the bar. Carlo bought the man a drink and spoke with him. The customer tossed back the shot of whiskey and shook his head.

Carlo turned around and nearly caught me peeking in the window. I scurried across the muddy road and waited in front of the store.

"Well?" I asked Carlo when they rejoined me.

He wagged his head. "I'm sorry darling. No one has seen or heard from him in months."

"I'm going to be happier when we get out of here," Father said. "Let's get an early start in the morning, I don't like the looks of that gambler and I'm thinking he recognized Clarissa. And he obviously is not fond of you, Carlo. Did you notice how he bristled when you asked him about Sam?"

I looked past Father as he spoke. The gambler, Augustus Pennyworth, stood outside the saloon, smoking a cigarillo, staring right at us.

I took the arms of my two men and walked back to the hotel. I'd asked Carlo previously about his history with Pennyworth without getting an answer. Whatever it was, Carlo didn't want to talk about it. Perhaps when we were alone, it would be a good time to ask him again.

Chapter 22

SONORA 1850

WELL GODDAMN, IF I DIDN'T HAVE ALL THE LUCK. THERE THEY WERE. HALF OF THE PEOPLE I'D NEEDED TO FIND. CAME RIGHT TO ME. WATCHED THEM WALK TO THE HOTEL.

WALKED DOWN TO THE BLACKSMITH AND STABLES. GREETED THE SMITHY. "MIGHTY PRETTY LADY CAME INTO TOWN WITH A COUPLE MEN. ARE THOSE THEIR HORSES IN THEM STALLS?" I ASKED IN A CASUAL WAY.

"YES, SIR. THOSE AND THEM." HE POINTED AT A PACKHORSE AND TWO OTHER ANIMALS IN THE CORRAL. TWO INDIAN SERVANTS CROUCHED ON THEIR HEELS WATCHING THE CORRAL.

"GOTTA HAVE 'EM READY TO GO AT DAWN." THE SMITHY SAID.

NOW I'D DIG UP THAT DEGENERATE. I'D NEED SOME HELP TAKING ON THE TWO MEN, MAYBE EVEN THE INJUNS WOULD BE WITH 'EM. ONCE

THEY WERE OUT OF THE WAY, I'D GET THAT SLUT TO TELL ME WHERE THE TWO BLONDIES WERE.

GETTING HER TO TALK COULD HAVE AN UPSIDE. HELL, THAT'D BE MORE THAN HALF THE FUN.

Chapter 23

We headed out at dawn. A mist lay lightly above meadows run riot with wildflowers. Birds chirped in oak trees, swollen creeks babbled, gentle breezes ruffled tall, green grass. It was a glorious morning to be alive and about.

In our enjoyment of the ride, Father, Carlo, and I pulled well ahead of White Owl and the carriers.

We were perhaps a mile in front when shots rang out.

The first one hit Father squarely in the chest.

The second hit Carlo.

I slid from my horse, picked up the revolver Father dropped, and scrambled behind the crotch of a large oak.

I aimed the revolver and looked for someone to shoot. I heard rustling, horses, and voices.

Father was perfectly still. No sign of breathing. A dark red splotch spread directly over his heart.

A glance at Carlo was all I could take. I prayed the blood on his head was a graze, but he wasn't moving. And with the next quick look, I saw all of his head covered with blood.

I forced myself to breathe. My heart pounded so hard it echoed in my head.

Heartbreak and anger overwhelmed my fear. Using two hands to steady the revolver, I shot in the direction of the noises.

I aimed toward the clump of trees from where I thought the shots had come and emptied Father's revolver.

I dashed for Carlo's weapons, a large knife and a rifle, dashed back behind the tree. Then I waited.

A man's voice yelled, "Don't ya kill her. I want her alive."

I hid Carlo's knife in my boot.

I shouldered the rifle. Placed it in the crotch of the tree. A small movement gave me a target. I shot.

A moan told me I'd hit someone.

One of the men who had captured the sisters, Sara and Susanna, stumbled from the trees and moved towards me. He dragged his left leg, both hands held blazing guns. I took aim, shot him cleanly in the heart. He lurched two more steps and fell face down in the grass.

There was a rustle behind me, a hand wrapped around my arm, and yanked me back from the tree. The rifle fell. I looked up to see the face of the gambler grinning at the man who stood behind me holding my arm.

"What've ya done with the girls?" the man yelled in my ear. With one hand he held my arm; the other slammed the side of my head and grabbed a hunk of my hair.

I lifted my foot, pulled the knife from my boot, reached back over my shoulder and plunged it into his neck.

Blood spurted over both of us, but he kept pulling my hair.

I kicked him repeatedly in the most vulnerable spot of his body. He slid forward to the ground taking me with him, covering me with his body. He passed out.

I pushed free and rolled way, into a pair of muddy boots.

I had no weapon left. I began to say good-bye to this world as I turned my face upward.

Before it had fully registered that I saw Sam's mining partner, Clem, standing above me, a shot hit him squarely between the eyes and he fell away from me.

White Owl and the two native carriers had hurried to the sound of shots. One had gotten Clem before I could find out if he knew anything about Sam, or even if he was with the gang of bad guys.

The gambler had disappeared.

There was nothing to be done for Father.

One of the native carriers checked Carlo's neck for signs of life. He ignored my pleas to touch my husband and lifted Carlo into the arms of the mounted native, White Owl. The warrior whirled his horse away from my begging arms, raced into the mountains with my husband's body.

We carried my father's body back to the rancho without stopping except to water the horses. By the time we arrived my numbness was wearing away.

The sound of doña Maria Elena's sobs was more than I could bear.

Lopa carried Emma Rose out of the hacienda and handed her to me, as though to remind me I still had someone to live for.

I held my baby girl and finally the tears came.

"Carlo?" Don Diego asked.

I shook my head. "I don't know, White Owl took him. He'd been shot, his head was bleeding. I wanted to . . . I don't know. It looked bad."

In my numb state, as we had ridden hard back to the rancho, I tried to tell myself that White Owl took Carlo to his people to heal him much as Lopa had carried me off to the mountains. But I knew it was possible that White Owl had taken Carlo so that his people could give him a proper send off, not a white man's funeral.

Don Diego shouted for his horse and his men. In a flurry of activity, he and six riders raced out the gates of the corral and toward the El Camino Real.

I doubted that it was still possible to catch the men who had disappeared after attacking us.

Lopa took Emma Rose and used her free arm to guide me to our bedroom. I crawled between the bed covers that smelled of my Carlo and allowed the sobs to break free. I cried until I had emptied the tears, and then cried some more.

Claudia came to my room carrying a steaming mug of brandy, lemon, and honey. "I'm so very sorry Clarissa. So sorry for the death of your father." She offered me the mug. "Drink this, if nothing else it eases the pain of crying too much."

I sipped the hot liquid, but I couldn't hold back the sobs long enough to drink it.

"Clarissa, White Owl will do everything possible to save Carlo," Claudia assured me. "Caring for Carlo is his duty and White Owl is a very wise man. And you know head wounds bleed a lot without being fatal."

I shook my head. "It looked bad," I sobbed.

Chapter 24

Doña Maria Elena came to my room. Black lace mantilla started on her head and covered her to her feet. Gone where the bright tiara head comb, scarlet sash, full fandango skirts, and contented smile that had lit her face since Father's return to California.

"My dear Clarissa, we must plan for your father's funeral."

I nodded, afraid to speak for fear the tears would start again.

"I have sent word to your brother, but of course, we can't wait for him to travel from England. Nor do we know if he is free to do so. The last letter your father received from him he said he had already assumed the duties of the Earl, of his grandfather who is too weak. I understand there is a very large rancho to be run?"

"The estate, in terms of acres, is smaller than this rancho, but in terms of people and buildings to be maintained, yes, it is a large responsibility. There are also political responsibilities in which I believe William has strong interest."

"I know that don Diego will want to honor your father, as will Chief Tenayakena so I will send word to them, but we must not wait past mañana."

I nodded. "Where is my father? Where is his body?"

"The casket is in the chapel."

Chapter 25

I said my goodbyes to my father.

I wanted to make him promises, but given the upheaval the discovery of gold had started in California, I didn't think I could promise to care for Rancho del Mar and its inhabitants.

The Americans had no respect for the Spanish land grants. Without Father's protection, without an American as head of the household . . . I was only a woman without property rights in much of the United States.

We buried Father the next day.

Neither don Diego nor Chief Tenayakena were present, but more than a hundred Californios and natives stood outside the tiny chapel while the priest prayed and eulogized my father.

For the first time, I understood the stability that my father's marriage had brought to the rancho. His strong work ethic had energized the people who took pride in their production of food and hides. The hides were traded for items the rancho did not produce and all had prospered under Father's management.

I glanced at Esteban. I didn't think he had it in him to take over, nor was that the plan. Before Father's death, plans had been set in motion for Esteban to travel to Spain, to Salamanca to study at the ancient university there.

I agreed it was best for Claudia and doña Maria Elena to accompany him.

Chapter 26

Two very long weeks went by with no word from don Diego. Long days, longer nights until Lopa's sleep potions would provide a few hours of relief from mourning. But in the next moment after waking, I would remember the men I had lost, the pain of grief would hit me anew.

Lopa, Emma Rose, and I watched a glorious pink, lavender, peach and golden sunset from the sand dunes. Lopa had urged me out of the house for walks with Emma Rose. She was learning to take steps, but in the sand, she needed to hold our hands for balance. Now she sat on my lap and pointed to the show of colors reflected in the ocean.

The sound of fast moving horses had Lopa and I jump in alert. Don Diego's horse crested the top of the dunes. I handed Emma Rose to Lopa and ran to meet him.

Don Diego jumped from his horse. "My lady, I do have news. Carlo does live."

My legs gave way; I slid to my knees on the cold sand.

"But he is very weak." Don Diego lifted me from the ground. "I did not come sooner because I wanted to bring you some news, and only a few days ago did we have any certainty that he might survive his wounds."

"Wounds? He had more than the head wound?" I asked.

"Yes, my dear."

"I must go to him. Will you please take me? Is he in the Valley?"

"Clarissa, he asked me to deliver a message. He wants you to go to William, to William's protection. California is not safe for you." He waved at my daughter. "Or, for Emma Rose."

I looked at my auburn haired, green-eyed daughter. "Because of her native blood? That's absurd. She's an American; so am I."

Don Diego shook his head at my suggestion that being Americans would protect us. "The idea of easy riches has brought bad men to our land. Once they learn how much hard work is required to get the gold, they try other means, criminal means to find wealth. You women on this land, in this prosperous hacienda, will be seen as easy targets for their greed," don Diego explained what I already knew.

"I can take care of myself." I had killed the men who had attacked and killed my father had I not?

Don Diego pointed at Emma Rose. "And your daughter?" He shook his head. "No Clarissa, we must face that you are not safe here. The security men your father hired are no longer available to us. I am to see you and doña Maria Elena and Claudia on to the ship that Esteban is sailing on."

I nodded. I had already decided that doña Maria Elena

and Claudia should accompany Esteban to Spain. But I wasn't going to leave my husband.

Don Diego took my hand in his. "I have a villa in Spain just south of Valencia, on a beach with a sea much gentler than this one. It was to be Carlo's one day. I give it to you now, to take your daughter to safety. Go to William, but when you grow tired of gray skies, go to Spain."

"Don Diego, I appreciate your generosity, but I will not leave my husband. I must go to him." I squeezed his hands. "Will you take me?"

He studied the sand at our feet. "I must not do that."

"Then Lopa and I will travel alone as we did once before."

"The world has changed. I cannot allow—"

I withdrew my hands from his. "Don Diego, I will go to my husband."

"The valley is no longer safe. The climb to where Carlo rests is too difficult. Emma Rose could not . . . Clarissa, please be sensible."

I turned to Lopa, tears streaming down my face. "Please Lopa, I must see him. What shall I do?"

"Come." Lopa took me in one arm, Emma Rose in the other and ushered us back to the hacienda.

Don Diego led his horse and his men behind us. He went directly to doña Maria Elena's rooms.

Lopa took us to ours. She placed Emma Rose in her crib and began to pack saddlebags.

"What will we do Lopa?" I asked.

"I know where are. Leave at dawn."

"And Emma Rose?"

"She must see her father." Lopa placed a knife in her belt, put my gun and my father's gun in holsters.

"Will we travel with just us three?" I knew I may not be thinking straight, but maybe a small group could slip into the valley safer than an armed contingent.

"Soon back." Lopa closed the door behind her and left for several minutes. When she returned she had with her the native who had carried my father's body back to the rancho.

"This Uwetaka, call 'im Taka. He strong, carry Rosa on back."

I nodded agreement to her plan. "Yes."

Chapter 27

I wore my English lady's riding jacket, split skirt, and hat. We dressed Taka and Lopa in Carlo's English clothes. Emma Rose rode on Taka's back in a basket Taka had spent the night fashioning.

We had not said farewell to anyone at the rancho, but had snuck out just before dawn, traveling light with just four horses, the extra horse to provide relief as our horses tired, and minimal water and food. And every weapon we could lay hands on during the long night.

Emma Rose slept in the carrier until late morning. Riding hard, we were already in the Pacheco pass leading to the valley by the time she awoke screaming for her breakfast.

We led our horses to the creek bed near where Lopa and I had camped on our first journey through this pass. We breakfasted without a fire, drank water from the creek, and remounted. We hoped to cross the valley without having to stop for the night.

Bright moonlight made passage through the tall grass possible as long as we avoided the trees. The howl of coyotes celebrating a successful kill kept us alert the first night.

The third day we finally reached the foothills of the Sierras where we made camp in a circle of oaks and rocks along a streambed. Even Emma Rose was tired enough that we were able to sleep through the dark night under the trees.

The climb to the higher caves above Yosemite Valley was treacherous. We had taken the horses to a high meadow plateau, and traveled on foot, hands and knees up the steep face. I didn't dare look down for fear the resulting vertigo would cause me to fall. I concentrated on my desire to see and talk to my husband and continued to put one hand above the other.

A rope appeared just above my head. I heard Chief Tenayakena's voice ordering men to assist us. "Put the rope around your waist, below your arms."

I did as ordered and soon received help pulling my body up the rock precipice. I was the last of us to reach the top of the cliff. Now I looked down at the valley below and realized we had just climbed the half dome that had always put me in mind of Lopa's face. Had I understood where we were to climb I believe I would have been frozen beyond my ability to move. I doubted I could ever do it again.

"Where is Carlo?" I asked before expressing my gratitude for the assistance getting up the rock face.

"Come." The chief led me through a rock wall into small cavern lit by sunlight streaming through a crack in the ceiling. Just beyond that area was a small niche. My husband, his head swathed in bandages and a leg raised in traction fashioned from a manzanita branch, lay asleep on a pile of skins.

"Oh," escaped from my mouth before I caught it.

I realized he was probably sedated with the same sleeping potion that Lopa had used to keep me still and resting while I recovered from my head wound.

I was quiet, but I did not control the flow of tears down my cheeks. I sat and watched him sleep until the light disappeared and I curled up nearby. I felt Lopa cover me with a fur, but otherwise I slept until the dawn brought light back to the room.

I sat up, gathered the fur around me against the dawn cold, and continued to watch.

Lopa brought me a hot herb tea and whispered that he knew I was there. He'd seen me when he'd been dosed with potion in the night.

"Is he angry?" I asked her.

"He not happy." Lopa smiled. "But he glad you safe."

I hoped that Emma Rose and my presence would aid his recovery, not hinder it. I still had hopes he would allow us to stay.

He groaned as he awoke, the sleeping potion having worn off.

"Clarissa," he whispered. "You are disobedient."

"Yes, my darling, I am." I smiled, restrained my desire to leap into his arms, brushed a soft kiss on his dimpled cheek.

"I owe you a spanking." He returned my smile.

96

"I'm looking forward to it."

Lopa entered the niche. "You must not make tired," she warned me as she spooned potion into Carlo's mouth.

"I need you . . . to sail with . . . doña Maria Elena." He held a finger against my mouth to still my protests. "You'll be . . . safer . . . traveling together . . . with Esteban."

"Esteban will be safer traveling with me, you mean," I said.

He started to chuckle but it obviously caused him pain. "That may be true . . . but then there's your tendency to get into trouble."

"Like spoiled rotten oysters trouble." We both smiled remembering what trouble resulted from that. Before we became lovers in Panama City, Carlo had to rescue me from ruffians at whom I had thrown tins filled with putrid oysters. Emma Rose was the result of the romantic interlude that followed the rescue.

"Exactly," Carlo whispered.

I kissed him again before Lopa led me out of the alcove.

In the lit cavern I saw my daughter with a rope tying her to the rock wall. I looked and remembered the steep rock face just outside the entrance to this room. I felt a maternal pain shoot through my body at the thought of the danger I had placed her in by bringing her to this place. They were all correct; this was no place for a toddler.

And it was obvious that it might be awhile before Carlo could be moved. How they had managed to get him to this place was unimaginable.

"Lopa, what is the matter with Carlo's chest?"

She explained but with her broken English it took awhile for me to understand that he had been shot in the chest in addition to the head wound—which fortunately had been more of a graze. He had also had sustained a compound fracture of his leg when he fell from his horse.

"Why here?"

"Valley not safe. Soldiers come."

I later learned that, in a horrifying example of man's heartbreaking inhumanity to his fellow man, the Governor of California had authorized the Mariposa Battalion to drive the indigenous people from the Yosemite Valley.

The Chief and a few warriors had managed to escape up the cliff. Most of the women and children had been cruelly herded out of their home. The men who had tried to protect the women and children had been shot and killed.

White Owl had eluded the soldiers to bring Carlo to his people and this hiding place, but he had since left the valley to search for his tribe to bring them to safety higher in the Sierra mountain range.

I understood why don Diego had carried the message that Rose and I were to leave California. If only he had explained. But I still would have insisted on seeing Carlo.

I wrestled with the question of what to do next. William would keep Emma Rose, Lopa and I safe, but what of Carlo? If we were to sail without him, it would be months, maybe more until he would join us.

And what if he were to get involved in the lop-sided battles between his peoples?

I knew he had planned to protect both his native cousins, as well as his Spanish, Californio, Scotch, French, and American family. How would he take sides? I knew he wouldn't run from this fight and thus knew I may never see him again.

And what of the child I now carried in my womb? Would my children ever really fit in anywhere but California? Would they long for the freedoms that California afforded her people? Where else would they feel the generous hospitality, love, and natural beauty that were abundant here?

I wanted to discuss all these questions with Carlo, but could I burden him with this?

"He awake," Lopa came to tell me.

I hurried to his side, knelt on the furs. "Carlo, I think I should go to San Francisco and wait for you there."

"Clarissa, it's not . . . safe place," he took a long but shallow breath. "The place has burned to the ground more than once . . . the elected officials, even the vigilantes are criminals." He grimaced as he raised his head to look me in the eye. "There will be no safe haven for you there."

"I think it is where Sam has gone, he would protect us," I tried to hold back the tears, catch a sob. "And I can protect us."

"My darling, go to William." He lowered his head to the fur pillow.

"I don't want to leave you." I took his hand. "And I want our son to be born in California."

Carlo smiled. "You are expecting?"

I nodded, smiled at my husband.

He groaned. "I can't believe . . . I can't even care for my family."

"You'll heal soon." I leaned over to place a kiss on his forehead. "Rest my darling."

Chapter 28

"Lopa, we'll go to San Francisco."

She looked at Emma Rose who was playing with a pile of stones. A rope tied her to Taka who sat next to her. Lopa nodded. "Go soon."

"When he wakes again, we must let him see Emma Rose."

"Chief Teniyakena give for you." Lopa handed me a bag containing coins and gold nuggets. "White man money."

"Where is the Chief?"

"He go." Lopa shrugged.

"Where?"

She waved her hand southeast and I understood he had gone to join the remnants of his tribe.

"Lopa, do you want to join your tribe?" I asked holding my breath for her answer.

Lopa looked at Emma Rose, then at me. "You my tribe."

"I know Carlo asked you to look out for me, I release you from your promise."

She studied my face, waved at Emma Rose. "You need me." She looked to the alcove where Carlo lay hopefully recovering from his nearly fatal wounds and nodded in his direction. "He my brother, you family."

I knew that Carlo was not literally Lopa's biological brother. They may have had some relative in common, but the truth was they were spiritually kin. And in someway I did not understand, just as White Owl felt responsible for Carlo's well-being, Lopa had devoted herself to Emma Rose, and to me.

I was uncomfortable with the idea that she had somehow become enslaved to me. Carlo had earlier admitted that he had asked her to "look after" me, but did that "looking after" have no end?

"Lopa, I very much appreciate all that you have done for me, for Emma Rose." I touched her hand. "I don't want to embarrass you, make you uncomfortable, but I want you to know that I love you and from now forward I want our relationship be as friends."

Lopa nodded. "We always friends." Her face lit up with a rare smile.

Chapter 29

The next morning Emma Rose pounded her father's face. "Papa," she burbled and then giggled, "Papa."

Carlo touched her face and said, "I love you kitten."

"Clarissa, if you insist on going to San Francisco," he sighed, closed his eyes. "I do have funds on account there." He rested for a few seconds before continuing. "Don Diego will help you . . . with papers."

"How will you find us?" I asked.

"Don Diego keeps offices in the city . . . Lopa knows."

"Will don Diego be okay?"

"Don't let his debonair charm . . . fool you." Carlo smiled. "He's tough under that suave refinement."

"I hate to leave you, but Emma Rose can't . . ."

"I know." He reached out, touched my hand, then my cheek. "Be careful."

Chapter 30

The next day dawned clear, bright, and bone chilling cold. Wrapped in furs with just her little face peeking out from the back carrier, Emma Rose giggled as we descended the face. I held my breath until we were all safely at the bottom where our horses waited on the plateau.

Moving quickly to avoid bandits and other trouble, Taka escorted us back to Rancho del Mar.

The hacienda was in packing chaos. Servants carried clothing to the courtyard filled with trunks, overflowing with gowns, furs, scarves, and shawls.

Doña Maria Elena greeted us with tears. "Will you travel with us Clarissa?"

I shook my head, hugged her. "We will wait for Carlo in San Francisco."

"Taka can go with you," she offered.

I shook my head again. "He should go to his tribe." I knew that Taka was gentle, caring, but he looked menacing, like a warrior. "I'm not sure he would be safe in San Francisco."

"Some of the natives will stay here with the foreman to run the rancho, but don Diego warns that our land granted by the King may not be honored by the Americans."

I waved at the activity in the courtyard.

"The trunks . . . you can't—" I remembered the trunks I had left behind on the Isthmus of Panama.

"We will sail around the horn to Spain. Come with us. You have many homes in Spain, and William would want you and Emma Rose to be near him."

"Thank you doña Maria Elena for everything," I leaned close to kiss her cheeks. "But we will pack our things and go to San Francisco."

PART THREE
Yerba Buena/San Francisco
May 1850

Chapter 31

Steep hills led to a harbor that held more abandoned ships than I could easily count. Most ships had been stripped of wooden parts that were used to build ramshackle buildings along the edge of the bay. Planks of wood had been placed between buildings over one enormous mud puddle.

It was no surprise that fire was a constant danger, but there were few remnants of burned out buildings to be seen. Presumably the remaining pieces of wood had been reused and the locations rebuilt. Saloons, gambling halls and brothels far outnumbered any other type of establishment.

Don Diego had insisted on escorting us three females to the city. He was no happier about my decision to remain in California than anyone else was, but he agreed that San Francisco might be the best place for us to wait for Carlo.

The man who had called for us at the rancho was not the Spanish grandee don Diego, but rather an American gentleman. Gone were his sombrero, serape, elaborate silver buckles and spurs. He wore a three-piece dark grey suit, cowboy hat and boots.

The carriage comfortably accommodated the driver and Susanna, Sara, Lopa, Emma Rose, and myself. An oxcart carrying the household goods that doña Maria Elena had ordered packed for our use followed the carriage. Don Diego and three of his ranch hands on horseback completed our procession that traveled past the opening to the now familiar Pacheco pass.

Half a day's travel north, we entered a vast forest of redwood trees whose branches reached far into the sky. The floor of the forest was carpeted with delicate leaves. As the wheels of the carriage crushed the leaves, a fresh, invigorating fragrance filled the air.

The girth of the trees was such that in some trunk bases rooms large enough to sleep our entire party had been hollowed out by fire yet the same trees still flourished far above our heads.

Don Diego's offices were not along the edge of the bay, but sat on a hillside plateau overlooking the gateway between the sea and the bay. The two-story building had offices on the first floor, a residence on the second. The balcony that ran the length of the second floor offered seating and a telescope from which to watch the activity of ships in the bay, horses and men in the city below.

While Emma Rose napped, Lopa, Susanna, Sara, and I wrapped ourselves in heavy shawls against the cool wind and relaxed in rocking chairs on the balcony. Don Diego's building sat on the edge of the sunbelt not far from the Mission Dolores. A heavy mass of dark grey fog covered the hills behind his property. Winds off the water and the fog kept the building cool but the east-facing balcony captured some warmth from the sun.

"Lopa, look, that wagon and horses are being swallowed in mud." I used the telescope to get a better look. The horses frantically tried to swim free of the heavy mud, but the weight of the mud added to the weight of the barrels filling the wagon pulled them down into the muck.

"Oh, please, someone save those poor animals! Lopa, what can we do?" My heart pounded as I watched men work to release the horses from the wagon. The rescuers had tied themselves to buildings to avoid being sucked into the mire, but they were losing the battle to save the horses. In fact, it looked as though some men were more concerned about the barrels. I couldn't watch anymore. What kind of men were these? I sat back down in my rocker and dried my tears with the handkerchief Lopa pulled out of her sleeve.

Don Diego cleared his throat to announce his presence in the doorway to the balcony.

"Oh, don Diego, I just witnessed the most horrible incident. A wagon and two horses were sucked into the mud. And it looked as though the men were more interested in saving the barrels than the horses."

Don Diego pulled a chair up to where we sat. "Dear Clarissa, as you have seen horses are plentiful in California. The barrels were most likely filled with whiskey, a very valuable commodity here in Yerba Buena. Forgive me, I forget to use the new name, here in San Francisco."

"I don't understand. Whiskey rather than helpless

animals? What heartless men."

Don Diego noticeably suppressed his smile at my naiveté. "My dear, there are many bad men that have come to our peaceful paradise looking to get rich easily and quickly. You must keep your distance from that part of town."

"But where are the shops?" I asked.

"You'll find everything you need between here and the Mission. Once a week, local farmers bring their produce to the mission grounds to sell. That market is growing larger every week. Now craftsmen also bring handmade goods— pottery, shawls, even flowers can be purchased there. And the chapel is convenient from here. You'll have no need to join the riffraff down by the water."

"Is that quicksand down there?" I pointed to the area below us.

Don Diego shook his head. "I understand that hundreds of ships abandoned by crews, by sailors that were lured by the gold fields, were at first shoved onto the beach and used for hotels, a jail, warehouses, stores and saloons. Many of the ships were scavenged for wood that had already been made into boards to be used in building those shacks you see below. Most of the abandoned ships were left to rot. And some were sunk intentionally to fill in the bay around the abandoned ships which resulted in the unstable land and mud."

I smiled at this gentle man. "We can't keep you from your home here. We are taking up all the rooms on this floor what with all the trunks that doña Maria Elena sent and the five of us women."

"Please do not be concerned. My men and I are comfortable enough in the backrooms downstairs. But I would like to begin building a home for you. We should pick out a safe spot near here. I recommend an adobe style, rather than the wood buildings such as the newcomers are building down there." He waved at the mess at the water's edge.

"There have been many fires that have wiped out large sections of that settlement." Don Diego shook his head and sighed. "Wood frame buildings move with the earthquakes that do shake the ground here periodically, but they burn easily. Brick does not burn, but brick buildings do not fare well in earthquakes. Our mud adobes with tile roofs seem to move fairly well with the shaking and, of course, do not burn."

"I love the adobes and tiles. And this balcony is heavenly."

"Your house shall have a balcony," don Diego proclaimed.

I nodded.

"And a walled garden." he added.

"Oh yes please, for Emma Rose to play in." I clapped with joy.

"And high walls will encircle the entire property for security," he said. "Tomorrow we will find the right spot between here and the Mission."

Chapter 32

True to his promise, the next morning don Diego took me on a tour of the area surrounding the Mission Dolores de San Francisco. Below the Mission, Dolores creek wound through land that sloped to the bay providing irrigation for orchards and fields of vegetables. The gentle hills immediately adjacent to the Mission were backed by larger, steeper hills that protected the area from the fog and winds off the ocean.

"Our little Yerba Buena has grown into a city nearly overnight." Don Diego took my arm as we strolled through the market. "And now we must remember to call her by her new name, San Francisco."

We wandered the area until we located a plot of land with a gentle slope and a small tributary of the creek. Below I could see a large portion of the southern bay, a peek of the larger bay, and only the more respectable parts of the fast spreading city.

"My men will grade a portion of this land to site the house and sitting garden. A low wall will surround the sitting garden but we must have a tall wall protecting the property edges." Don Diego waved his arm to indicate that location. "Although this is a warmer, sunnier portion of the hills, you will need a fireplace in every room. Is our traditional room layout suitable for your needs?"

"May I provide a sketch of the rooms?" I smiled at don Diego. "And how do I pay for this?"

"I'll arrange with proper authorities a deed for the land which will likely be better held by an American. Our Spanish land grants are no longer held valid without substantial legal investment." He returned my smile with a touch of sadness, then shook it off.

"I want to compensate the current owner." I said.

Don Diego smiled. "Of course, and that will be appreciated. And Carlo, uh, Charles has instructed me as to which of his funds are to be used to build your home. Which reminds me," he drew a small pouch from his waistcoat. "You'll need spending money. My housekeeper will introduce you to furniture makers and importers of furnishings." He pressed the pouch into my hand.

He bent his hand at the wrist to point at the bay below. "Ships of the importers are forced to wait their turn often for many days to unload their goods, and those goods are quickly bought up. Not only are goods scarce in the fast growing city, but also the many fires have repetitively destroyed carpets, curtains and such. You'll need connections to obtain quality goods."

Don Diego escorted me back to the second floor of his offices.

Sara and Susanna practiced reading aloud to each other

in soft voices while Emma Rose and Lopa napped in the quiet afternoon. The quiet house felt empty without Emma Rose's sweet voice filling the air. An aching longing for Carlo haunted me at these quiet moments.

I tiptoed to the balcony. This building being closer to the newer portion of the city, the view from the balcony showed the wharves, the line of ships waiting to dock, the chaos of the mud streets, and men the size of ants moving from building to building on wood planks.

I used the telescope with some trepidation as to what I might see, but I still hoped to one day catch sight of the frizzy grey head and beard of my dear friend Sam. Scruffy headed, bearded men were visible below through the telescope, but unlike the gold field's populations, the majority were freshly barbered with beards neatly trimmed or reduced to moustaches and hair barely visible beneath their hats. Faces of moving men were hard to catch in the lens. I concentrated on the looking at the manner of walking hoping to recognize Sam's gait. I wasted the quiet afternoon with no luck, but tomorrow I would try a different time of day.

Chapter 33

As I knew I was not to have access to the main part of town and once our new home was complete, I would no longer have a view of the area populated by most of the miners, I spent a portion of each day searching the telescope for my friend Sam.

As my desire to locate my friend had already brought disaster to my family, I kept my activity secret from all but Lopa.

I had varied the time of day using all daylight hours but soon began to concentrate my efforts during the early morning hours, as I knew Sam to be an early riser.

On a beautiful May morning, I enjoyed the sunrise over the east bay while I sipped my coffee and began my search of the city. Emma Rose slept until later most mornings with Lopa hovered nearby her. Those mornings provided quiet in which to concentrate on the method I had devised to ensure I thoroughly covered the area.

On several occasions I believed I had spotted my friend's gait only to be disappointed when I managed to train the scope on the subject's face. On this morning I once again saw a man who walked like Sam. With trembling hands, I worked to focus on his face.

"By all that is holy, I think that's him, that's Sam," I exclaimed.

I rushed to change from my morning robes into an ensemble appropriate for the city. Pinning a hat in place, pulling on my gloves, I schemed as to how to travel to the area without upsetting don Diego.

The landau we used on outings with don Diego required a driver so that was out. A small carriage that I could drive was kept in the nearby stables, but remembering the horrifying scene of the horses and the wagon in the mud, eliminated that idea. I would simply ride my favorite mount sidesaddle as I had always ridden prior to becoming a Californian. I pulled off dainty slippers in favor of riding boots.

"Lopa, I'm heading off for a ride on this beautiful morning," I whispered into the room where she sat watch over sleeping Emma Rose.

Lopa raised a suspicious eyebrow at me, shook her head.

"Okay." I couldn't lie to Lopa. It was pointless because she always seemed to know the truth anyway. "I think I saw Sam."

She nodded; a faint smile traveled her face.

I ran to the stables, located an English style saddle and was attempting to attach it to my horse when the stable boy gently brushed me aside and expertly saddled the animal. He walked us to the mounting block and helped me aboard.

He lifted his sombrero, "Buenos dias, Señora."

I hoped this sweet young man would not be punished for aiding me. I pulled a coin from my pouch, handed it to him but he waved my hand away

"No gracias, Señora, no necesario." He smiled, flourished his hat in a deep bow.

Vowing to see to it that no disfavor fell on this young man, I urged my horse down the dusty trail. I rode through the Yerba Buena herbs that once covered all the hillsides of a sleepy mission settlement and into the madness of a city born of avarice.

Chapter 34

Where to leave my horse in the chaos? The wobbly planks of wood lay on top of mud looked much too precarious to even walk him along. I led him back to a blacksmith's livery stables on the edge of a plaza above the muddy area.

This man readily accepted my offered coin.

"He doesn't need feed, but water him please. I should not be more than an hour or so," I said in my lack of foresight.

I tread cautiously along the planks grateful for the last-minute change to boots from my dainty slippers. Mud oozed on all the board edges and in the cracks. I saw no other women, and even men were scarce in this early morning hour.

Nearly every establishment on this main avenue appeared to be a saloon with raucous sounds of music, laughter, and shouts broadcasting through the doorways of all despite the hour. Drunks teetered out of the entrances, leered and even grabbed at me.

Boarding houses and public baths lined the side streets.

A large canvas tent that served as a church was empty but the window of the brothel next door was already occupied by a scantily clad woman offering her services. I blushed at the sight and hurried along nearly missing the next plank in my haste.

I watched my feet for several steps. When I looked up again, I saw a newly built saloon and gambling house pretentiously identified by a bold sign as the United States Exchange.

I peeked in the window seeking Sam's frizzy gray hair. Several gray-haired men were to be seen so I ventured in the grand double door entrance. The smell of freshly sawn wood still filled the air despite the added fragrance of whiskey and tobacco smoke. The music provided by a player piano was barely audible above the din of men's voices.

I was no more than three feet inside the door when the sound of the piano was plainly heard as the voices were suddenly quiet.

One man called out, "Ha-a-l-loo young lady." Similar catcalls echoed from all parts of the room.

Panic raced through my body. What had I done?

Chapter 35

I remembered the days spent in the gold fields and held my head high giving these men my most arrogant, aristocratic glare.

But these were not the innocents of my previous experience. These ruffians were drunks, crooks, gamblers, and disappointed miners. My act did nothing to discourage their advances.

I began to fear for the safety of my unborn child. Perhaps if my condition had been more apparent . . . but I doubted that even that would stop these degraded men. If only I had thought to carry a pistol in my reticule. I held back tears as one man grabbed my arm; another reached out to squeeze my breast.

The arm grabber swung at the breast squeezer.

Momentarily I was freed of their unwanted attentions as they brawled on the sawdust floor, but from behind me an arm around my waist lifted me off the floor.

The sharp report of a gunshot followed by a second one caused most of the men to duck under tables or throw themselves to the floor.

A young man I did not immediately recognize, as he was now clean shaven as he had not been when I last saw him in Clementine, walked towards me and addressed the man who still held me aloft from behind my back. "Sir, kindly unhand the Lady Clarissa Wells," he shouted loud enough for even our ears shocked by gunfire to hear. "Lady Clarissa Wells," he repeated and punctuated the statement with another gunshot fired into the ceiling.

The arm that had held me dropped me onto the floor and swung at the young man.

More gunshots rang out. More fisticuffs turned the gambling hall into an enormous brawl.

I scurried on all fours out the door as punches were being exchanged above me.

Chapter 36

Once outside, I stood, smoothed my clothing, brushing off sawdust and stumbled away from the entrance.

At the corner of the building, I stopped at the intersection of Kearny and Clay trying to recall the direction of the plaza near the livery stable. Montgomery, Washington, if only I'd paid more attention. Was the square on Washington Street?

I shook my head as though to clear my thoughts, to shake off my confusion.

My hands were trembling. To calm myself, I forced a deep breath.

My lungs were filled with smoke, my ears with the crackling of a fire.

I looked up.

The roof of the United States Exchange was on fire, flames reaching high into the sky.

Sparks flew in all directions. Adjoining roofs soon burst into infernos.

Smoke pricked my eyes like needles.

Men fleeing flames pushed past me.

Shouts of frightened people and the crash of falling timbers replaced the sound of music, laughter and pugilists.

Showers of burning splinters fell onto the wood planked walkways and ignited hundreds of hot spots leaving a choice between being burned or sucked into mud.

I lifted my skirts, ran down a side street, ducked into an alcove to avoid being trampled by maddened horses released from burning livery stables. I watched as the herd plunged down the street but failed to spot my horse among them.

I ran in the direction the horses had come from and, with relief, found myself in the plaza near the stables.

My relief was short lived. As I watched in horror, the fire jumped the plaza and continued to ignite building after building.

In surrounding burning structures, countless firearms discharged from exposure to the intense heat.

Screams of burned and injured convinced me to give up my plan of locating the stable where I had left my horse. I ran.

I ran up the street in hopes of out running the flames that jumped from wood building to wood building as though igniting a pile of matches.

Buildings would be farther apart if I could escape the flat fill land, I reasoned. I took an upslope turn; tore off my burning jacket and then my hat as I raced toward what I hoped was open land.

Several misturns and dead-ends later, I stopped to wrap my scorched face with cloth torn from my petticoats.

I tried to see a directional clue in the sky but smoke obscured the sun. Winds off the ocean were lost in smoky swirls fed by and feeding the fire.

The cloth over my mouth and nostrils failed to stop suffocating smoke. A vast sheet of flame covered the burning district most of which was behind me. Forced by the wall of flames and the thunder of falling ruins, blinded by gray smoke and sparks, I rushed up what I prayed was a hill above the fire.

An eternity later, I emerged from the storm of smoke and flame onto a hillside populated by other escapees. Men carried wounded shot by the heat discharged firearms, aided burn victims to climb the steep slope, and dragged bodies out of the flames.

The position of the sun told me it was noon. Less than four hours had passed since I had left my horse at the stables.

I forced myself to climb higher until I could breathe clean ocean breezes and look down on the ruins of more than three hundred burnt out buildings.

I collapsed in a heap.

Chapter 37

A cool, damp cloth wiped my face. Water dribbled onto my lips. I sucked the moisture.

Lopa pulled me to sitting and poured water into my mouth.

Cool fog streamed over the hills behind us. Below were blackened, smoldering ruins.

"Emma Rose?" I muttered.

"Rosa good. Don Diego's Juanita have Rosa."

"Casa?"

"Good." Lopa reached out to support me. "We go home."

I leaned on her, stumbled back to don Diego's building.

A cool tub of water soaked away some of the black soot.

Lopa bathed my singed hair and body. She rubbed her magic unguent onto my burned limbs, neck and face.

Before I slept, I made her a promise. Knowing that my foolishness had caused yet another disaster, I swore I would give up looking for Sam. If fate brought us together again, so be it. I would give up endangering my family for a purpose born as much out of boredom as friendship. And now I had, by my actions, started a disastrous fire.

Chapter 38

One week after the "Second Great Fire," as the disaster was called, another danger of this beautiful bay shook us from sleep two days in a row.

I had felt the ground shake at Rancho del Mar but that rolling motion hardly compared to the sharp jolt that threw us from our beds and china from shelves.

At the first occurrence, Emma Rose screamed in terror as the adobe bounced and the rumble roared. That night she still clung to me so she and I shared a bed with Lopa on her skins on the floor of the bedchamber.

I held her tight against me when the rumbling sound warned me again the next morning. This motion was a slightly gentler, but still a terrifying jolt.

Don Diego's words as to the mud adobes faring better in both fire and earthquake rang true as we surveyed the damage to wood and brick structures. Fires started by the shock were quickly extinguished, but brick buildings lay in heaps and some wood structures had leapt from their foundations. The mud adobe we occupied had new cracks that were quickly repaired by workmen smoothing new mud over the thick walls.

Grateful for don Diego's good advice, I went to thank him carrying my still clinging daughter with me. I knocked on the thick wood door of his study.

"Clarissa, dear child, I hope our Mother Earth's attempts to throw us off have not shaken your resolve to live on this beautiful site." He took Emma Rose from my arms.

She wrapped her tiny arms around his neck. "Pa, Pa," she said in her sweet voice. Don Diego was a fine stand-in grandfather.

"Shall we see how your new home has survived?" he asked me.

"Yes, please," I said.

The three of us walked to the property we had registered with the town council as belonging to me, and to my husband, Charles Anthony, as Carlo would be known in San Francisco.

One section near the creek had been dedicated to the making of mud blocks. A stock of blocks lay in the sun drying. Nearby men shaped clay over their thighs making curved tiles for the roof.

Workmen had framed the U-shaped building with heavy wood timbers, which would later be covered by mud. Fireplaces built with smooth river rock were being assembled in each room and even in the courtyard in anticipation of cool foggy mornings and evenings. The kitchen was to be included in the main house, as I had no plans for a separate outbuilding.

There was no sign of damage from the two

earthquakes.

"Don Diego, I already love my new home and I am grateful for not only your sage advice to build an adobe, but also for the builders and your supervision."

"It is my pleasure."

"I don't understand why the Americans insist on building wood and brick structures when the mud adobes are demonstrably better at surviving in this location. Don't they see the Mission Dolores that has survived nearly a hundred years of shaking and burning?"

"I believe they see our adobes as primitive mud huts and their wooden and brick houses as modern," don Diego said.

"But the thick walls keep heat in when it is cold outside, heat out when it is hot outside. The heavy timbers do not easily catch fire, and the tile roofs simply shed flying embers. And the mud seems to shake with its mother earth. Plus, you have the sense not to build on unstable ground, but on earth that sits on bedrock." I shook my head at my fellow American's foolishness.

"Speaking of American's, I've been concerned about something don Diego. Are your properties granted by the Spanish King secure?"

Don Diego smiled. "I appreciate your concern, but please know that Carlo and I transferred all of our family's properties to Charles Robles Antione in 1847. Carlo's great grandfather was a Frenchman who swore away his allegiance to the French King in 1779 to become an American citizen."

"Have you any word as to Carlo's recovery?" I held my breath waiting for an answer.

"I'm sorry my dear. I have not received any messages." Don Diego took my hand, placed it on his arm. "But Carlo was healing. Do not fret."

"Are they still in Yosemite?" I asked.

Don Diego hesitated, looked away from my eyes. "I doubt they would be."

Chapter 39

Our new home was beginning to look like a building. The walls were in place and being whitewashed while curved tiles were being layered onto the roof. The low wall of Emma Rose's garden was in place although the gate had yet to be installed.

Lopa and I worked the soil at the base of the wall while Emma Rose played in the freshly scythed grass. Doña Maria Elena had given us seeds for a variety of plants. The vegetables—peas, beans, lentils, onions, carrots, red peppers, corn, potatoes, squashes, cucumbers and melons, Susanna and Sara planted in the kitchen garden, but flowers would decorate this entrance garden.

Lopa had tended several cuttings from Castilian Roses, a pink and very fragrant sort from Mexico. What had been pieces of stems stuck in terra-cotta pots had leafed out. The roses would flank the gate. The hollyhocks would be against the wall, the sweet peas on the wall with the pinks and nasturtiums on the ground. The bulbs of the white lilies would be planted in pots in the courtyard where the deer could not get to them.

A carreta, an ox-cart with solid wooden wheels,

arrived carrying a handsome table made from long, thick planks of redwood. This first piece of furniture was so heavy it took four men to place it in the center of the courtyard. Picturing the family gatherings with my loved ones seated at the twenty-foot long table triggered the familiar heartache for Carlo.

I was surprised again that my longing for him was not strictly felt in my heart.

I knelt and attacked the soil with renewed vigor.

"Ma, Ma, Ma, Ma," Emma Rose chanted as she often did when I was near.

"Mama's busy, Emma Rose," I answered.

"Lo, Lo, Lo." Her voice was louder. "Lo, Lo. Ma, Ma, Ma."

Lopa rushed to Emma Rose's side, picked her up. Turned to me. "We go inside," she said quietly.

"What? Okay, you two go inside, but stay away from where the men are working on the roof." I forced my shovel into the dirt, pulled a large rock free.

"You come."

I turned to look at Lopa and Emma Rose.

Lopa nodded towards something behind me. "Move slow," she said.

I turned to see what she nodded at and froze.

An enormous grizzly watched the three of us from less than twenty feet away. Even with all four paws on the ground he was taller than the garden wall.

"Will he come after us?" My voice squeaked.

"You no run."

"I understand, but maybe you and Emma Rose should go first," I whispered without looking away from the giant animal.

"You no move."

"There is a rifle near the table in the courtyard."

"No rifle."

This was no time to debate Lopa's usual reluctance to kill any creature.

"Rifle no kill. Bear big."

I understood, shooting a rifle at this creature would be like trying to bring down a lion with a stick. It would only serve to anger him.

I heard the sound of fast moving horses coming toward us. Were they chasing the grizzly?

I remembered the bear that had been entered in a fight by young gauchos at Rancho del Mar but this bear was easily twice the size of any we had seen previously. Even bigger than those in Yosemite.

"Lopa, walk into the house." I was worried that either the men on the roof or those moving toward us would startle the bear, frightening him into moving towards us.

The grizzly raised his front paws and stood to his full height.

I stood tall, glared at the animal. Even as frightened as I was, I had to admire this magnificent animal.

The horses were moving slower. Perhaps they had spotted the animal. I was afraid to look away from the bear to see where the horses were.

From out of my line of sight, flew first one then

several lariats lassoing the giant and pulling him to the ground.

"Don't hurt him!" I shouted turning to look at the riders.

The familiar laugh from a long-haired, bearded man had me running toward the riders.

"Carlo!" I ran to his arms as he slipped from his saddle.

Chapter 40

"It's estimated that bear weighs five hundred pounds." Carlo informed me from where he soaked in the tub of warm soapy water. He chuckled at recalling me standing off the five-hundred-pound monster.

"Clarissa, my darling, I must say, the day I saw you on that dock in New York, fussing because your skirts might be soiled by the muck," Carlo laughed, "I never would have foreseen that prissy, delicate lady climbing half dome, threatening a grizzly bear, riding the width of California— all the brave, but foolhardy things you have done since you became a Californian."

He reached his arms out to me, "Come here my sweet."

I leaned toward him.

He wrapped wet arms around my waist and pulled me close. His mouth sought mine.

Without concern for wetting my garments, I fell onto him. But my petticoats were so cumbersome once they were wet, I couldn't manage their weight. I struggled to get them off.

"Relax, I can help you." Carlo stood and pulled me up to standing. He loosened my skirts and let them fall into the tub. He pulled my blouse over my head and we embraced.

Carlo slipped one arm under my bottom and the other around my waist. He stepped from the tub and carried me to our bed.

He stood naked and looked down at me. "In New York, I thought you were the most ethereally beautiful thing I had ever seen. But now you are even more beautiful than you were that day on the dock. That young lady was a child. Now you are a woman."

He ran his hand down my shoulder, caressed each breast and continued to my hip. "A voluptuous woman. And I couldn't love you more." His hand rested on my rounded belly. "When is our child expected?"

"I'm not sure. I have yet to consult a doctor but Lopa knows."

"Yes, I'm sure she does." He lay down next to me and pulled me toward him. Gentle kisses soon turned to passionate crushes of lips and tongues.

By the time he entered me, I was arching with need to feel him. But after two thrusts, he withdrew.

"What are you doing?" I moaned.

"It's been too long." He smiled into my eyes as he held his body above mine. "My body is too pent up to pleasure you." He rolled next to me, slipped one hand below my bottom and the other on top of my private parts. Fingers from the bottom hand slid inside while the other hand caressed until my body shuddered with waves of bliss.

"Now?" I asked.

He smiled and placed his legs straddling my hips. "Yes, now." He groaned as he slid his organ into mine.

Chapter 41

In the month since Carlo had joined us in San Francisco, he had supervised the completion of our new home making several improvements to my plans along the way.

He had added a fountain opposite the fireplace in the courtyard, windows overlooking the bay in the sitting rooms, shelving to his library and procured books to fill those shelves.

He had aggressively traveled to the ships in the harbor waiting to unload their goods thereby obtaining intricately patterned, hand knotted silk rugs; French Havilland china; a silver tea service; fine fabrics for upholstery; and even silk for my new ball gown.

Carlo looked at my décolleté, raised an eyebrow. "Dresses cut that low are really acceptable? Are you sure? This is a grand ball for sixty of the most respectable ladies in the city we are attending tonight." "Have you seen dresses like that anywhere but on Maiden Lane?"

"I have yet to spend time on Maiden Lane," I teased. "But yes, I have, at the dressmakers, several of the ladies planning to attend tonight were having dresses sewn with the same décolletage as my ball gown."

"How many of them fill out that "décolletage" like you do?" He grinned.

It was true, the décolletage of my ball gown bared more than my neck and shoulders. My pregnant décolleté also consisted of swollen breasts visible to just above my nipples.

"I thought you like my breasts like this."

He leered at my chest. "That I do, the changes in your body when pregnant make me feel like I'm getting two women in one wife. A slender one, a voluptuous one." He raised both eyebrows, grinned at me. "But I don't like the idea of sharing the sight of my wife's breasts with other men." Carlo frowned.

"There won't be many occasions for a dress like this so you needn't be overly concerned. I believe this is only the second ball in this city," I said.

"And from what I understand, this is the first ball to which gentlemen would take their wives. Do you have a wrap? Can't take you out into the cold summer night half naked."

I handed him my matching silk cape and Carlo wrapped it around my shoulders stopping to kiss my neck before turning me around to fasten the tie.

The July nights were surprisingly cold. Summer had proved to be a lot foggier than spring. And where we were headed to the St. Francis Hotel on Dupont Street would be even cooler than the Mission as our neighborhood was known.

The driver had pulled the landau up to our front gate. Carlo lifted me aboard.

We passed through an area of dark, lit only by the moon. Carlo took advantage of the privacy afforded by the dark to sneak his hand under my cape, reaching into my gown to tease my nipples with his fingertips.

"Careful," I whispered. "You don't want to expose everything, do you?"

"No worries, I'll take care of that." Carlo pulled the front of my dress up and lifted my skirt. His fingers found the bare skin above my stockings, stroking my inner thigh.

I squirmed, worried where his fingers might go next. "Darling, I don't want to arrive at my first ball disheveled."

"Your first?" Carlo moved his hand down my leg. "Surely you attended balls in New York."

"My first grown up ball."

"Oh yes, you are grown up." He chuckled. "And out." He removed his hand from under my skirt, smoothed my gown, and adjusted my décolletage as we drew close to Dupont and Clay Street.

Carlo lifted me from the landau and completed the job of making sure I was put back together. He bowed before offering his arm. "My lady."

A liveried doorman opened the wide entrance and pointed the way to the ladies' cloakroom.

I greeted the women I knew from my fittings at the dressmakers.

"Isn't it wonderful to have this grand hotel?" Mrs.

Martin gushed. "Now we will have a proper tea room for our ladies' outings."

"If it doesn't burn down before we can organize such an outing," commented Mrs. Stewart.

Smiling, I nodded agreement to that sentiment. I stood before the mirror and checked that my dress revealed no more than planned, tucked loose strands back into my upswept hairdo.

Chattering voices behind me caught my attention when I heard the word "Zorro." The Spanish word for fox? I was surprised to hear anyone speaking Spanish in this group.

I pretended to examine my face, looked into the mirror at the women behind me to see who was speaking.

"My husband says that the masked men are not common criminals, but caballeros, Spanish gentlemen," said a woman I did not know.

"The masked man who saved my daughter and I from Black Bart did not have a Spanish accent," said an elderly woman resting on the divan. "But he was definitely a gentleman. My daughter was quite taken with him, a fine figure of a man."

"Oh pshaw, gentlemen do not wear masks on the street. A common ruffian like so many of the men who have arrived here recently."

"My maid says that the Spanish Fox is a legend, a man that never dies, that he has been protecting the poor for fifty years," said another lady. "Quite the romantic figure, well thought of by the natives."

"My maid says he is a native, an Indian."

"My French maid insists he is French, he spoke to her with a Parisian accent."

Obviously, my husband had been busy with more than buying furniture. Was he acquainted with every young woman, every maid in the city? My anger was quickly replaced by fear for him. He had a family now; responsibilities. What was he thinking?

Carlo awaited me in the line for the grand march, which had formed on the wide staircase leading to the second-floor ballroom. "Smile my dear," he ordered, "and remember to call me Charles should you introduce me to your lady friends."

"Mister and Missus Charles Anthony." The ball master announced as we joined the procession around the edge of the dance floor. Once all one hundred and twenty couples had been introduced and seen by all in the promenade, the orchestra played a waltz.

"You do look exceptionally lovely tonight my darling, but I can't wait to get you home and out of that dress," Carlo whispered in my ear as we glided across the ballroom floor. "Care to join me on the balcony for a preview? Perhaps a glass of champagne?"

"Don't you like to dance?" I asked.

"I find it difficult holding you like this without . . ."

He held me closer than correct for the waltz. Even through the many layers of my ball gown skirt, I felt the stiffness. Surely, he could not have the energy for attending other women with the same attentiveness he had shown me in recent weeks.

"Let's have the champagne." I smiled into his eyes.

Chapter 42

Carlo ran his hand over my ever-expanding belly and planted a kiss where he hoped the baby's head was located. "No more lovemaking my darling," he said to me.

I groaned my disappointment collapsing back onto the pile of down pillows.

"I don't think there's room for me in there anymore my sweet." His lips brushed my mouth with a sweet caress.

I wrapped my hands through his black hair and pulled his mouth tighter to mine. My tongue darted into his mouth; my hands ran down his back to his bottom eliciting a groan from him.

He pulled away; lay back on the pillows next to me.

I turned on my side, slid down the featherbed and took him in my mouth.

"My God, Clarissa what are you doing?"

I looked up from my task to see that his grin belied his words. He may have been shocked but he wasn't unhappy. My lips and my hand stroked until his face contorted, his back arched with spasms of pleasure, his seed spilled into my mouth, onto his belly. His arms pulled me so my head rested on his chest.

Several minutes went by before he spoke. "I'm not going to ask how you learned to do that."

I looked at his face to see if he was still shocked and saw his smile lit his green eyes and exposed his dimples.

"In the never-ending list of surprises you provide, that might have been one of the best." He murmured against my lips as his hands found my pregnant breasts. The child in my belly did not dissuade my body from yearning with desire. The ache between my legs had me squirming with need.

Thankfully, Carlo's hands slid along my thighs to my knees and spread my legs open to his touch. His hands traveled to my sex.

With a delicate touch his thumb found the spot that sent a jolt of sensation through my body. Gently, gradually his thumb increased the pressure of the circles that built waves of pleasure tingling from my head to my toes. My back arched as my body strained for release of the building tension.

His fingers stroking inside, fingers rubbing outside soon brought relief as tiny explosions of pleasure flowed through my body. I collapsed into my husband's arms and enjoyed the quiet moments before the household awoke.

The patter of small feet outside the thick wood door of our boudoir jolted Carlo into action. He reached for the white duvet at the end of the bed and pulled it over our bodies.

Our daughter Emma Rose flung open the door, ran into

the room and pounced on the bed. "Mama, Poppy." She squealed as she jumped on her father. "See Poppy, I careful Mama's tummy." She wiggled between our bodies. "When baby come?" she asked.

"Soon." I hoped. The swollen feet, the pull on my back and the waddle that was my walk were all growing wearisome. I brushed back auburn hair and kissed my daughter's cheek. "I think I hear Lopa calling you."

Emma Rose slipped her little arms around my neck and returned my kiss before she slid from the bed and ran out the door she had left ajar. "My baby come soon," she squealed to Lopa.

I reached for the robe on the settee and wrapped it around my cumbersome body.

Carlo pulled on trousers and opened the shutters at our window overlooking the garden. Welcome sunlight flooded the room. "A beautiful day, perhaps we should take Emma Rose on a picnic in the redwood grove. Are you up to that my darling?"

The last few days had found me in the throes of "nesting," a symptom I recognized from my previous pregnancy as an indication that my body was ready to expel this child. A review of the nursery and the entire estate yesterday had assured me that all was ready to greet our new baby.

Carlo had completed construction on our two-story adobe two months earlier and together we had furnished each room and the garden patios.

Carlo had rowed out to ships in the harbor that were

awaiting their turn to dock, so that he had first choice of goods arriving from around the world. Our wood floors were carpeted with silk and wool rugs from the Orient. Our windows draped with Italian silk. Our walls decorated with oil paintings from Europe. Our library shelves filled with books from everywhere.

He had directed local craftsmen in the making of tables, four-poster beds, armoires, chairs of all kinds, and cradles. One cradle resided in our bedroom, another in the sitting room, and the largest in the nursery.

The nursery was painted a soft butter yellow to brighten the room against the typical San Francisco fog. Susanna, Sara and I had sewn baby clothes that were now washed and neatly folded in the dresser. Two rocking chairs, a daybed, and a low dresser topped with a changing pad, and a crib filled with stuffed animals awaited the arrival.

The gardens too had flourished under Carlo's direction. The courtyard was now filled with hanging pots over-flowing with blossoms. A spectacular display of color and green bordered the patio of the walled pleasure garden.

I sighed with satisfaction and dressed to spend the day with my husband and daughter.

Chapter 43

From my resting place on the floor of the redwood grove, I watched Emma Rose and Carlo play hide and seek as he pretended not to see her dart from one massive trunk to another.

Her shrieks of delight and giggles alone would have made her easy to follow.

In my womb, my other child flipped somersaults as though anxious to escape and join the fun. He, or she, had been very active for weeks, kicking and tumbling much more than his sister had.

The dense cover of delicate, golden brown leaves beneath our quilt provided a soft bed. I took a deep breath enjoying the fresh scent of the forest, snuggled into the pillows, and dozed off to the pleasant sounds of giggles, breezes in the trees and the gurgling creek.

Cold air, damp fog, and strong winds disturbed my sleep. When I opened my eyes, I was surprised at how dark it had grown. I did not see or hear my husband and daughter. Panicked, I jumped to my feet and was hit by a wave of dizziness. I reached out to the closest tree trunk for support until my head cleared.

"Carlo? Charles?" I called. "Where are you?"

Wind rushed through the trees. No one answered.

"Emma Rose? Carlo," I yelled.

The grove of trees no longer seemed pleasant. The wind, the wisps of fog, the cold and the dark felt threatening. Had something happened to my family?

"Charles," I screamed. "Where are you? Answer me!"

I stumbled from the quilt and hurried down to the creek. I hoped to find them catching tadpoles or searching under rocks for interesting insects, but there was no sign of them. I called out to them again.

Another wave of lightheadedness hit me; I tripped over an exposed tree root and fell.

When I realized I couldn't stop the fall, I twisted to my side, tried to land on my bottom, to avoid falling on my baby. Carlo said I must have screamed as I fell. I don't remember that, only how hard and sharp that slab of stone was when I landed on my hip.

At first, I felt only my racing heart and the wooziness. Had I harmed my baby? I was afraid to move for fear I would fall again. A dull ache started in my hip joint then pain shot down my leg. I tried to stand, but my legs refused to cooperate.

From above I heard Carlo's voice calling to me, but I could only whisper an answer. The black grew larger, the light smaller.

Chapter 44

I awoke in my bed.

Lopa's face was bent over mine. She smiled.

"My baby?" I asked.

"Baby good," she answered.

"Carlo? Emma Rose?"

"Carlo, Rosa good."

I raised my head and turned to get out of bed. My hip and leg hurt. I winced.

Lopa pushed my shoulders back onto the bed. "Stay."

"I want to see Carlo."

"I get." She turned and left the bedroom.

Outside the door I heard the sound of Emma Rose crying.

Carlo entered with Emma Rose in his arms. "See Mama is fine. She and baby will be alright."

To me he said, "You scared the hell out of me. I heard you scream then I couldn't find you." He scowled. "The doctor is on his way."

"Lopa said the baby is well."

"I want the doctor to check on you." He rested a hip on

the edge of the bed. Emma Rose squirmed in his arms. "We aren't in a remote valley now. We can take advantage of the availability of medical professionals."

"I trust Lopa."

Carlo smiled. "I trust her too. You know that. But it won't hurt to get a second opinion. Plus, I want the doctor to attend the birth, so he might as well get acquainted with his patient."

"I don't need, or want, anyone but Lopa."

"Well, Lopa says you have to stay in this bed until the baby comes. Do you want a second opinion on that diagnosis?

I nodded.

Chapter 45

The doctor concurred with Lopa regarding complete bed rest.

And I hated it.

Well, the first two days weren't bad. I read, cuddled with Emma Rose who napped in my bed. I even knit baby blankets.

Emma Rose grew bored with keeping me company in my bed. Lopa charged Sara and Susanna with keeping Emma occupied with games and outings so that I could rest.

My hip had an ugly bruise on it, but the doctor said it was not broken. I was extremely lucky in that nothing was broken, but it hurt to move around so I lay quiet.

By the third day I was restless and felt otherwise fine, so I wrapped myself in my robe and wandered out to the garden. The sky was blue, the flowers bright in the sunshine.

Lopa found me bent over to smell a beautiful pink Castilian Rose.

"Bed," she ordered and pointed the way to my bedroom.

I whined but returned to my bed.

Chapter 46

I lounged on the chaise Carlo had moved to the garden. I still felt restless, but the baby had stopped moving and Lopa assured me that meant he was ready to come out soon.

The first twinge of an ache at the bottom of my womb was a welcome relief to my boredom. Carlo noticed me wincing with pain and carried me to our bedroom.

An hour later, I wished I was bored again.

Lopa and the doctor agreed that although my delivery was progressing slowly, all seemed to be going well. Slow did not make it any less painful.

Two hours later, Lopa suggested that I walk around the room and the doctor agreed with her suggestion.

I walked between pains, but after ten days in bed I tired easily. I returned to my bed an hour later. I cried when the doctor decided it was safe for him to check on other patients. How long could this go on?

Miraculously, as soon as the doctor left, the pains came closer together. I felt an urge to push, but Lopa said, "No push, breath." She coaxed me to take deep breaths and release them slowly. She peeked under the bedclothes. "No push."

When that pain subsided, she left the room. I could hear her in the hall speaking with Carlo. "Get doctor."

"Susanna, give Emma Rose to Sara. Have Jorge help you find the doctor," Carlo said. "Sara, take Emma to the kitchen. See if Cook has something the two of you can do for him."

"What's wrong?" Carlo asked Lopa.

"Must turn baby."

"The baby is breech?"

"No. Sideways. Can't come out."

"You can turn him?"

I didn't hear what she answered.

She returned with a knife in her hand that she hid behind her back when she saw my eyes widen at the sight.

The pains were now coming close enough together that it felt like one. I soon lost awareness of anything but pain and an over whelming urge to push this child out of my body.

But Lopa continued to say "No, no push."

She tossed the bedcovers onto the floor and pushed my knees into the air. When she shoved her hands into my womb, I lost consciousness.

As I slid in and out of blackness, I was only vaguely aware of voices and activity in the room, but even in the haze of pain, I was scared. What was wrong? Was my baby all right?

Chapter 47

Lopa paced the room, a bundle in her arms.

"Baby?" I whispered. Oh God please let my baby be well.

Her smile flooded my heart with relief.

She laid the bundle at my side. "Baby boy good."

Wrinkled red skin, puffy eyes, sticky brown hair—my son was one of the most beautiful sights I'd ever seen. Ignoring the hurt that came with any movement, I took him in my arms and held him to my breast.

Carlo entered, sat on the edge of the bed. He smiled, but his face looked strained.

"What?" I asked.

He shook his head. "Our son is healthy. You should sleep. Rest. Let Lopa care for the babe."

I pulled the baby tighter to me. "What will we name him?"

"I was thinking of Edward, after your father."

"After my father?" My pain of losing Father was still too fresh. "Could Edward be his middle, his second name?"

"Certainly." Carlo said. "Did you have a name in

mind?"

"No, just something new," I whispered, "not a re-
minder of the past."

He nodded.

"What's wrong?" I asked, as he still looked anxious.

Carlo shook his head, but his eyes were filled with
tears.

"What? I demanded.

"Nothing now that you are both alright." He smiled,
wiped his eyes. "I was afraid, afraid that I had lost you."

Chapter 48

When Lopa stuck her hands inside to turn the baby, she discovered he had the umbilical cord wrapped around his neck. The result of all those somersaults no doubt. If she hadn't had to turn him, his cord would have strangled him.

So, we were lucky, I told myself as I held my son to my breast and tried not to think of what might have happened had Lopa not aggressively dealt with the problem.

"No more babies," Carlo said the next day after the birth. "We have a boy and a girl. It is enough and I can't lose you.

"Don't be silly." I looked at the babe at my breast with his tiny hand wrapped around my little finger. I treasured the joy of suckling my child. "I wasn't in danger."

He shook his head. "I had to help Lopa until the doctor got here." He sighed. "I couldn't stand . . ." He shook his head again. "You lost a lot of blood . . . and . . ."

"I'm recovering. Lopa makes me drink that awful smelling potion, to build my strength. She convinces me that I must drink it for the baby's sake." I reached for my husband's hand. "I am not fragile. But we needn't worry about more babies for a while. I'm content for now."

I smiled into his green eyes, pulled him closer. "I don't fuss at you when you ride off to your caves and don that black outfit of yours. I know you put yourself in danger each time, but I also know it is important to you."

"Once you are stronger," Carlo said, "I want to move you and the children to my rancho. It is nearly ready for our family, and this city worries me. While you were busy having . . . there's been another massive fire. And these vigilantes are causing more trouble than they solve."

Chapter 49

Emma Rose chased butterflies that fluttered from flower to flower. Tall hollyhocks towered above rose bushes. Pink, white and yellow hollyhock blossoms topped stems that reached above the garden walls, but the butterflies favored the nasturtiums that covered the beds and the sweet peas that climbed the walls.

I enjoyed watching my daughter from my chaise on the patio. Our baby, Theodore Edward Wells Anthony, slept in my arms.

Sara gathered sweet peas for the fragrant bouquets she scattered in rooms of the house. Susanna practiced playing her ukulele and serenaded us with her sweet voice.

The morning fog had burnt off leaving a perfect blue sky with wisps of white clouds over the distant mountains.

I took a deep breath expecting to enjoy clean refreshing air. I was surprised by a faint flavor of smoke. It was early in the day for barbecues.

Lopa passed through the gate separating the pleasure garden from the vegetable garden carrying a basket overflowing with carrots, peas, onions, red peppers, and corn.

Carlo had hired a cook, a Chinaman named Won Toy, but Lopa did not like him or his cooking. The kitchen was the scene of endless squabbles as Lopa continued to make her own dishes to feed our family. The cook fed the staff and was assured by Carlo that when I recovered and we began to entertain, the cook would be able to take charge of the kitchen. I wasn't too sure how that was to work out as Carlo had told Lopa and I that when I recovered, we were to move to the rancho.

Lopa stopped to check on Teddy and me. She smiled. "Baby sleeping good."

"Do I smell smoke?" I asked her. The odor had grown.

She turned to look over the garden wall towards the city. She dropped her basket and took Teddy from my arms. "Go inside now."

I struggled to stand while Lopa ordered Sara to take Emma Rose by the hand and lead her into the house. She handed the baby to Susanna.

Once I had managed to push myself to my feet, a glance in the direction Lopa had looked shocked me.

A sheet of flames stretched a half-mile across the district of wooden structures bordering the bay. A lack of strong wind allowed the massive plume of dark gray smoke to rise high into the blue sky.

From experience, I knew a large fire created its own windstorm. That self-generated wind plus even a light breeze off the water would drive the flames through the low-lying district and up the hills into the residential areas.

Lopa returned to my side, took my arm. "Go inside now." She supported me and took me into my room, helped me climb into bed. Sleeping Teddy was placed in his cradle next to the bed. I could hear the thump of shutters being closed against the increasing amount of smoke.

"Lopa, are we safe here?" I asked.

She nodded, pulled a blanket over my legs.

"Where is Carlo?"

She shook her head.

"Have you seen him today?"

She continued to shake her head.

I tried to recall what he had whispered to me when he left our bed early this morning. I was nursing the baby and had paid little attention to his plans. Had he gone to his rancho?

No. I remembered. He said he and don Diego were checking on the construction of two buildings in the city. My God, were they in the path of the fire?

Chapter 50

"Lopa?" I called as I attempted to ease from my bed. "Lopa."

"What you do?" she scolded. "Stay."

"I think that Carlo and don Diego are down in that fire." I cried. "We must send someone to help them. Send a cart and two strong men to the construction site."

Lopa shook her head. "You stay. I do." She hurried from the room.

I leaned back on my pillows and tried to quiet my racing heart. I remembered all too clearly the horror of being caught in one of the countless fires that wiped out large portions of the city several times a year. The fire I was caught in months ago had destroyed three hundred buildings.

Granted, many were little more than shacks thrown up in a hurry to replace the buildings destroyed in the previous fire. San Franciscans continued to build layer after layer of wood structures on top of the ashes. In desperation, early on in the population explosion that resulted from the rush for gold, ships had been moved ashore to be used as housing, saloons, gambling halls and brothels. Few of those ships had survived the fires; their burnt and melted hulls served as foundations for the new buildings.

I hoped the buildings Carlo and don Diego were constructing used traditional California adobe. But unlike the brush fires that swept past adobe ranchos, the city fires were intense with more fuel for the heat and smoke either of which were deadly. Even in an adobe building, they would not be safe.

Lopa returned to the room. "Men go. You rest."

Chapter 51

The minutes that turned to hours passed excruciatingly slowly.

Even the joy of holding and nursing my babe did not distract me from my worry.

I kept telling myself that Carlo and don Diego were resourceful and competent. But I also knew that they were both generous with their aid to others. If anyone needed a rescue, they would not hesitate to jump in harm's way. Of course, many victims of the fire would need their assistance.

Lopa brought the foul-tasting potion she insisted I drink each day together with lunch. She took Teddy from my arms and placed him in his cradle.

"Am I not strong enough to come to the table?" I asked.

"You stay with baby," she answered.

"Is the fire still burning?"

Lopa nodded.

"Any word from Carlo?"

Lopa nodded. "Men, cart back."

"Why didn't you tell me?" I sat up intent on getting out of bed.

"No." She blocked my path. "Not Carlo. Carlo good."

"What are you saying? I don't understand. The men and the cart came back without Carlo?"

"Si."

"Why did they come back without him? Did you not tell them to go get him?"

"Si."

"Lopa, get out of my way. I have to know what is happening." I sat up, swung my legs to the side of the bed. "Stand back."

Rather than move aside, Lopa took my arm and helped me from the bed. She supported me as I made my way to the front of the house, to the balcony overlooking the garden and the entrance gates.

In the distance, the fire was still burning but it was smaller. Behind the front edge of flame, blackened ruins sent up streams of smoke. Scattered pockets of flames licked at the reduced remaining fuel.

Below the balcony, Jorge and Rafael, the two men sent to rescue Carlo and don Diego, unloaded injured from the oxcart. The doctor, aided by Sara, Susanna, and our cook Won Toy, attended the half dozen burned and injured who lay on blankets that covered our patio in the walled garden.

I called to Jorge. "Where are Carlo and don Diego?

Jorge looked up from where he and Rafael had just laid another burned man on the patio. "They are safe, Señora."

Right, pulling people out of the fire. How long will they be safe?

Chapter 52

Lopa helped me to a chair on the balcony. From there I could watch for Carlo's return and monitor the fire. Fortunately, a broad swath of open land was between our adobe and the city. Don Diego's offices and warehouse were between us and the main district of the fire, but they too looked to be out of reach of the flames. Any sparks would land on the tiled roofs that were impervious to fire.

I wondered why Carlo had not mentioned that he and don Diego were building in the city. Granted I had been more than a little distracted by my preparations for baby's arrival.

To my great relief, I recognized the two soot-covered horsemen as my husband and his uncle Diego as they made their way through the herb-covered hillside to our entrance gates.

I waved as they drew closer. Carlo's smile revealed a band of white teeth in contrast to his blackened face and neck.

When he reached our gates, he called. "Let me get some of this black off me and I'll be up to see you.

Meanwhile, I believe you are supposed to be keeping your feet up, are you not?"

The doctor looked up from where he sewed a forehead gash and nodded his agreement. "Mrs. Anthony, I must insist that you remain abed to prevent hemorrhaging. And I could certainly use assistance from Lopa."

Lopa led me back to my bed and hurried down the stairs to the garden.

I looked forward to Carlo telling me of his day. And now I could find out what he was constructing in the city.

Chapter 53

I heard faint voices in the hall outside my bedroom. It sounded like Carlo's voice and Diego's accented English. They often spoke English when they didn't want the servants to understand their conversations.

"Who do you suppose he works for?" Diego said.

"I'm guessing Augustus, but I don't know why . . ."

"It was a close call, if we hadn't chased him off when we did, we would have lost the lot."

"All the more incentive to get a less flammable warehouse completed," Carlo said. "I need to check on my wife now, but at dawn tomorrow I'll have all hands at the site. And I'll have Jorge round up more men to make adobe bricks and tiles."

Carlo forced a broad smile as he entered my boudoir. "My darling wife." He carefully perched on the edge of the bed. "Please follow the doctor's instructions."

"I don't think I'm that bad off. I wish everyone would stop treating me like an invalid." I pouted.

Carlo brushed back a tendril of blonde hair that had escaped my braid. "I'm sorry you don't like your treatment.

It's only that we were all frightened at the difficulty of Teddy's birth, and we love you. I can't stand the thought of losing you." He took my hand. "Please promise to do exactly as the doctor orders."

I thought I knew my body and my limitations better than the doctor, so I wasn't going to be tricked into a promise I might not keep.

I changed the subject. "How many people did you and Diego rescue from the fire?"

Carlo smiled at my ploy but never the less he told me of the woman and her children who were on the second floor of a ramshackle structure in Chinatown, an elderly Chinaman next door, horses from a stable, but he failed to mention rescuing his warehouse.

"What are you building?" I asked as soon as Carlo finished his tale of rescues.

"A warehouse, for one." He lay on our bed with Teddy on his chest.

"A warehouse?"

"Yes, hopefully a less flammable one. In purchasing furnishings for this house, I found that the captains of the ships are impatient to unload and get out of here before they lose their crew. The number of abandoned ships in the bay scares the hell out of them. Also, they have to wait too long for their turn to use the limited number of docks. Eventually we will build more piers, but for now we are getting excellent prices for the goods from the waiting ships and those goods need to be stored."

"You are becoming a merchant?" I smiled at my handsome husband.

"Your family will disapprove?" he asked with a scowl.

"Perhaps some will, but no one that matters." I kissed his cheek that still had some remains of soot smears. "Will you build a shop?" It was difficult to imagine Carlo and don Diego as shopkeepers.

"For now we will sell from the warehouse." He rubbed Teddy's head, attempted to smooth down the dark brown hair that stuck up like an Indian's Mohawk.

"What else do you build?"

"My friend, Domingo Ghirardelli, wishes to have a factory in which to make chocolate."

I clapped my hands in delight. "How wonderful! I love chocolate. Are you building that?"

"I'm assisting him. He wishes to build with bricks—even though Diego advises against such building materials because of the earthquakes. But Domingo envisions his factory in brick. And because we are already dealing with the ship captains, Diego and I are exchanging hides for the bricks the ships use for ballast."

"Brick buildings won't burn as readily as the wood," I said.

"This is true. And he wants a building that will house his store and factory on the ground floor and his family on the second floor." Carlo kissed the top of his son's head. Teddy had fallen back to sleep.

"How did you get involved in this chocolate factory?"

"My wife loves chocolate, what else could I do?" Carlo grinned at me with that smile that always made my heart swell. "And, since Domingo's wife and children are waiting in Peru for him to provide a home for them here in San Francisco, I sympathize with his desire to have them with him. I want my family with me always."

"He's from Peru? Ghirardelli sounds Italian."

"Originally from Italy. But in search of the best chocolate, spices and coffees, he ended up in South America."

"Chocolate. I do love chocolate. How soon will you complete this building?"

Carlo chuckled. "I'll see if I can't bargain to get paid in chocolate!"

Chapter 54

The next morning my breakfast was served with cinnamon laced hot chocolate. With enough chocolate, and my children by my side, I was content to stay abed for several more days.

I read to Emma Rose until she fell asleep at both naptime and bedtime. Fortunately, she did not mind me repeating stories over and over, but I was soon begging Carlo to find more children's books. I also needed more reading material.

"Really, you really have read every book in our library?" he asked

"No, not every book. I don't read Russian. Or Chinese. I do reasonably well with French, Spanish and Italian. But I have no interest in the collected works of Copernicus. Or any of the medical books. Or books on construction. I've tried but they just do not distract me from being trapped in this bed." I had skimmed through the medical books looking for answers as to how long I would be trapped in this bedroom, but had not found any useful information. And my head was soon spinning with the Latin words I had never learned.

"My poor darling, I'll fetch the doctor in the morning," Carlo promised.

"Tell me more about the activities in the city."

Carlo looked at me, frowned, and was silent.

"What's the matter? Is all the news bad? I haven't seen a newspaper for days. Have the California Sun offices burned?"

Carlo sighed, his green eyes squinted. "A vigilante committee has formed."

I sat up, leaned over to grab his arm. "Are they after you? After the fox?"

"No." He forced a smile. "As a matter of fact, I am a member of the committee."

"You!" I returned his smile. "Is this a ploy to hide your identity?"

"No, every upstanding citizen was invited to join. Don Diego and I are among two hundred members. Respectable members of the community are tired of the arson, the looting, and the extortion. And we don't have enough honest lawmen to handle the numbers of evil-doers who have arrived here expecting easy money," Carlo said. "Oh, and Uncle Diego has dropped using the title 'don' for now. We have to get accustomed to calling him Uncle instead."

"Is it that bad to be of Spanish heritage in California now?"

"Maybe just better not to use the title."

Chapter 55

Three nights later, I awoke late into the night to discover that Carlo had not yet come to bed. I placed Teddy in his cradle and walked to the balcony. Perhaps Uncle Diego and Carlo were enjoying cigars on the patio.

I felt well enough to enjoy some freedom of movement even though the doctor had cautioned me to allow myself more recovery time. He also forbade sexual intercourse until Teddy was six weeks old. I wondered if that mattered since my husband had said "No more babies."

I was pretty certain I could dissuade him from that edict.

I walked onto the balcony. There was no sign of anyone in the patio. I went to the top of the stairs. No sounds from downstairs. I was half way down the stairs when Lopa caught me.

"What wrong?" she asked.

"Where is Carlo?"

She shrugged to say she didn't know just as the clock struck two.

Two in the morning! Carlo did not stay out this late.

"Did he say anything about going to the rancho?"

She shook her head.

"Well, where the hell is he?"

"Go bed. I find." She led me back up to my room. Teddy was fussing. She picked him up and handed him to me once I was settled in bed.

I was burping the well-fed baby when she returned.

"Jorge say hanging." She motioned towards the city.

"What!" I leaned over to place the baby in his cradle, threw off my nightgown. I grabbed clothing from the wardrobe. Without concern for what the pieces were, I pulled on a skirt, blouse, and jacket. And riding boots while I quizzed Lopa. "Who?"

She shrugged.

"Where?"

Another shrug as she watched me dress. "No Carlo," she said.

"Are you sure? Do you know that? Or are you just trying to calm me?"

She didn't even bother to shrug. She shook her head. "No go. No good. You sick." She reached for my arm, but I shook her off.

"Watch the children," I cried as I ran down the stairs to look for Jorge.

I found him in the stables preparing to unsaddle his horse. I seized the reins from his hands, catapulted myself into the saddle. Jorge's saddle was not designed to accommodate a lady but I was not at all concerned about riding sidesaddle. It was the middle of the night. Who was going to see my legs showing beneath my skirts? And quite possibly my husband was in danger of being hanged. Legs be damned.

"Jorge, who is being hanged?

"I don't know Señora," he answered.

"Where is Carlo? Is he there?"

"Si Señora, he is there. At Portsmouth Square."

"And Uncle Diego?"

Jorge shrugged, did not answer.

I turned the horse and rode hard down to Montgomery Street then to the square. As I got close, I saw crowds headed down Sansome, California, Clay and Montgomery Streets converging on the plaza. Several of the prominent members of the eighty-strong vigilance committee were stationed at the adobe customhouse on the northwest corner of the plaza.

A wretch of a man with a hangman's noose around his neck was being pulled along the ground by the end of the rope by a score of heavily armed men. As they neared the adobe, the local authorities made a feeble attempt to stop the procession.

I recognized some of the men waiting at the customhouse as being well-respected, prominent members of the community. More respected and reputable than those who were the so-called authorities and thus the interference was merely symbolic.

The authorities stood back as the man was dragged and the rope was thrown over a beam that projected from the adobe. The prisoner was a strong-built, healthy man, and his struggles, when hanging, were very violent for a few minutes.

Although I could now plainly see that the man was a stranger, not Carlo or Diego, I still hated the sight of his vain attempts to survive.

The crowd, of near a thousand people, remained quiet until well passed the end of the man's struggles.

From horseback, I could search the crowd until I spotted my husband's dark hair and broad shoulders to one side of the adobe. Even from this distance, I could see that he looked as unhappy as I felt. I rode to a nearby street, circled around to the north west of the plaza and to his side.

"My God Clarissa, what in the world? What are you doing here?" His strong arms lifted me down from the saddle and I collapsed against his chest.

I whispered into his neck, "I was so afraid."

He held me back so he could see my tear-stained face. "You thought you needed to rescue me?"

I nodded, choked back a sob.

"Oh, my darling." He pulled me close, lifted me into his arms.

"Who was that man?" I asked. "What did he do to deserve that?"

"We need to get you home, back to bed," Carlo said. "We'll talk about this tomorrow."

"Did he kill someone?"

"Tomorrow," Carlo repeated.

Chapter 56

"I was so afraid," I said as I leaned over to where my husband had pulled a pillow over his head. I picked up the pillow. "Please don't disappear in the middle of the night without telling me where you are going ever again."

"Believe me, if I had any idea you would come looking for me, I would never have done that. I should've realized with the babe waking you in the night, you would notice my absence." He lifted his head, kissed my lips. "I'm sorry. I'll try not to frighten you like that again."

He smiled, brushed back my hair. "How were you planning to rescue me?"

"I didn't have a plan," I admitted. "As I rode, I promised myself that the next time I needed to rescue you, I would at least make sure I had a pistol with me."

Carlo laughed.

"Do not laugh at me." I scowled at him, punched his arm and blinked away tears.

He failed to stifle his laugh. In fact, he laughed even more. So much that he couldn't talk when he tried to say he was sorry.

"Charles Anthony, you have no right to laugh at me. I could rescue you if I had to." I started to pout, but thought better of it. "But maybe you aren't worth saving!"

He rolled over, pulled my body against his. "Has it been six weeks? Oh, I don't know if I can keep my hands off you another month." He groaned, ran his hands over my back and bottom.

I put my arms around his neck. "Carlo, you must promise not to take foolish chances. I know this Spanish fox stuff you and don Diego do is important to you both, but you have other responsibilities now." Anger made me cry even more. I backhanded tears off my cheeks.

He chuckled.

"Dammit Carlo, stop laughing. This is serious. The thought of you being dragged through the streets at the end of a rope scares the hell out of me!"

"Clarissa, darling. Please don't cry." He licked tears off my face. "I am careful. I do not do anything that would give cause for me to be hanged. My uncle and I do not steal. Or murder. We scare bad men into doing the right thing."

"What did that man that hanged do?"

Carlo released me, turned onto his back.

"Did he do something so terrible, so heinous that you don't think a fragile female can bear to hear it?" I asked.

"No."

"So, what did he do?" I demanded.

"Look Clarissa, you have to understand who he is . . . er, was. He was part of a gang of criminals known as

Sydney Coves or Sydney Ducks. Former convicts from the penal colonies in Australia."

"Ducks? Coves?"

"The first colony was in Sydney Cove," he explained. "Anyway, that area of San Francisco called Sydney Town where the worst of the saloons and houses of uhm, ill repute—"

"Carlo, I know about houses of prostitution, whore houses. And I'm pretty sure I walked through Sydney town once."

"Right." He frowned probably because he was remembering the months I spent alone with Lopa, fending for ourselves, associating with whores. "Anyway, these convicts got to California pretty quickly when word of the gold got out, and once they realized how much work was involved in mining, they looked for easier methods of making money. Quite a few of them returned to San Francisco and reverted to their old ways—thieving, murdering, arson, and looting. They settled in the area near the harbor now known as Sydney Town."

"This man was a duck?"

"His name was Jenkins, John Jenkins," Carlo said.

"Ducks? Why duck?"

"Well, it's believed that this gang from Sydney Town have purposely started some of the six fires we've had so that they could loot while everyone else was busy fighting or escaping from the flames. Someone said, in response to their belief that the Sydney Town gang had set the fire, 'The Sydney Ducks are cackling in the pond.' And now whenever there's trouble on a large scale, that phrase is repeated."

"So, what did this Duck, this Jenkins do that was so horrible?"

"Truth be known, what he did wasn't so horrible, but the vigilante committee decided to make an example of him. It seems that the only thing these Sydney Ducks are afraid of is the gallows. If the authorities put one of their gang in jail, they rescue him. The Ducks take care of their own."

"What did he do?"

"He stole a safe, carried it off. When he was chased he put it in a row boat and took it out into the bay."

"What was he going to do with it in the bay?" I asked.

"Hard to say, because he managed to lose it into the water." Carlo laughed. "A bit of a bungler, huh?"

"Doesn't seem like a hanging offense," I said.

"I agree." Carlo frowned. "But grand larceny is punishable by hanging per California law. I did have to agree with the committee's opinion that we have to do something about these Ducks, although I'd rather deport them. Per Mexican law, anyone convicted of a crime, is not allowed to settle in California."

"So why not deport them?"

"One, there are an awful lot of them, a few thousand at least, hard to round them all up. Two, it's thought that they will just come right back. The committee wants to convince the most criminal of them that they would be better off somewhere else by hanging any of them caught breaking the law. They intend to keep on hanging until the Ducks get the message that they won't be tolerated."

"So there will be more hangings?" I asked.

"I'm afraid so, my darling." Carlo hugged me. "But I do not plan to participate again."

"Will that make you suspect?"

He shook his head, but I was afraid.

Chapter 57

Nearly a month to the day, from the date of Jenkins's hanging, the sound of the three rings of the Monumental Fire Company's bell signaled the next meeting of the Vigilante Committee.

The next day another man from Sydney was hanged. Carlo had attended the so-called trial and in addition to the burglary the Duck was caught in the act of doing, all heard the man confess to killing a Yuba County Sheriff. Needless to say, the vigilante committee had found him guilty of murder.

A week later, Carlo was pleased to inform me that fourteen Ducks had been deported back to Australia and several more had been ordered to leave California.

By December, the population of Sydney Town had been significantly reduced as the evildoers got the message and left the city. There had been no more fires like the one in May that had destroyed two thousand buildings. On that particular day, the wind had kept the flames away from Sydney Town. Whether that was a coincidence, or good planning on the part of the Ducks could only be a matter of opinion.

Things had quieted down, but the district had no less cheap saloons, gambling halls or brothels. Slightly more upscale entertainment was to be found on the blocks bordering Sydney Town. And it was to a music hall in that vicinity that Susanna went to seek a position as a singer. Unfortunately, she did not bother to explain her errand to any of us including her sister Sara.

Sara came to my sitting room, peeked in the door to see Emma Rose playing with building blocks on the floor at my feet, and baby Teddy on my lap.

"What is it Sara?" I asked. "Join us if you like."

"Thanks, but no thanks. Just looking for Susanna," Sara answered.

"Is she helping Cook or Lopa in the kitchen?"

"No, I checked there."

"Did you try the flower garden? Perhaps she is picking a bouquet?" I asked.

"I'll look. Thanks."

I listened to her step lightly down the staircase and thought about how much her mental state had improved since Lopa rescued her from captors a few years ago. She did not speak, not a single word for the first months that she was with us. Susanna, her older sister, assured us that Sara could speak; that she wasn't mute. But that was before two men had killed their parents and brothers and carried off the girls. The young girls had been mistreated in ways I couldn't stand to think about.

I heard the front gate close. I carried Teddy with me to

the balcony.

Susanna walked up the road from the city, Sara ran to meet her. I couldn't hear what they said, but I imagined Sara scolding her sister for going off without her. They hugged, joined hands and skipped up the slope to the gate.

When I asked what that was about, where Susanna had been, they both just giggled.

It was two nights later that Susanna disappeared again.

Chapter 58

The doctor had finally agreed that my health had improved and I was no longer in danger. I was thrilled to be released from my prison bed.

I had looked forward to dressing in real clothes, not bed gowns and robes, but my dressing room was soon littered with dresses that did not fit. I wondered if I would ever again have the small waist that did not require a corset to be stylish. Even when Lopa pulled tight the ribbons of a corset, the waists of my gowns could not be fastened. And I couldn't breathe.

"Oh Lopa, am I to be a shapeless lump forever?" I whined. "I don't remember being this fat after Emma was born."

Lopa smiled as she picked up discarded clothing from the chaise lounge. "No glass," she said.

She was correct. Our sweet cabin in Yosemite had no mirror, no looking glass. And we had very few articles of clothing. I had worn loose fitting clothing both during and after my pregnancy. With a sigh, I pulled a peasant style blouse over my head and stepped into a skirt with an adjustable sash.

I looked at my reflection in the chiffonier mirror. I looked like a blond peasant señora, but I was comfortable and anxious to get back to life. I went downstairs to join my family for breakfast.

Carlo, Emma Rose, Lopa and I were enjoying a leisurely breakfast in the courtyard filled with the music of the fountain, the fragrance of the blossoms, and the warmth of sunlight. I nodded at the empty seats meant for Sara and Susanna. "Where are the girls?"

Carlo and Lopa exchanged glances. Carlo spoke, "To be honest darling, while you spent the last weeks in your boudoir, we did not have formal meals. It was catch as catch can, eating on the run in the kitchen."

"Lopa, I thought you told the girls to come for breakfast. They would enjoy the hot cocoa," I said.

"Knock on door, say breakfast," Lopa answered.

"I'll see what is keeping them." I climbed the stairs to the room shared by the sisters.

Sara opened the door, her face wet with tears.

I took her in my arms. "What is the matter?"

"Susanna did not sleep in her bed."

"Where did she go?" I asked.

Sara shook her head indicating she didn't know.

I pulled a handkerchief from my skirt pocket and offered it to Sara. She wiped away tears, blew her nose.

"Come have some hot cocoa, and then we'll find her." I tried not to think of what could have kept Susanna from returning home.

A sweet domestic scene greeted our return to the courtyard; Emma Rose playing in the fountain, Lopa rocking the baby in her arms, Carlo enjoying a cigarette with his coffee. I told myself that too much seemed right with the world in that moment for something dire to have happened to Susanna. There must be an innocent explanation.

"Come sit. Sip this cocoa." I showed Sara to her seat, took a biscuit from the basket, and put it on a plate in front of her. "The biscuits are delicious, especially with the raspberry preserves."

Carlo gave me a questioning glance. I shrugged, looked at Sara spreading jam on her biscuit. He nodded in understanding that we would wait until the child had eaten to quiz her.

Sara ate one biscuit, reached for a second. She and her sister had been starved into skeletal thinness when Lopa rescued them. They both had been eating as though they were enjoying their last meal ever since. Both had filled out some, but Sara still looked much younger than her actual age.

She spread butter and preserve on a third biscuit. "Met a countess."

I knitted my brow to look at her questioningly.

"She met a real countess," Sara repeated. "Countess Landsomethun'." She bit into the biscuit.

"Lola Montez?" Carlo offered.

"Yes, that's the one." Sara nodded.

"Is she Spanish?" I asked.

"Pretends to be a Spanish dancer. But she's not much of a dancer, and I doubt she is Spanish," Carlo said.

"Is she actually a countess?" I asked.

Carlo nodded. "That part of her story is true."

I looked a question at him.

"King Ludwig of Bavaria made her a countess when he was besotted with her," Carlo explained, "She was not only his mistress, but had such a strong influence that he allowed her to interfere in his governing. Brought about his downfall."

"And she's here? In San Francisco?" I asked.

Both Sara and Carlo answered yes.

"Is Susanna with her?" I asked Sara.

"Maybe," Sara answered hopefully.

"Where?" I asked.

Sara shook her head.

Carlo thought for a moment. "Most likely she is staying at the St. Francis hotel. I'll go by there."

"I'm coming with you," I said.

Carlo smiled, looked at my clothing. "Darling, I find your peasant attire charming, and I'm sure more comfortable than the usual ladies' corseted dresses, but . . ."

"I don't care, I want to see this woman, this countess. And this is the only thing that fits me."

Chapter 59

Lopa helped me into one of the gowns I had worn in my pregnancy. As I had mostly worn what Carlo dubbed "peasant attire" for the last four months, it was in fact the only gown I had worn. And it was a silk evening gown.

She pulled the ribbons of the corset tight. I couldn't breathe. When she helped me into my dress, it was impossible to wear with my milk full bosom overflowing the décolletage. I wrapped a shawl around my shoulders and chest, which covered my exposed breasts as long as I kept it in place. But now instead of looking like a peasant, I looked like a whore. The fabric and cut were inappropriate for daywear.

"Lopa," I said, "What am I to do? I can't go out like this."

She nodded in agreement and pulled one of my afternoon dresses from the armoire.

I struggled to get out of the evening gown. Lopa yanked it off me and helped me into the afternoon dress. It, as was expected, was impossible to hook or button.

Lopa used a needle and thread to sew the opening with

a gap of a few inches. She then took a cape from the cupboard and placed it over my shoulders hiding the sewn together gap.

I looked in the mirror, twisting my neck in an effort to check each angle. I felt awkward, but I no longer looked like a peasant—or a whore.

I hugged Lopa. "Thank you. You saved me again."

"What happened to my little peasant girl?" Carlo asked from the doorway as he offered me his arm and led me to the carriage.

Carlo drove Sara and me to the St. Francis Hotel at the corner of Clay and Dupont. En route, he cautioned us both to remember to address him as Charles.

Even though the hotel was near Portsmouth Square, it had thus far managed to survive the numerous fires that ravaged the district.

When we arrived at the hotel, I was grateful to have taken the time to be properly attired. Ladies arriving for lunch in the dining room greeted us. I introduced Sara to a group of my new acquaintances while Carlo inquired for the Countess at the reception desk. He handed his calling card to the bellman that was sent to her room to see if she was receiving.

The bellman hurried back down the stairs. "The Countess will be pleased to receive you, sir." Carlo pressed a tip into his hand.

Removing his hat, Carlo greeted the women with wishes for a good day. "Excuse me ladies, I must steal my wife and ward away." He offered his arms to Sara and me.

We walked up the broad staircase of the hotel built hurriedly in 1849. It surely did not compare well to the grand hotels of Europe in which the Countess must have stayed, but it was the best the city had to offer.

We reached the first landing. I turned to look at the bustling activity of the lobby. A short, blonde man whom I recognized as the gambler named Augustus Pennyworth glared at the three of us from the bottom of the stairs. I shook off the shiver that his glare sent up my spine.

Sara was visibly nervous as we waited at the door to the suite. Rather than the maid I expected, the Countess herself opened the door.

She threw herself at my husband. "Carlo, querido." I knew enough Spanish to know she had called my husband "darling". She chatted on in what I recognized as Castilian Spanish, but Carlo pulled out of her arms and answered her in English introducing his wife and ward.

She did not appear pleased to see us, barely nodding in answer to his introductions.

She ignored Sara and me and continued to address Carlo in Spanish while grasping his arm.

"My wife does understand some Spanish, but Sara very little," Carlo said politely.

"Oh, pardon please, come in, be seated." She swept away from the door into the small sitting room of her suite. "It is a pleasure to meet Carlo's family. Please call me Lola."

To Carlo she said, "We have not seen each other for many years. I believe we last saw each other in Paris, no?"

Her English held a trace of an Irish lilt. Her deep brown eyes and dark hair could pass for Spanish, but could just as easily be black Irish. Ironically, the Countess was attired in a fancy, beaded version of my peasant clothing. No doubt part of her Spanish dancer persona.

"Yes. I agree. It has been some years, but you are looking as young and beautiful as ever," Carlo said. "It is a pleasure to see you, but I'm afraid this is not a social call. We are looking for Sara's sister, Susanna. Has she visited you?"

"Oh, that girl has a lovely voice," Lola answered.

"So, she has been here?" I blurted.

Lola turned to look me over. I could see she dismissed me as uninteresting. She turned back to Carlo. "You live here in the city?" she asked him.

"Yes, and we would be delighted to entertain you at our home. But at the moment, we are concerned about Susanna. Do you know where she is?"

"Perhaps she is at the music hall nearby here," Lola said.

I sighed. In this neighborhood, the so-called music hall would be a saloon. No place for a young girl.

My sigh caught Lola's attention. She gave me a glance, turned back to Carlo. "This girl, Susanna is quite petite, like her sister here, but she is not a child, correct?"

I glared at my husband, stood.

"Do you know which hall that would be?" Carlo asked.

"I believe it would be one just the other side of the square," Lola answered.

"Did you take her there?" I asked, but Lola ignored me.

Instead she took my husband's face between her hands and kissed his lips. He smiled and rose from his chair. "Please excuse us Lola. We are concerned for Susanna's safety and wish to bring her home as soon as possible." He took the hand she extended, kissed it. "Once we have resolved this concern, we will send an invitation. Thank you for helping us."

Carlo ushered Sara and me out of the suite. As we walked down the stairs, I was silent, but Sara asked, "Will we go to the music hall next?"

"I think not. I believe it would be best for me to take you ladies home and I will continue the search for her."

I did not bother to answer. I agreed we should return Sara home, but I had no intention of staying there.

Chapter 60

Carlo insisted I stay at home. I insisted I would not do so.

"If you do not allow me to accompany you, I will follow on my own," I repeated stamping my foot.

"You are a stubborn pain in my ass," Carlo snarled. "I can do this much more efficiently without you. Don't you agree that time is of the essence?"

"Then why do we not take Jorge and Rafael with us?" I asked.

"Because they are likely to be unwelcome and get into trouble themselves."

"I am coming with you. Stop wasting time arguing." I refused to get out of the carriage.

"Fine, stay where you are." Carlo opened the front gate for Sara. To my lack of foresight, I saw him head for the stables.

"Damn." He was planning to ride into town. I couldn't do that in these clothes. The flounces in my skirt would not allow me to sit on horseback. I climbed to the driver's seat, picked up the reins and prepared to follow him. I waited for several minutes to no avail. I'd been tricked.

To my disappointment, he did not use the road in front of our gate. On horseback he was free to cut through fields. I turned the buggy around and headed down the road. I knew the way to the Square. I was sure I could find the hall to which the Countess had referred.

I left the horse and buggy with the doorman at the hotel and walked across the square. I saw Carlo exit the saloon closest to the square and hurried to catch up with him.

"I take it she wasn't in that saloon?" I asked him.

He turned at the sound of my voice. "Goddamn it, Clarissa." But he took my hand and placed it on his arm. "Are you never going to behave like a lady?"

"But you forget, I am officially a Lady, a titled English Lady. I can behave in any manner I like and still be a Lady," I said into his ear. "If the Countess can behave as she does and still mingle with royalty, surely I can step foot into a saloon and still be accepted by San Francisco so-called society."

He answered me with a scowl.

I entered the next hall on his arm.

"We are looking for our ward, Miss Susanna," Carlo said to the bartender. "Has she been here?"

"No."

"She is small, blonde, and fancies herself a singer."

"I said no."

Carlo raised his voice over the din of gamblers and drinkers. "I am offering a hundred-dollar reward for information as to the whereabouts of our ward Susanna. She is petite, blonde, and sings."

"Plays a ukulele, does she?" came a deep voice from across the room.

"Yes," I said

"Sir, do you know where she is?" Carlo asked.

A grey bearded man dressed in denim overalls walked to us. "I believe I do. A sweet little thing, she doesn't belong around here. Come with me. I'll show you where I saw her last."

Chapter 61

We followed him out of the hall, down the wood planked walkway, and past several saloons. The sign above the door where he took us said "Music Hall", but it looked very much like the other saloons with the exception of a small raised platform that served as a stage. Like most of the other saloons, the makeshift bar consisted of planks of wood laid across barrels.

The bartender asked Carlo, "What's your pleasure?"

Carlo repeated, "We are looking for our ward, Miss Susanna."

The bartender looked us over. "What for?" he said.

"We want a word with her."

"Says she's eighteen, not underage. Is she lyin?"

I realized we didn't actually know her age. Nor did she, but we had all assumed she was around that age.

"We just want to speak with her, to make sure she is alright," I said. "Her sister is worried about her. I want to put her sister's mind to rest."

The bartender stared at me. "You one of the temperance ladies?"

"Look, we would like to speak with her. We would rather not have to get the authorities involved," Carlo said.

The bartender yelled at a woman sitting on a man's lap at a poker table, "Sal, get that singer gal."

"I'll take my hundred now," said the man who led us to this saloon.

Carlo paid the man his money.

Sal returned pulling a frightened Susanna by the arm.

I ran to Susanna, hugged her, whispered, "Are you alright?"

Chapter 62

"Am I in trouble?" Susanna whimpered. "I din't mean to stay away so long." She hung her head, studied her feet.

Carlo and I looked around the room; saw that every man stared at the three of us. Carlo took Susanna's arm. "Let's talk about this at home. Where is your ukulele?" he asked.

She nodded her head towards the door she and Sal had used to enter the saloon.

"Let's go." He motioned to me to follow. We entered a storeroom furnished with two stools. Susanna's ukulele rested against the leg of one stool. Her cloak was on top of the second stool.

We collected Susanna's ukulele and cloak and Carlo escorted both of us to the buggy I had driven.

"Wait here while I fetch my horse," Carlo ordered in an annoyed tone. He wasn't happy with either of us.

I watched him walk away, and then turned to Susanna. "You scared the hell out of your sister, and me, and everyone else in the household."

Her face was wet with tears.

"We care about you."

She stifled a sob. Once she started talking the words poured out of her so fast I had trouble following. "We started practicin', the Countess and me, an then she brought me to that music hall, an I played an sang an they liked my singin', then it was so late, she said 'sleep in my sittin' room', so we went back to her rooms an then today she brought me back here, an promised she would come for me after I performed tonight, an have a driver take me home so's I could explain. I jus lost track of the time yesterday, it was so excitin' to have a real professional entertainer take a interest in me."

"Hold on," I said. "You were with the Countess last night?"

"Yeah."

"Miss Lola, that countess?"

"Yeah, she says I could have a career like she did. She's a dancer. Specialty is a spider dance. She showed me, it's kinda strange, but she's been all over the world dancin' and havin' a excitin' life. Oh Clarissa, I love you, an' Lopa, an' the babies, an' Sara, but I wanna life."

"I understand Susanna." I bit my tongue rather than comment on Lola's exciting life.

Carlo rode next to us, "You know the way home from here?" he asked.

I nodded.

"I'll follow you." He was still annoyed with both us.

We were silent on the drive home. I wondered what Lola was up to. It seemed likely she knew Susanna was

Carlo's ward and she was using her to get his attention. Carlo knew Lola was in the city, but it seemed they had not seen each other. Was all of this a ploy to get him to come to her?

Chapter 63

"Carlo, how did you know the Countess was in the city?" I asked.

"People talk about flamboyant personalities like her. Let's deal with Susanna's situation before we get going on the subject of Lola." He turned to Susanna who sat on the settee with Sara. Sara had locked her arm through Susanna's.

"So young lady, you want to be an entertainer," he said studying Susanna's face. "You do realize that life will bar you from parts of society?"

Susanna looked at him with a puzzled expression.

I had an idea that society was not a concept she had given much thought to, and if she had, the station of an actress was perhaps above what she had expected before we had taken her under our protection.

"Carlo, I think you need to explain," I said.

"Very well," he sighed, hesitated a moment. "I thought to see you and your sister well married to men who will care for you, provide for you. Now that Clarissa is well again, I planned to entertain, take you with us when we attend social outings, balls and such. There is not yet a season here for young ladies, no debutantes, but I thought we could give a ball in your honor, to launch you . . ." He stopped speaking noticing that Susanna looked even more puzzled.

"But, I like to sing an play," she muttered.

"Ladies sing and play for gatherings of friends."

Susanna looked down, "Who would have damaged goods such as me?"

My heart ached with the knowledge that this was her opinion of herself.

"Oh, my darling girl." I choked back tears. "You can't be held responsible for what was done to you." But I knew that even though what I said was how it should be, I was lying. The men who had held her and her sister captive had abused them sexually as well as emotionally. They had mostly recovered from the emotions that had crushed their spirits, but I was uncertain how prospective husbands would view them.

She must have known it too, because she did not look up.

"Susanna, sweetheart, few of the people in this city are pure," Carlo said. "Most everyone here has secrets, pasts they are escaping. This place represents a new beginning, a clean slate, for everyone . . . including you."

She looked at Carlo as he spoke, but clearly was not convinced.

"Here's something else to consider, the men in this city greatly outnumber the women." Carlo smiled at her. "A woman as beautiful, gracious and talented as you will have numerous suitors."

"I don't wanna husband who will only have me 'cause he has no other choice." Susanna pouted. "An' I don't think I wanna husband anyway."

"I'll make a deal with you Susanna, now that Clarissa is well, we will organize an afternoon salon. You start deciding what pieces to play, and we will work with Cook on a menu and invite people for Saturday afternoon. Give you a chance to see what choices are available to young ladies. If you enjoy the afternoon, we will plan a ball in your honor."

Susanna nodded without looking up from her hands.

"And if you still want to be an entertainer, I will see to it that you find a suitable theatre in which to perform. Definitely not a saloon."

Chapter 64

"No, I do not think we should invite Lola. I'm quite certain the Countess is the kind of woman who would steal everyone's attention away from Susanna," I said.

Carlo and I were sitting side by side at his desk in the library. "Besides, you have yet to explain how you know her."

"In Paris, we were both students," Carlo said. "She and a couple of English Lords were scheming to make her a famous dancer. They made up her name and her dance, which is not really a dance so much as an act." He set down the pen he used to write our guest list and placed his hand on my shoulder.

"Were you involved with her?" I asked pulling away.

"Do you mean was I sleeping with her? Or did I think I was in love with her? The answer to both is no. I would have had to get in a long line to do either." Carlo smiled at me. "I do believe you are jealous." His hand left my shoulder, traveled to my waist, drew me closer to him.

"I did have the thought that perhaps she came to this city looking for you." I looked into his eyes. Could I tell if he lied to me?

"How would she know I was here? If not for you, I would be hiding out at my rancho and she never would have found me." His hand found my breast. "I think we should take a break from our task." He looked at the sofa that flanked the fireplace.

"Perhaps she heard some gossip?" I offered.

Carlo withdrew the pen from my hand, slipped an arm beneath my bottom, and carried me to the sofa. "I love this clothing style you have adopted. A sash that is easily untied," He pulled the sash from my skirt. "No corset to struggle with." His hand slid up from my waist to tease my nipple with his fingers.

My body immediately reacted with a surge of thrill between my legs. "Carlo, Lola definitely behaved as though she expected you to call on her. She knew you were here."

He raised my shirt, licked each nipple in turn.

"Are you trying to distract me from this subject?" I stuttered.

"It seems to be working." He looked up from his task, grinning. "Darling, I have no interest in that woman, but I would be happy to discuss her with you . . . some other time." He pulled my blouse over my head. His mouth captured mine; his tongue flirted with mine. His hand slipped beneath my skirt, eased down my pantaloons while his tongue distracted me.

"Is the door locked? I managed to say against his mouth.

"Yes, my darling," he whispered.

"You planned this?"

"Yes, my darling."

He stood to remove his trousers, glanced at the door, strode to turn the key, and returned to my side.

"You lied," I whispered.

"Yes, my darling."

He shut me up with deep kisses that captured my tongue and took me a to another world of passion. His fingers worked their magic between my legs. His manhood filled the aching void.

It was a long time before we returned to list writing.

Chapter 65

The dressmaker's shop was too small for the number of women and the amount of cloth crammed into the space. This was the fourth shop she had occupied since I visited her to have a gown made for the first ball in the city.

"Charles insists that Susanna have a new wardrobe." I perched on a tiny stool that was the only seating. "He says I have been having dresses made for them as though they were children. That is appropriate for Sara, but Susanna needs an afternoon dress, an evening gown, a riding habit, a cape, and a morning gown. Is it possible to complete the afternoon dress within the week?"

The tiny dressmaker was the same woman we first met in the Sierra's. Both of us had improved our circumstances since those days. Mary was much in demand and now had two Chinamen assisting her with the sewing. The men worked in an adjacent room out of sight of the ladies who were her clientele.

"I'm going to have to find more help." She smiled. "I will do the dress for Susanna, but what about your wardrobe? I can see it needs up dating." She lifted the cape

I now wore over the dresses that could not be hooked at my waist.

"Because I'm fat now?" I scowled.

"Women's figures mature after childbirth. In time your waist will re-appear, but your bust and hips may remain fuller." She inspected the dress I wore under the cape. "Send in your favorite afternoon dress to be refitted, we'll add some gussets."

She pulled the measuring tape from around her neck and measured my waist. She made a note in her tablet. "Shall we do the new style for the evening gown?"

"The new style?" I asked.

Susanna and I both gave her our full attention.

"Crinolines," the tiny seamstress said as she continued to measure my new body size. "To make the skirt fuller. The hoops take some getting used to managing. One has to sit just so to avoid the skirt flying up. I think we should use flounces for the afternoon dress. And then make a supply of pantalets to use under the hoop skirts."

"Flounces seem a good idea," I agreed.

"What's a flounce?" Susanna asked.

"A large ruffle on the skirt, usually done in layers of at least three, gives the skirt fullness. Oh, here's a drawing of a flounced skirt." The seamstress pointed to the drawing of a dress hanging on the wall. "That drawing was one of the few things I salvaged from the last fire. I don't have a drawing of the crinoline skirt, a client showed me a drawing she had, said it was all the rage in New York."

"We are going to need a lot of dresses, aren't we?" I

smiled at our little dressmaker. "You'll need a lot of helpers if every woman in the city is to want the new style."

"Yes, the Countess has already ordered Spanish dancer skirts with the crinoline."

"The Countess?" I asked.

"She is a friend of your husband, correct?"

"Yes," I answered. "Well, an acquaintance."

"She was very curious about you. Asked a lot of questions. Between us, I think she was disappointed to learn he is married, and to such a beautiful lady."

"She asked me about you also," Susanna said.

"Really?" I said. "What did you tell her?"

"That you're not only beautiful but in fact the sister of uh English lord. An' kind, an' generous, an' that your husband is mad for you." Susanna's grin changed to a frown. "I suppose that were why she showed uh, interest in me."

"My sweet girl, I think she appreciated your talent," I said.

"I think she din't even know about my talent when she invited me to her suite. I must learn to be more careful about the company I keep. Right?"

Chapter 66

Susanna, beautiful, ethereal in pale blue to match her eyes, floated into the parlor. Susanna and I were clothed in our afternoon dresses. Carlo had managed to acquire a piano and arranged for a pianist to accompany her. A dainty chair accompanied by a small table that held her ukulele sat next to the piano.

The flames of a crackling fire reflected in the silver tea service. Cook had made tea sandwiches, scones, and tiny cakes, which were displayed interspersed with roses on a tiered server. Our guests were to choose from tea, coffee, punch or champagne. Cook, in a pristine white apron, watched over the tea table.

I had tried to coax Lopa into one of my unaltered afternoon dresses. It would only be slightly short on her, but she refused to participate in our tea party. "Watch children," she insisted and they stayed upstairs in the nursery.

This was to be our first entertaining in our new home. I hoped it would be the first of many as even the anticipation was fun. I asked the pianist to play softly to provide background music. I checked my upswept hairdo in the mirror above the mantle, strolled to the window to watch for our guest's arrival.

Carlo had invited young men he deemed suitable. I had invited lady friends, Mrs. Stewart, Mrs. Taylor, and Mrs. Roberts, all of whom I had met at the dressmakers. I had asked that they each bring a guest in order to broaden our social circle.

Mrs. Stewart and a young man I took to be her nephew alighted from a buggy at our front gate. Carlo had asked Jorge to be stationed there to assist our guests with their horses and carriages. As we did not have a butler nor a housemaid who spoke English, Carlo greeted guests at the front door and escorted them to the parlor.

I introduced Susanna to each guest as they arrived. When each guest had been served and comfortably settled, I coaxed a nervous Susanna to take her place next to the piano.

She arranged her flounced skirt around the chair, picked up her ukulele, and gave her audience a quick smile, before launching into her signature song, *"Oh! Susanna."* Once she began to sing, *"Oh don' cha cry for me,"* her nervousness disappeared.

The occasion was proceeding pleasantly, when I saw an unwelcome sight in the front garden. Countess Lola attired in her customary Spanish dancer garb walked up the path to our front door. What was she doing here? Had Carlo invited her even though I had said not to do so?

I forced a smile and motioned to Carlo to look out at

the garden. He slipped from the room and went to the front entrance. He stepped outside to greet her, but even with the door closed, I could hear her shrill voice. "Carlo querido, I came to pay my respects to your charming wife, but I see you are enjoying tea."

From what I heard of the conversation, it was clear that Carlo felt obliged to invite her to join us. I prayed she would not cause a scene.

Her very presence distracted from Susanna's recital. Realizing she had lost her audience, Susanna lay down her ukulele at the end of her second song. Polite applause was punctuated with murmurs of curiosity about our unexpected visitor.

Carlo introduced Lola as Countess Landsfeldt to each of our guests. Lola greeted each of the women with disinterested politeness, but flirted with every man.

Susanna was no longer the center of attention, but Mrs. Stewart's nephew, Stanley went to her side. "Miss Susanna, may I fetch you a punch?"

Susanna smiled, nodded, but continued to watch the Countess work her wiles on the men in the room. Stanley returned with the punch, told Susanna he had enjoyed her singing, and asked if he could call on her the next afternoon. She said, "Of course," with little enthusiasm.

Within minutes of Lola's arrival, our lady guests began to thank us and make their departures. Mrs. Stewart whispered, "My nephew seems quite taken with your husband's niece. I presume she is not seeing . . . er, is not spoken for?"

"No, in fact, we are planning to give a ball in her honor as soon as a suitable location is found." I replied.

"Oh, how wonderful, it will be our first debut," she exclaimed and kissed my cheek.

I had seen the last lady to the door and returned to the parlor where young men encircled Lola.

Susanna whispered, "She's old in't she? How does she do it?"

What I wanted to know was how did she know we would be providing an audience for her today?

Chapter 67

"We could decorate the courtyard, tent the garden." I suggested as Carlo and I discussed where to hold a ball for Susanna's debut. "Maybe we should wait until the Countess leaves the city. Do you have any idea when that will be?"

"My darling, how many times do I have to tell you? I had no idea she would turn up yesterday." Carlo grinned. "But I know how I could make it up to you."

"How did she know we were entertaining?" I wondered aloud.

"Small town gossip. She probably heard about our tea party at the hotel. Or at your dressmaker's?"

"Oh yes, the dressmaker's," I said. "Damn."

"Perhaps you have to make it up to me?" he said, still grinning. "Let's continue this conversation upstairs?" His fingers played with the tendrils of hair on my neck.

"Carlo, be serious." I pulled away. "We need to make some decisions, send out invitations. It's not like a tea party. We have to give weeks of notice so that all the ladies can have their gowns made and there is a shortage of dressmakers in this city."

"If we have to give several weeks notice, there's no guarantee whatever location we choose won't have burnt to the ground before the ball," Carlo said. "So, I say we tent the garden. Now that's decided, upstairs with you."

He slid his arms beneath my bottom, nibbled at the back of my neck and carried me up the staircase. He kicked open the door to our bedroom, tossed me on the bed, and kicked the door closed again while he stripped off his clothing.

"Do you think the garden is big enough? Maybe we should use the corral?" I sat up to talk.

Carlo plopped on the bed next to me. He flung an arm across my shoulders and gently pushed me back to the feather mattress. He wrapped both arms around me and pulled me close kissing my mouth to stop me chattering. His fingers slipped under my blouse, tweaked my nipples. But as soon as his mouth moved from mine towards my breasts, I thought of another idea for the ball.

"Carlo, what if we decorated the stables?"

"Dammit woman, I'll build you a hell of a ball room if you'll just shut up about it while I ravish you."

Chapter 68

There was no ball.

Susanna begged us not to try to pass her off as a lady. "That man, Stanley, I . . . I don't wan' uh husband. I don't wan' ta . . . I am grateful for all you have dun for me, for my sister. An' uh ball an' such, you do for Sara. She fits in."

Carlo and I spoke with her at length, but to no avail. She was not comfortable with the people we had invited to the tea party, and she could not imagine that style of life. She understood we were concerned for her safety and health. Carlo told her horror stories of girls who were forever banned from society. To which she answered with the Countess as an example of an exciting life.

"If you are determined to be an entertainer, please allow me to escort you to various music halls, see you settled in to safe living quarters." Carlo said.

Susanna grinned. "Oh, that would be won'erful."

"Is that possible, safe living?" I asked thinking of the endless fires not to mention shootings and other violence.

Carlo placed his arms on both of our shoulders. "I'll make inquiries. We'll do our best."

Chapter 69

Over breakfast the next morning, Carlo announced, "I have found a couple of possible situations. The best is Bella Union Theatre."

Susanna smiled, danced around the courtyard.

Sara was silent, sad-faced.

My heart sank, but I forced a smile. "It will be alright, Sara. She's only going across town." But I knew that she was in fact going to another world, one that it would be best that Sara not visit. "Let's make an agreement to have Sunday afternoon supper every week. Susanna can fill us in on all of her adventures."

"Oh yes, every Sunday," Susanna sang. Sara smiled weakly.

I insisted that I accompany Carlo and Susanna.

"I am so excited," Susanna smoothed the deep red skirt of her riding habit. In the run up to our tea party, Mary had managed to complete all the dresses we had ordered for Susanna, so at least we would be seeing her off with a presentable wardrobe. The ball dress, done in the latest fashion with a full crinoline skirt, would do well for performances.

The gussets Mary had added to my jacket made it possible to button.

Carlo assisted us into the buggy and he drove. I hoped that the wardrobe, and the arrival with reputable guardians would send a message to the scoundrels that inhabited the world Susanna was to enter; a message to treat this young woman with respect. I was still hopelessly naïve.

Carlo took us to a tall wood building near Portsmouth Square. The proprietor pleasantly requested that Susanna audition.

She pulled her ukulele from its new case and began a rendition of her theme song,

"Oh! Susanna, Oh don't you cry for me,

Cos' I've come from Alabama, Wid my banjo on my knee"

As her sweet and true voice filled the empty hall with the sounds of the nonsensical lyrics, she looked far more at ease in this setting than she had been while singing for our guests in the parlor. The three of us including Jake the proprietor clapped our appreciation.

"Nice, young lady. Howa bout a ballad?" Jake asked.

Susanna smiled, "I just learned uh new one. The Countess taught me uh German song."

"Let's hear it." Jake said.

"How can I leave thee! How can I bear to part!

That thou hast all my heart, Dearest believe!

Thou hast this soul of mine, so wholly is it thine

That I can love no-one but thee alone."

A man holding a broom, another with a hammer in his hand entered the hall and stood at the back listening. Two women in dressing gowns came from the side of the stage and quietly moved to the front where they could see who produced these glorious sounds.

"Blue is the flow-ret called the forget me not,
Ah! Lay it on thy heart, and think of me."

Instead of concentrating on her hands on the ukulele, Susanna smiled at her growing audience between choruses.

"Should hope fade with the Flow'rs, love's wealth shall still be ours."

Her face glowed with happiness even before the clapping began and the proprietor announced, "I'd be happy to have her."

"We have rooms upstairs, she'd be welcome to live there," he added.

Carlo asked to inspect the rooms while Susanna and I chatted with the two women.

"Do you like it here?" I asked them.

"It's good," the one named Sheila said. "Jake is fair with wages and keeps unwanted attentions away from us."

The other woman nodded her agreement to Sheila's statement.

"Let's step outside," Carlo said when he returned from inspecting the rooms. "Please excuse us," he said to Jake.

We stood on the planked sidewalk.

"The rooms are clean, furnished simply with bed, chair, table and chest. There's a bathing room at the end of the passageway. The women have the floor to themselves,"

Carlo reported.

"What was the other place?" I asked.

"This one is definitely the better choice of the two," Carlo said. "That's why I brought you here first."

We went home to pack Susanna's things.

I'd learned a lesson about thinking I knew what was best for someone else.

Chapter 70

We fell into a routine of Sunday suppers early enough that Susanna could spend a few hours with the family and still return to the theatre in time to dress for her performance. The Countess taught her how to do her make-up for the stage. The high fashion ball gown Mary had sewn gave Susanna a presence that set her apart from the typical entertainer.

Perhaps it was her respectable appearance, or the efforts of the theatre owner, which made it socially acceptable to attend by even the most highly regarded families. Her performances were soon sold out for days then weeks ahead and acquaintances applied to Carlo for assistance in securing admission tickets.

Susanna flourished, glowing with her happiness. Bouquets of flowers were replaced by increasingly more elaborate floral arrangements filling the rooms of the girls and overflowing into the halls. But Susanna, while she graciously thanked her admirers with notes, refused their personal attentions.

Mary was kept busy designing new gowns for Susanna

and the other ladies who wished to emulate her look. Sara and I arranged our fittings to coordinate with Susanna's giving us the opportunity to catch up on her life without the men being present. We were all thrilled with her success.

Everything was going so well for our family. We were all very happy in our new home.

Chapter 71

"It's after four," Sara whined as she continued to pace the courtyard floor as she had been doing for the last hour. "She's two hours late."

"She's probably rehearsing and forgot the time," I said, but I was concerned also. I looked at Carlo with what I hoped was an imploring message in my eyes.

"I'll go fetch her," he said. "Or at least verify that she is okay." He stood, asked Jorge to join him. I wondered why as they headed for the stables.

"Sara, let us play with the babes." I picked up baby Teddy, took Emma Rose's hand, and motioned to Sara to follow us to the garden.

The Sunday afternoon sun had burned away the morning fog, and softly lit the flower border and the children's play lawn. Sara soon joined Emma Rose in chasing the butterflies attracted by the glowing blossoms.

I was content to watch the two girls frolic while I nursed the baby, but when the sun became low in the sky and a cool wind chilled the air, I began to worry again.

I noticed Emma Rose shiver. "It's time to go inside

girls." I led them into the parlor where Lopa had lit the fire.

Lopa set a tea tray for the three of us on the table in front of the fireplace. Emma Rose snagged a cookie. She gave me a guilty look as she took the first bite.

"Sandwich first," I reminded her.

Sara used the teacup to warm her hands, but made no move to take a sandwich. Her blue eyes looked at me with worry. "It's been a long time, they should be back by now," she said.

As if answering her concern, we heard the sound of horses headed towards the stables. Sara dashed from the room before I could head her off.

I handed the baby to Lopa, followed Sara.

Jorge handled the horses. Carlo walked towards us shaking his head.

"You didn't find her?" I asked.

"No," he said, "But we know she is with the countess so I'm certain she is safe." His eyes belied his assurances.

"I will look for her myself," Sara said.

"I won't allow that for several reasons," Carlo said. "One, the evening is not a safe time for you, or any young lady, to be on the streets of the city, and two, Jorge and I have already looked for her in more places than you could ever access. Tomorrow, in the morning, you and I will go to the theatre. I'm sure we will find her there practicing her ukulele."

Sara looked at her feet, muttered something I couldn't make out, but she returned to the parlor and picked up a sandwich.

Carlo took my arm, pulled me with him into the court-yard. "She must not wander in the city," he said quietly.

I looked at him, waited for an explanation.

"A ship from the Orient has been quarantined in the harbor," he said, "but not before a few passengers dis-appeared into the city."

"Quarantined?" I asked.

"Cholera."

Chapter 72

It was assumed that the missing passengers had hidden in what was being called Chinatown, a portion of the city that bordered Sydney Town and Portsmouth Square. It was overcrowded with a population comprised of the Chinese who had come in expectations of growing rich in the gold fields. If they had grown rich, they hid it well. But then they would be smart to do so.

I wondered if the early arrivals were shocked at the bigotry with which they were met in America, the land of immigrants. While my mother who came from England was welcomed even in the highest society, the Chinese were badly treated by nearly everyone except the Californios. Granted mother's father being an Earl might have had some influence on her reception. But it was obvious to all that a European background helped one assimilate successfully.

Very few Chinese women had arrived, and there was talk of limiting future immigration of Chinese women in an effort to control the growth of the Chinese community. Why any of these people would want to be in this hostile place was difficult to understand. Their lives in China must have been horrible.

Finding the latest arrivals in the crowded ghetto was impossible. Best choice was to steer clear of the area as Carlo warned everyone in our household to do.

"But Chinatown is literally next door to the theatre where Susanna lives," I said when we were alone.

"Yes, unfortunately it is, but I will keep Sara in the carriage except when we enter the theater directly," Carlo said. "And do not even think of demanding to go along. You are not yet fully recovered and you must consider your children."

I nodded, but when they left the house the next morning I found it torture to stay behind. I paced the floor, tried my best not to imagine horrifying scenarios. But the longer Sara and Carlo were gone, the more my panic grew. Lopa found me pacing, wringing my hands, and suppressing tears.

"Feed baby," she said and motioned to the rocking chair indicating I should sit. I sat and took the baby.

"No good for baby," she said.

I understood her abbreviated language. My worry was not good for the baby. I didn't believe, as she did, that my moods could sour my breast milk, but I did see that the baby was aware of my upsets. I took several deep breaths and tried to think pleasant thoughts.

Chapter 73

Carlo came home without either of the girls. He asked Lopa to take the children out of the parlor and told me to sit down.

"Susanna is ill."

"What?" I said. "Please not with Cholera."

He nodded, "I'm afraid so."

"Oh, dear God." I tried to breath. "Sara?"

"She refused to leave her sister." He collapsed into the chair next to mine. "I couldn't dissuade her. And she is correct, without care, Susanna will not survive."

"And you? Are you not also in danger?"

"I think not. One, I was not exposed, I only looked into the room from the hall, and two, I have been exposed to the disease before without falling ill. Perhaps I am immune."

I reached for his hand. He withdrew from my reach, moved across the room. "To be safe I will keep my distance from you and the children. I think it would be wise for me to go to the rancho."

"But should you fall ill, there will be no one there to care for you."

"There would be, but perhaps I should stay close. In case I am needed," Carlo said. "I'll stay in the stables."

Lopa stood in the doorway. "Children sleep," she said. "I go."

"Lopa, you aren't going to Susanna," I said. "Please."

"I no sick. I care, I know." She exited, headed for the kitchen.

I followed her. She was packing a basket with jugs, herbs, and her secret ingredients. She filled the jugs with water.

"Surely, they have water," I said.

She pointed to the water in the jugs. "Water clean."

I looked at Carlo.

"You know, there is a theory that unsanitary water carries the disease." He shook his head. "I don't know from where she gets her wisdom, but I know from my travels that the important care for Cholera patients includes keeping them hydrated."

Carlo took several jugs from the shelf, carried them to the well. When he returned he said to Lopa, "I'll load the wagon and take you to the girls."

Chapter 74

I heard the wagon return hours later. From the door to the garden, I saw the flare of a lantern in the stables. I ran to the light, "Carlo, where are you?"

He emerged from one of the stalls. "I'm right here darling, but I think you should keep your distance. I couldn't stand it if I were to infect you."

I swallowed the scream of sudden terror I felt. What if I were to lose the girls? Or Lopa? Or, oh god help me, Carlo? In a flash I remembered how frightened I was when I first left Rancho del Mar. Alone, pregnant, no idea where I was going. What would have become of me if Lopa had not followed me?

And now, how would my children survive without Lopa and Carlo to take care of us? Could I survive the broken heart? I shook the fearsome thoughts from my head.

"Is Susanna going to be alright?" I asked.

"I think she has a chance. Lopa knows to keep her hydrated, and Susanna is tougher than she appears," Carlo said.

"But don't people usually die from cholera?"

"Not always." Carlo masked his grim look with a forced smile. "Young, otherwise healthy people often survive."

"What about Lopa? She's not young." In truth I had no idea how old Lopa was. Her wisdom was that of an old woman, but her strength was that of a girl.

Carlo looked at me with longing in his eyes. "I wish I could take you in my arms, reassure you that everyone will survive." He shook his head. "But I will keep my distance, please go inside. You will have to care for the children on your own. Even feed them because Cook, Won Toy has disappeared into Chinatown. I believe he is also tending sick."

I kissed my hand and blew the kiss to my husband. "I love you. Please take care."

I walked back, checked on the children asleep in the nursery, looked out the window and saw the lantern dim, then go out in the stables. I crawled into the cot in the corner of the nursery and begged God to spare my loved ones.

Chapter 75

Three days later Uncle Diego entered the garden where I played with my children. His serious countenance frightened me before he spoke. I held my breath expecting bad news.

"Is it bad?" I asked rising from where I had sat on the bench.

His smile was softened with sadness. "Many people have died, but Lopa taught Won Toy how to deal with the dehydration the sickness brings, and between them they have saved lives. They force water into the mouths of the sick when the ill have no strength to drink on their own. Carlo and Jorge have carried clean water to Lopa and Won Toy."

"Are they well?" I asked.

"I believe so but as I am an old man, Carlo will not allow me to come close," Uncle Diego said. "And you too have been quarantined, no?"

"Yes." Really my circumstances were a reverse quarantine, but I understood what he meant.

"Carlo thinks I should take you and the children to his

rancho. Farther away from the sickness."

"No." I immediately regretted my rude answer to this kind man who had always shown me respect and affection, but I did not want to be exiled even farther away from my loved ones.

"Carlo fears that you will not be able to stay away from the ill."

I almost smiled at the realization of how well my husband knew me. I was having trouble resisting the temptation to see for myself how they were faring. Then the wording of Uncle Diego's statement alarmed me. "Is someone besides Susanna ill?" My heart stopped while I waited for his answer.

"I'm afraid so my dear." He lowered his gaze to his feet. "Sara is quite ill."

I sat down hard.

Uncle Diego took my hand. "Are you feeling alright?"

I nodded.

"Susanna appears to be recovering. And Sara is young. She will be recovering next."

Chapter 76

I refused to accompany Uncle Diego to the rancho.

I waited for Jorge to return to load the wagon with water, and when he did, I ran to ask him for news.

"Señora," he said, "please stay back."

"Please tell me, is Carlo well?"

Jorge nodded.

"Lopa?"

He nodded.

"Susanna?"

"Better."

"Sara?"

He studied the jug, then the ground.

"Tell me," I demanded.

He shook his head.

"Is she worse?"

"No sé."

"What do you mean, you don't know? Is she recovering?"

"Señora, por favor. Don Carlo not allow me in sick rooms. I take wagon with water to the street. Lopa and don

241

Carlo take water inside."

"I want to go with you."

His eyes grew large. "No, no Señora. Por favor."

I realized I couldn't go at that moment. I must find someone to care for the children, but surely I could do what Jorge did and see Carlo and Lopa and learn how each of them fared. If I didn't go into the sick rooms, I wouldn't carry the disease. Besides, Carlo said it was carried in the water . . . or at least maybe it was.

Surely one of the household staff was still here. I went to find a housemaid.

Chapter 77

I found a maid, took her to the nursery, but by the time I returned to where Jorge had been loading the wagon, he was gone. I suspected he left without completely filling the wagon in order to escape my demand to ride along. I saddled my horse and rode toward the city.

In the distance, along the road, I saw a cloud of dust raised by a galloping horse. I reined in my horse when I recognized my husband bearing down on my position. I was in trouble.

Damn I refused to be treated like a child. Now I was going to be chastised, and worst of all, I knew I deserved it.

Carlo stopped twenty feet away from me. "Clarissa, what are you thinking? Do you want to leave your children motherless?"

I failed to stop the tears that sprang to my eyes. "I just want to know what is happening."

Carlo took a deep breath, sighed. "Susanna is recovering, she will be fine."

"Is she well?" I asked.

"She is weak, but she will be well."

"Uncle Diego said many have died."

Carlo nodded. "Hundreds actually. But it seems that if the sick survive the first twenty-four hours, they have a good chance to get well."

"And Sara? When did she become ill?" I asked.

"She showed symptoms yesterday."

"Lopa?"

"She is fine, she is careful to only drink water untouched by the ill, clean water from our well, food from our farm."

"Then why is Sara ill?"

"I believe she drank contaminated water before Lopa warned her not to do so," Carlo answered. "But there is no certainty that water or food spread the disease."

"And you? Are you well?"

"I'm fine darling."

"Won Toy?"

Carlo shook his head. "I don't know, we have not seen him, he has disappeared into Chinatown. But he knows to use clean water, his messengers retrieve water Jorge brings from our well."

"When will you all be home?"

"Once Sara is past danger, we will bring the girls to recover in their rooms in our house if you promise to keep your distance. And, of course, the children will be kept away," Carlo said.

"Tomorrow?"

He shook his head. "A few days."

But it was less than a few days.

Chapter 78

Carlo carried a sobbing Susanna into the courtyard and up the stairs to the bedroom she had once shared with her sister. He held his hand up to motion me away from both of them. But I couldn't stand to watch my darling Susanna weep without comforting her.

"Please Carlo. Surely you wouldn't bring her here if she were still contagious." I opened the bedcovers. Carlo placed her in the bed, and I smoothed the covers over the sobbing young woman.

"Clarissa, I'm so sorry." Susanna moaned between sobs. "All my fault." She pulled the quilt over her head and wailed. "I've killed my sister."

I looked to Carlo, "What has happened? Sara died?"

He nodded.

"But Lopa saved Susanna, why couldn't she save Sara?"

Carlo bit his lip, shook his head.

"Tell me."

He motioned to the doorway; I followed him to the hall.

"We don't know how this disease works," he whispered. "Sara was weaker, maybe tired from caring for . . ." He shook his head. "Sara quickly developed the glassy, sunken eyed look of the seriously dehydrated. I believe that is what kills."

I wanted to melt into his arms, forget this was happening, but he kept me at arm's length.

"Sara just didn't have the reserves to withstand . . . I'm sorry my darling, I know you love these girls as though they were your own." He reached to wipe a tear from my cheek. "But you and Lopa saved them from a cruel death once. You gave Sara good years. Joyful years she would never have had."

I turned, returned to Susanna's bedside, and brushed her pale blonde hair off her face. I held her, sobbed with her until she cried herself to sleep.

Chapter 79

Susanna stayed with us for six weeks, until she regained her strength. And until the disease had run its course in the community.

For the first month, she did not pick up her ukulele nor did she join in the children's songs.

Lopa and Won Toy returned tired but in good health. Their earlier jealousy was behind them, having allied against the disease that swept through much of the city. Lopa even allowed Won Toy to prepare food for the children.

The one plus side to the horrible events; it appeared that the cholera had chased the Countess from our city.

We settled into a quiet domestic routine with the antics of our growing children distracting us from our grief. Emma Rose was more than usually affectionate with Susanna, showering her with kisses and hugs whenever Susanna looked sad.

Carlo continued to mention moving our household to his rancho, but he understood that we did not wish to be far away from Susanna once she returned to the theater.

Carlo appeared reluctant to be far from his family. He and Uncle Diego moved their business meetings with lawyers from Diego's offices to our parlor and library.

I worried about the continual meetings with lawyers, and since Carlo seemed to think the way to keep me from worrying was to keep me uninformed, I eavesdropped from outside the door.

"It will be expensive to pursue all of these cases," I heard one of the lawyers say.

"Yes, I agree," Carlo said. "We must choose which ones we have the best chance of winning, the ones with the most documentation. The others, we negotiate settlements. Doña Maria Elena has no plans to return to California, so I say we sell her property and the others with the similar circumstances."

"But Carlo," don Diego addressed his nephew in Spanish, "Rancho del Mar should by all rights belong to your son now."

"Uncle, let us speak English for the sake of our associates," Carlo said.

Diego grunted his agreement, continued in English. "Your wife's father held title to Rancho del Mar, thus title passes to his heirs. William has already waived his claim in favor of your children."

"Clarissa's father took title to the rancho strictly to protect doña Maria Elena's interest and I will not take advantage—"

A lawyer cleared his throat to interrupt Carlo. "That particular title will be easiest to maintain. We have good paperwork, for the most part specific boundaries, and it adjoins your rancho on the boundary that is most questionable."

"Very well, then I must raise the funds to pay doña Maria Elena for the land," Carlo said.

"I say we sell the land I hold title to," Uncle Diego said. "My rancho is now far from my only family, my dear nephew, his wife and children," Diego explained to the lawyers. "My land lies close to the southern border neighboring Mexico. I am seldom there now."

"Then you will have title to Rancho del Mar," Carlo said.

"No, nephew, I will provide the funds for doña Maria Elena, and I will manage the rancho, but title will be Teddy's."

Carlo must have nodded agreement. "Settled. Now what will we do with these others."

"Not so fast," said a voice I didn't recognize. "I don't think that will work, that won't satisfy the commission."

I spotted Won Toy carrying a tray of refreshments intended for the men in the library. I hurried away from my listening post, but I vowed to quiz Carlo. What in the world was this discussion about?

Chapter 80

The children and I enjoyed the afternoon sun in the garden. Carlo approached from behind my chair, caressed the back of my neck. I stiffened at his touch.

"Why do you keep secrets from me?" I said

Carlo sat in the chair next to mine. "Secrets?"

"Don't," I snapped.

"My darling, you know my secrets," Carlo said. "I shared my complicated ancestry with you, my responsibilities to my uncle, my activities to protect those who cannot protect themselves."

"You don't tell me about your businesses," I said.

"When you asked about the buildings, I explained," Carlo said.

"Only when I asked. You don't share your concerns with me."

"Why would I want to worry you?"

"Carlo, I am no longer ill. You need not protect me. I worry more when I know you are keeping things from me. Like these meetings with lawyers. What is the matter?"

Carlo sighed, took a deep breath.

"Is it really bad?" I asked.

"Oh, my darling, no. It is not really bad. It is just complicated," Carlo said. "I am sorry. I did not realize I was causing you to worry even more by not sharing my concerns."

"So?"

"When Spain relinquished California to Mexican rule, those residents of California who were born in Spain were ordered to leave the province."

"Really? But many of your friends and family, the people I have met here in California were born in Spain," I said.

Carlo nodded. "Yes. In fact, only the clergy, the Jesuit and Franciscan priests, paid much attention to the order."

"That's why the missions no longer have Spanish priests?" I asked.

Carlo nodded again.

"But that was many years ago. Obviously, no effort was made to enforce the Mexican order. So, what does that order have to do with ownership of the ranchos?"

"You were listening to the meeting?" Carlo grinned. "You sneak, you will pay for that."

"You're not funny Charles." I glared at him even though his grin and the implication that I would pay with sexual favors stirred a reaction between my legs. "I have a right to know what is going on in my own home, with my own family."

"Yes, I will explain. Doña Maria Elena was one of the many Spanish born who refused to leave their homes.

251

When the United States took control of California in 1848 the Treaty of Guadalupe Hidalgo provided that the Mexican land grants would be honored, but your father foresaw that there may be complications for those landowners who held Spanish grants."

"I know that was why Father took title to Rancho del Mar. He told me he thought an American would find it easier to hold onto the land. But why is that an issue now?"

"American officials went to Monterey and took the provincial records of the Spanish and Mexican governments."

"So, they know that Rancho del Mar was a Spanish land grant?"

Carlo scowled, nodded.

"Is that why you and Diego are concerned now?"

Carlo shook his head.

"What is it?" I demanded.

"A new law has been passed. It is called, *"An Act to Ascertain and Settle Private Land Claims in the State of California."*

"That's not a good thing, to have it resolved?" I held my breath awaiting further explanation.

"Backers of the California Senator who pushed this law through the United States Senate did not have resolution in mind," Carlo said.

"They are trying to get the land?" I asked.

"Yes."

"Do you know who these backers are?"

"Not yet, but I have suspicions."

Chapter 81

"Don, uh, Uncle Diego, I think I recognize that man." I nodded at the back of a short man with sandy blonde hair.

Diego and I watched the proceedings of the Board of California Land Commissioners from the balcony at the rear of the hall. Carlo and our lawyers were to present titles to our land to the board for confirmation.

I was certain the short man was Augustus Pennyworth. If I was correct, his presence did not bode well for our confirmation to proceed without complication. I suspected Pennyworth hated Carlo. From the time I first noticed him, as we journeyed to California, he had demonstrated his determination to impede Carlo at any opportunity. Carlo had yet to explain why.

Our lawyer handed papers to the secretary of the board. Six members of the board were seated at a long table on a dais at the front of the room. Each man glanced through a stack of papers that had earlier been placed at each chair. The secretary handed our additional documents to the chairman.

"Mr. Anthony?" the chairman said looking at Carlo.

"Yes, sir." Carlo stood.

"This all appears to be in order." The chairman turned to the members of the board, "I recommend—"

Pennyworth poked the side of the man next to him. The man stood, "Your honor, I beg the board's indulgence. There is further information I believe has been purposely withheld from the board."

A buzz of conversation filled the hall. Diego and I exchanged glances and sucked in deep breaths.

"Who are you, sir?" the chairman asked.

"Jefferson Atticus, attorney at law."

"Representing who?" the chairman asked.

"Interests of justice, sir."

From the balcony, I could see two of the board roll their eyes. But the chairman was interested. "What is this information, sir?"

"Mr. Anthony intends to lay claim to two grants both consisting of several thousand acres."

Our lawyer jumped from his seat, stood at Carlo side. "Sir, may we know who is Attorney Atticus's client?"

The chairman ignored our lawyer's question, addressed Carlo, "Is this true Mr. Anthony?"

"I hold title to an additional land grant inherited from my family. Rancho del Mar was granted to my wife's father. My son will inherit—"

"Who is your wife's father, sir?"

"Edward Wells."

"An American?" the chairman asked.

"Yes, sir."

"Why is he not present?"

"He is deceased. My wife and her brother inherited. My brother-in-law has assigned his interest to our son Theodore."

Our lawyer handed a paper to Carlo. Carlo offered the paper to the secretary. "This is his affidavit."

"I want to see the papers for the grant held in your name," the chairman announced. "We will adjourn the public meeting while those papers are presented and studied."

Chapter 82

Carlo's attorney provided the proof of title to the Antoine property, Rancho de La Cruz and a map of the boundaries. The two ranchos adjoined on the northeast boundary of Rancho del Mar. Unfortunately, due to the hilly terrain through which the boundary ran, and the close relationship between the families of the owners, the exact boundaries had never been clearly defined.

Carlo and his team of lawyers had not considered the boundary between the two to be of importance, but after a great deal of back and forth including objections by Jefferson Atticus the commissioners concluded that the boundaries must be properly marked and surveyed before the grants could be confirmed.

Our attorney whispered to Carlo and me as we exited the court, "I am sorry to say, sir, that I fear that the next argument to be presented by the attorney Atticus will be to question if Mr. Wells fulfilled the requirements of the Mexican colonization laws."

Carlo sighed, turned to me. "I am sorry darling. It seems that we under estimated the difficulty of these confirmations."

"Augustus Pennyworth is behind this. He sat behind Attorney Atticus," I said to Carlo once we were alone. "Please tell me why he is determined to harm you at every turn. I've told you he was there the . . . when you and Father were shot."

"We have no proof that he was involved."

"But I would swear he was there."

"Darling, I'm sorry to tell you, the word of a woman and two natives will not convince the courts to try him."

I sighed.

Carlo pulled me into his arms. "Clarissa, I promise you I will preserve Teddy's right to Rancho del Mar."

I considered Carlo's statement and worried how much time, money, and anxiety it would cost our family to retain ownership to property that might prove to be nothing more than a burden of responsibility. I decided to think about that later. Instead I asked Carlo the question that had bothered me for a long time.

"What does Pennyworth have against you?"

Chapter 83

Carlo refused to provide a clue as to Pennyworth's motivation for his endless determination to destroy Carlo. He insisted I imagined Augustus Pennyworth's vendetta.

"Carlo, do not be pigheaded." I stomped a foot. "You are foolish to ignore that he is out to get you."

"It is not personal, it is the land that he wants." Carlo poured a brandy for each of us, handed a goblet to me. "I am sorry it has been a difficult day. Drink your brandy and relax now."

I sighed. Was it the difference between men and women? Carlo was so brilliant in business, in construction, in managing, but seemed to be blind to the very personal ill will of Pennyworth. To me, all relationships were always "personal".

Carlo smiled at my frown. "Darling, I should never have invited you to the board meeting, had I foreseen the difficulties. Please do not worry. I will take care of this." He ran his fingers across my neck causing a tingle to run down my spine.

I shook him off, refused to be distracted, but my effort

was for naught. His mouth replaced his fingers. He nibbled at the back of my neck, ran his hand around to my breast. His thumb brushed my nipple through the fabric of my gown. The tingle ran to between my legs. My breathing grew deeper.

The grin that usually charmed me annoyed me when I realized that once again he had won the argument with seduction. But my desire overcame my annoyance and I allowed him to lead me to our bedroom.

Chapter 84

Carlo's mouth captured mine while his hands unfastened the row of tiny buttons on my velvet jacket.

In my impatience, I attempted to help him, but he pushed my hands away. "I want to enjoy every moment of unwrapping my beautiful gift," he murmured against my neck.

His fingers slipped under my camisole to caress my full breasts.

My fingers reached for the fastenings of his breeches.

"No, no distractions from my enjoyment of each moment," Carlo whispered against my mouth. "Let us take this slow. Nice and slow."

My hips were already writhing with desire. Slow! Was this torture in retribution for having scolded him?

The corset that fashion required was not easily removed, and not necessary to be removed in order to enjoy consummation, but my husband insisted that he loosen every lace, unfasten every hook until the torturous contraption fell to the floor. Next his fingers slipped beneath the waist of my pantalettes, his hands cupped my butt cheeks and pulled my hips against his.

Anticipation was building desire that again had me reaching for him. He slipped his arms beneath my legs and my shoulders, picked me up, and placed me on our bed. His eyes held mine as he teased me by slowly stripping his clothing from his body. Again, I reached for him intending to capture his manhood between my fingers, but he withdrew and approached the foot of the bed.

He crawled between my legs and buried his face. His tongue found my center of desire, his fingers slipped rhythmically in and out of my wet. Thrilling sensations built a tension that released showers of starry explosions. When I grew overwhelmed with sensations and tender to the touch, I begged him to enter and fulfill the ache.

PART FOUR

Rancho de La Cruz
July 1852

Chapter 85

Carlo and Uncle Diego concluded that it would be wise to live on the ranchos until the grants were confirmed. Remembering the charm of Rancho del Mar, I was pleased.

"We should ride out and take a look at what you want to take with us when we relocate the household," Carlo said.

"I can hardly wait to see your rancho."

"I hope it does not disappoint. It has always been a working ranch, not grand like Uncle Diego's. Or as homey as Rancho del Mar. That's why I wanted to build it out a bit more." He took my hand in his, fingers caressing my palm. "I want you to like it. Just tell me what you want."

I grinned. "I can do that."

He planted a kiss on my cheek, then my lips. He pulled on the ties of my negligee. "Get into riding gear, before I get too distracted."

My heart ached with love as I watched him walk away to supervise the loading of carts and wagons with the household goods we were to take with us. Two women servants had arrived from the rancho to assist with packing.

Lopa and Won Toy ordered them about.

I hurried to dress. By the time I reached the stables, Jorge waited on the seat of one wagon, Jose on the cart. Carlo held the reins of our horses. He helped me mount and the two of us rode ahead first through agricultural fields and then through golden grass dotted with clusters of oak trees.

Three exhilarating hours of hard riding later, we entered the refreshing cool of a dark grove of tall redwood trees. Carlo spread a blanket over the forest floor lined with fragrant leafs. A creek outlined by bright green ferns burbled nearby.

Carlo unpacked wine, chicken, and peaches from his saddlebag. He uncorked the wine. "Sorry. No glasses." He handed me the bottle and I took a swig.

He patted the blanket next to him and I sat.

The chicken and peaches smelled so good, I suddenly realized I was starving. I bit into the chicken. Offered a bite to Carlo. He grinned and pulled off a chunk with his teeth. We shared three pieces.

Carlo passed me a fat peach. When I bit into it, he licked the juice of the peach that ran down my fingers. Then he licked the juice from my chin, my mouth. Although it was the tastiest peach I'd ever eaten, it was soon forgotten when Carlo loosened my riding jacket, slipped his hand under my skirt. Fingers caressed my thighs then teased my lady parts. His teeth nibbled my breast. All until I was writhing with desire.

He stood me against the giant trunk of the tree and

knelt before me. His mouth found the magic spot, his fingers slipped into me. I lost awareness of everything but the building pleasure that soon sent waves of tingling sensations through my body. He lifted me onto his manhood and repeatedly slammed us into the tree until he groaned with release. He gently returned me to the blanket.

I collapsed onto the blanket, watched the rays of sun dance through the branches, and sighed with contentment. Carlo lay at my side. Dreamily, I thought he had stopped worrying about me having more children.

I drifted into sleep, but soon felt Carlo leave the blanket, repack his bag and lead the horses to the creek for water.

"My lazy darling, we still have a ways to go before dark." He offered me his hand, pulled me up, and helped me refasten my clothes before I mounted my horse.

We rode out of the redwoods and crossed slopes covered with golden grass and oak trees.

An allée of young pine trees lined both sides of a road leading into a tight canyon. The pines were flanked by orderly rows of an orchard. On one side, the first row of trees was heavy with peaches, the next with apricots. The other side looked to be small budding apples.

Carlo raced up the road and opened a gate.

I hurried my horse to where he waited with a broad grin on his handsome face. A gurgling fountain sat in the center of a broad, tiled patio that was surrounded by two wings of an adobe house.

I hid my smile with a forced scowl and a raised

eyebrow. "A primitive little ranch, huh?"

"I have done some work to it," he admitted still grinning. "But there is much still to be done." He held his arms up to me, lifted me to the ground. We walked the horses to a barn that sat farther up the canyon.

When the horses were unsaddled, fed, watered and let loose in the corral, Carlo led me back to the house. One wing housed the kitchen and rooms for the staff, the other had four bedchambers simply furnished with beds and cupboards. Each room had but one small, shuttered window. The center or bottom of the "U" held the sitting room and dining room. Carlo opened the shutters of one window to let light into the room. All of the rooms needed rugs, upholstered furniture, and linens to be comfortable.

"Jorge is bringing some rugs and a sofa, but I know we need more furnishings. We can purchase those together?"

I nodded. "Of course. The children will love it here. Is it safe for them to run free here?"

Carlo hesitated. "We will make it safe," he answered.

I looked at him with a raised eyebrow.

"Each spring, we kill every rattlesnake and mountain lion that is close to the corral or house. Perhaps we will hunt a larger area before we bring the children here."

"Will you show me your caves?" I asked.

"In the morning? They are some distance from here." Carlo looked down the road expecting Jorge and Jose to arrive with the furnishings, but the sound of horses was coming from behind us farther into the canyon.

"Go into the house," he ordered.

When I hesitated, he said, "Now."

"Come with me?" I asked.

"Go."

I hurried into the sitting room and peered out the only unshuttered window at the cloud of dust headed out of the canyon towards our hacienda.

That amount of dust meant several riders, but Carlo waited to meet them by himself. Where were Jorge and Jose?

I hurried into the kitchen looking for some kind of weapon. I picked up a rifle leaning against the back door, checked to see if it was loaded, and returned to the sitting room window. As I stood watch at the window, I reminded myself to breathe.

Carlo had walked to the back of the house, to the rear gate. He faced the fast approaching horsemen with his empty hands at his side.

Chapter 86

Silhouettes of six riders bounced above a cloud of angry dust.

I placed the rifle barrel in the corner of the window opening hoping that it would be unnoticed, but ready should I need to defend my husband.

As they drew closer I recognized the short rider leading the pack, Augustus Pennyworth.

Why does this man haunt us?

Carlo greeted the men as though they had paid us a social call. "Good evening. How can I help you gentlemen?"

His question met with grunts, no answer that I could hear.

He invited them to water their horses, offered the men water to drink. But no one dismounted.

"Anthony," Pennyworth growled. "You have horses in a box canyon up there." He gestured towards the hills behind him. "Several of the herd are black."

Oh, Holy Mother, they had found the Spanish Fox's horses, the black stallions that Diego and Carlo used only when they masqueraded as the Fox.

I waited for Carlo to chew them out for trespassing on his property, but he remained cordial. "Perhaps a whiskey?" he asked ignoring Pennyworth's comment.

"What are those horses doing hidden in that canyon?" Pennyworth asked.

Carlo shrugged as if the horses held no significance. "I have a pretty decent brandy you might prefer."

"If this property is being used for illegal activities, it will be confiscated.

With relief I heard the sound of wagons approaching the front gate. Jorge and Jose, thank heavens.

But then I saw Carlo stiffen at the noise. Why did their arrival concern him?

Chapter 87

I ran to the front patio to alert Jorge and Jose. They chatted in Spanish as they unfastened the horses from the wagon and cart.

"There are men here, with Pennyworth. In the back," I warned them.

Jorge drew his gun, motioned Jose to go around the house from the opposite side, waved me back inside.

I ran back to the window. Carlo was still offering refreshments,

One ugly, dirty man had moved his horse closer to Pennyworth. He tossed a pointed knife from hand to hand, stopped to use it to clean his teeth. He grinned at Carlo when he caught sight of me in the window.

Two of the men on horseback looked to the corner of the house, pulled guns from their holsters. Jose stepped around the corner making his presence known. "Everything okay boss?"

"We are fine, Jose. The gentlemen do not care to have refreshments. They are leaving."

Jorge rounded the other corner. I pulled the rifle into

my arms, trained it on the man with the knife.

"Good day gentlemen."

Pennyworth glared at Carlo, glanced at me, then at Jose. Horses neighed, stomped on the patio. I could see the indecision on his face; he didn't know how many men had arrived. He nodded at Carlo and pulled his horse around the house. The group of men followed.

I ran to the front patio and watched the riders gallop down the tree-lined road. Carlo, Jorge, and Jose joined me.

"Better get these horses watered," Carlo said. "I want to check on the herd, and we will have to move them and the gear by first light."

"Full moon tonight jefe."

Carlo nodded. "Good." He turned to me. "My darling, you will have to go with us. I cannot leave you here alone."

Finally, Carlo was letting me into to his life, his other life.

"We will eat, rest the horses, and leave once the moon gets high."

Chapter 88

Carlo dug through a trunk in the bedroom until he found a dark wool serape for me to wear over my riding jacket. He helped me pull it over my head, brushed my breast with a grin, and patted my behind. "You must stay close to me on this ride."

"Is it dangerous? Where we're going, will there be danger?"

Carlo shrugged. "Most of the animals will be asleep."

"Bears?"

"Maybe we will see one or two."

"Wolves?"

"Possibly, definitely we will hear, maybe even see, coyotes, but they will keep their distance from us."

"Are you worried about those men? Pennyworth?" I asked.

"Yes, they could be waiting to follow us to the caves." Carlo nodded. "I'm pretty sure that is what they are looking for."

"How would they know?"

"Rumors."

"Who knows about the cave? Who would tell?"

Carlo shook his head. "My father kept his knowledge of the caves quiet. He only took trusted servants there. And only Jorge and I moved Diego's gear there. But the caves are no secret among the native tribes."

"But they wouldn't tell someone like Pennyworth," I said.

"It is a rather extensive network of caves stretching many miles. One entrance, the west entrance, is not far from here, but the east entrance is a full day's ride away. It's possible that others have stumbled upon an entrance." Carlo pulled a felt hat from the trunk. "Let us get moving."

The full moon lit Jorge and Jose at the corral where they held the four-saddled horses. Carlo helped me mount. "Your hair reflects the moon light like a torch." Carlo brushed my hair back and placed the dark hat on my head.

"We will check on the herd first," Carlo said as the others mounted. "It is possible that Pennyworth left men at the herd, waiting for us to lead them to the caves. So proceed with care, keep an eye out for trouble."

Chapter 89

Moonlight reflected off two dappled greys. Eyes and teeth appeared to float in five black shadows that flitted toward us in answer to Carlo's low whistle. As they drew close, I recognized three of the stallions that had once been hidden briefly at Rancho del Mar.

Jose and Jorge circled the makeshift corral looking for signs of men lurking there. Jorge pulled his horse next to Carlo. "No sign of anyone jefe."

"Regardless, I think it best to move them," Carlo said. He looked at the moon gauging its position in the sky to determine how much longer we would have the benefit of the bright light. "Let us do that first, while we have the light." He turned to me to explain. "Light will not matter in the caves."

He lifted the rail and the seven horses walked through the improvised gate. They followed Carlo like dogs follow their master. Jose and Jorge rode behind them as protection rather than herding.

We rode to the mouth of the canyon, followed a stream past two contributory creeks to a third creek. We rode up the canyon from which the creek emerged. Shimmers of moonlight reflected off a delicate waterfall that marked the vertical wall of rock at the end of the canyon. The herd followed Carlo into the canyon while Jorge and Jose strung a rope between trees at the entrance.

Carlo murmured reassurances to each of his horses and then lifted the rope so that we could exit. We retraced our route passed the original canyon to a narrow canyon just beyond.

We left our horses tied to a low tree branch and scrambled over piled rocks on foot. A slit in the rock formation hid behind a massive outcrop. We each turned sideways in order to get in to a narrow passageway that soon let into a large cavern.

Jorge and Carlo lit torches they had taken from the entry wall. The light revealed a grotto filled with tapered columns rising from the floor and hanging from the ceiling. A magic but spooky place.

I shivered from the cold damp.

An alcove almost hidden by the columns contained a trunk, several small pouches, a pile of swords and rifles.

"How would anyone ever find this place?" I whispered. My whisper echoed off the damp walls.

Carlo shook his head. "I found this entrance as a child."

His echo was joined by the sound of squeals that grew in volume.

I looked at Carlo. "What in the world? Rats?"

"Bats. I hope you are not afraid of them because we

are going to move these things into the part of the caves where thousands of them live." He pulled a black scarf from the trunk and wrapped it over my hat, around my neck, and over my face up to my eyes. "That will protect you from the guano."

"Guano?"

"Bat droppings."

Lovely.

Jorge and Jose slung pouches over their shoulders and picked up the trunk. Carlo also picked up pouches, handed me two small ones, slung the rest over his shoulders, and carried the weapons.

We exited the back of the cavern again edging through a narrow passage into still another cavern. We climbed through that cavern into another.

The sound of water moving explained the slippery surfaces over which we climbed.

The squeals grew louder; so intense that conversation was impossible.

The next narrow passage opened onto a grotto thick with flapping wings and small black bodies dive- bombing us. The torches illuminated the ceiling covered with black bumps of bats at rest.

We slid on bat droppings through the cavern into a deeper alcove where we deposited the trappings of the Fox. From there we climbed through multiple stinking caverns until we were finally greeted by fresh air. Carlo and Jorge extinguished the torches and stowed them behind a mass of guano-covered stalagmites.

I stumbled over stalagmites slick with droppings and found the source of the fresher air. Exiting the cave, I ran into the sharp branches of manzanita that caught my scarf, hat and serape. Carlo grabbed my arm, pulled me back against the rock wall, and led me from behind the shrubs. He carried my hat and scarf. I shook my head when he offered the filthy items. We hurried away from the caves and the bats.

The four of us were well down the canyon before we spoke. I turned to look behind us.

The exit was hidden behind manzanita shrubs but the flight of masses of bats out into the night sky made the opening obvious.

"Wouldn't it be easy to spot that opening?" I asked.

"Very few of the critters venture out in daylight," Carlo said. "And at night, well, I doubt the merely curious would care to climb into that cave."

I doubted Augustus Pennyworth fell into the "merely curious" category.

Chapter 90

I trashed every garment I had worn into the caves. I found a comfortable peasant blouse and skirt in an old trunk at the rancho. Could these clothes have belonged to Carlo's mother? I promised myself that I would be able to wear only riding gear and peasant blouses once we relocated our household.

I slept well into the next day.

While I was asleep the men had unloaded the wagon and the cart of the furnishings. The sitting room now had two tall-backed leather chairs drawn up to the fireplace. A sofa divided the sitting area from the dining table. Linens were piled onto the table. Cookware was being put away in the kitchen.

"Good afternoon sleepyhead." Carlo handed me a mug of coffee. "Shall we make lists of what else we need here?"

We spent a pleasant, lazy day touring the house and property making lists of not only what we needed to bring, but also what repairs and improvements needed to be made in order to make the location practical for our children.

"Were these clothes your mother's?" I asked Carlo

once the list-making task was complete.

He shook his head. "I do not remember her ever wearing white, or anything that casual. And I do not think my mother spent much time here."

"I thought that the Spanish ladies always wore white, until they wore black that is."

"My mother was not a Spanish lady." Carlo looked away signaling this was not a subject he wished to discuss. "I would like to get an early start in the morning. I will bring workmen to start the fencing and walls as well as another load of furnishings as soon as we can organize. I want to get settled here before the rains start."

"Will our family be safe here?" I asked.

"I will make it safe," he promised.

Later I realized I had asked the wrong question. I should have asked if our family would be safe anywhere.

Chapter 91

We rode back to the city at first light. I gave the redwood grove a wistful look as we passed in haste.

The grounds of our hacienda were quiet. Even though the skies were blue and the garden sunlit, Lopa and the children were not playing there. The dogs did not rush out to greet us. And when we stabled our tired horses, we noticed that all of the horses were already in their stalls rather than in the corral. No one was in sight, but I heard dogs barking inside the house.

Carlo and I exchanged questioning looks at the lack of the usual activity.

"Please take care of my horse, darling. I want to check on the children," I said.

"Wait," Carlo answered. "I will go with you."

We hurried to the garden gate where Carlo lifted the bar that was typically used to lock the gate at night. I pushed past him and ran to the door to the courtyard.

Just inside, Diego and Won Toy each held a dog with one hand and a pistol in their other. Diego sighed upon seeing us, collapsed into a chair.

"The children, where are the children?" I asked as I rushed up the stairs to the nursery. Lopa sat in the rocking chair with Teddy in her lap. Emma Rose ran to my arms. I hugged her to me.

"Lopa, what in the world?" My eyes filled with tears at the relief of finding my children and Lopa. I kissed Emma Rose on both cheeks, leaned over to kiss Teddy, and patted Lopa on her shoulder. "What is happening here?"

Chapter 92

"Man come," Lopa said. "Many riders. Hit Won Toy."

I had no patience for trying to decipher what she was saying. I put Emma Rose back where she had been playing with her dollhouse and rushed downstairs. Uncle Diego spoke in Spanish too fast for me to catch more than an occasional word. "Vigilante," was perhaps the worst one.

"Carlo," I said fighting to control the panic that welled up at the thought that perhaps the vigilance committee had turned its attention to Carlo and Diego. "Please, in English. Tell me."

Carlo hurried to my side, put his arm around me. "Relax darling. It will be okay."

"Dammit Carlo, I'm not a child. Tell me now, what happened?"

Don Diego spoke in English, "I apologize my dear Clarissa." He placed the pistol on the tabletop. "Lopa had the children in the garden. That man, the one who was in court with the lawyer Atticus, came with several riders. They stopped at the gate, yelled for me to come out, but I was not in the house. The children cried. Won Toy went

284

out to see what the noise was. When I came out of the stables, I saw one of the men push Won Toy to the ground, kick him, and grab his pigtail. I picked up the rifle we keep in the stables to protect the horses from predators. I shot over the attacker's head. He walked away from Won Toy, pulled a gun from his holster. Lopa had carried the children inside, came back with a pistol in her hand. She shot a pistol out of the hand of the man who had attacked Won Toy and then all of the men pulled out guns. The stable boy and one of our vaqueros, how do you say, uhm cowboys, came to the garden with guns. The riders rode away." Diego took a breath. "That is what happened."

"What was the thing with the vigilantes?"

Diego and Carlo exchanged looks.

"What?" I shook off Carlo's arm. "What about vigilantes?"

Diego looked at Carlo who nodded back.

"The sheriff came by later and said that Pennyworth was speaking to a meeting of the vigilance committee, attempting to drum up support for arresting Won Toy, Lopa, me and even Carlo."

"On what grounds?"

"That we had shot at his man."

Carlo pulled me back into his arms. "Darling, when Jorge and Jose arrive, I am going to go see if the committee is meeting. Please go up with Lopa and see to the children."

"I'm coming with you." I looked down at my peasant attire, at Carlo's dusty riding gear. "But first we will get cleaned up."

Chapter 93

Lopa helped me get into a corset and crinolines. I dressed in my finest aristocratic day dress and jacket. We dressed my hair and pinned on my new hat.

I insisted that Carlo wear his frock coat and hat.

Jorge drove the new landau that Carlo had bought on a whim, thinking it would be a treat to take me out for a date with a driver perched high above us. I remembered these fancy carriages from visiting London.

Unfortunately, our first outing riding in the landau was not a celebration. I raised my seldom-used parasol and hoped we looked sufficiently intimidating to crush any efforts of Pennyworth's to incriminate our family.

Jorge pulled the landau up in front of the hall. The sound of voices raised in anger drifted through the double doors that stood ajar.

Carlo turned to me. "My darling, I understand your wish to speak to these men, but I believe it would be more appropriate if you were to wait here with Jorge. I have never seen a lady in one of these meetings."

"You have seen women?"

Carlo frowned, shook his head. "Not a lady."

"I'll stay at the back."

"Surely you do not believe that you will not be noticed."

"I'll be quiet, I'll stand slightly behind you." I glared into his eyes. "I am coming in there, help me out of this contraption."

I took Carlo's arm, climbed up the entry steps and through the double doors into the meeting hall. The large room was crowded with men several of whom were yelling at the speaker. I expected the speaker to be Pennyworth, but in fact it was an associate of his, an even more slimy, sleazy dandy who was in fact a gambler and swindler.

The room quieted. Committee members politely made way for Carlo and me to walk to the front of the hall.

Pennyworth's associate stood there with his mouth agape. Carlo smiled at him. I smiled at the gathering.

"I have heard a shocking rumor that this man," Carlo indicated Pennyworth with a nod, "and it seems his associate, have accused our cook, and our housekeeper, and even my uncle of unjustified violence in defense of our home."

Mr. Stewart stepped forward. He removed his hat, bowed towards me. "In fact, Mr. Anthony, he accuses you of being this bandit, this man the Spanish Fox."

Carlo chuckled. "That's a good one." Carlo smiled, shook his head. "Did he explain much about this Fox?"

A buzz of quiet comments went through the room.

"Look here, others of you may know more than I about

this Spanish Fox. But here is one thing I do know. He first appeared in California more than half a century ago. That is, as I recall being told the legend, as a child, it was more than sixty-five years ago that he first was seen." Carlo grinned at Mr. Stewart and the board. "Just how old do these men accuse me of being?"

The buzz grew louder.

"Did they perhaps suggest that I might also be Santa Claus?"

That drew a roar of laughter.

Mr. Stewart stepped forward and slapped Carlo on the back. Several men held out their hands to shake Carlo's hand.

Pennyworth and his associate slipped through the crowd and out of the hall.

We stayed to chat with the men we knew. I asked Mr. Stewart to greet his wife for me. "I must have her to tea soon."

Once we were back in the landau, and well away from the meeting hall, I asked Carlo, "Do you think that will take care of the rumors?"

"For now," he answered. "I hope."

Chapter 94

Carlo invited me to sit in on his planning meeting with Jorge and Uncle Diego. Carlo had decided to send them back to oversee the improvements needed to his rancho while he stayed with his family until it was time to move the household.

"A wall to enclose the patio. Another to enclose a play garden. Locks on the gates," Carlo said. "Darling, what are your requests?"

"A door from the parlor to the back garden, the play garden. We will need more bedchambers. Perhaps a guest wing." I smiled at Uncle Diego.

"I intend to sell my rancho in the south and live at Rancho del Mar," Uncle Diego said.

Carlo looked at his uncle. "I know we agreed to that plan, and while Rancho del Mar will be your official residence, I will feel more comfortable if you spent a great deal of time with us." Carlo turned to Jorge, drew lines on the plans on the table. "A guest wing, here across the front of the patio."

Uncle Diego nodded his agreement to the plan. "I must

get started on my trip south first thing mañana, tomorrow. I'll send a few of my staff with Jorge, and I'll bring my vaqueros from the south to work both ranchos." He stood, addressed Carlo. "I must go to my offices, work out who will go where. I will send four of my best men to keep watch here until you have Clarissa and the children safely moved."

Carlo stood, embraced his uncle.

Uncle Diego bent to kiss my cheek. "Adiós, my dear."

"Will he be safe?" I asked Carlo as Diego went out the gate.

Chapter 95

Despite the tension of threatened danger, Carlo and I enjoyed the next few weeks gathering furnishings for our new home.

Won Toy provided a long list for his kitchen and led forays into Chinatown for some of the items. There we were able to find silk fabrics for pillows and beautiful carpets as well as furniture fashioned from bamboo and other reeds.

Lopa supervised the packing of the children's favorite toys and books. She ordered the housemaids to wash and pack the new linens and cookware. She insisted I stack piles of books in the library so that she knew which ones to pack.

Diego's four men took shifts keeping watch. Their presence and the excitement of preparations provided distraction from any worries of danger. The cheerful household looked forward to this new adventure.

We were ill prepared for the bad news Jorge brought the night before we planned to leave for the rancho. He and two vaqueros galloped to the garden gate. Jorge jumped from his horse and ran into the house. The vaqueros went to the barn and emerged with a wagon.

"Jefe, where are you?" he yelled in Spanish.

Carlo ran to the courtyard. Jorge exclaimed in rapid Spanish. Carlo answered him in Spanish. The expressions on their faces made it clear that something bad had occurred.

"What?" I asked.

"They were ambushed at the redwood grove." Carlo said. "On their way to help us move to the rancho."

"Are they okay?"

"No, two men were wounded, one killed." Carlo said as he walked to where he kept his guns. He strapped on his holster, picked up a rifle. "We are going to get the wounded. Take them to the doctor. Diego's men will stay here with you and the children."

"Carlo, please be careful."

Chapter 96

Carlo returned in the middle of the night. "The wounded will recover. They are sleeping at Diego's offices.

"Will we still leave in the morning?" I asked him as he climbed into bed.

Carlo groaned. "We organized Diego's men to guard the offices and this place as well as some to ride with us. We need everyone to be rested so we will leave at dawn the day after tomorrow."

Six wagons, two carriages, twenty horsemen set out at first light. We arrived at the Rancho de La Cruz without incident. I was surprised at the number of armed men awaiting our arrival. I wondered if anyone was left at Rancho del Mar.

I was thrilled to see Uncle Diego with arms out stretched at the entrance gate. Emma Rose scrambled to be let down from the carriage and threw herself at him. He put her on his shoulders and gave her a tour of her new home ending in the nursery where he had placed a rocking horse and an elaborate dollhouse. Her squeals of delight brought smiles to everyone's faces. Even the armed men, who had looked so serious and ferocious until that moment, grinned and chuckled.

"Thank you, Uncle." I wrapped my arms around his shoulders and noticed how frail he had become. "Emma Rose, and soon Teddy, will enjoy the toys."

"Toys gathered dust. My wife collected them with hopes, hopes for children that never were. She would be happy to see our nephew Carlo's beautiful children." Diego smiled at the children in their new nursery.

Carlo carried a rocking chair, placed it in the corner next to the window of the nursery.

I sat in the chair, Lopa handed me Teddy.

"I want to help place the furnishings." I knew that Carlo remembered where we had planned to put each piece, but the placing was the fun part. I did not want to be relegated to the nursery.

Carlo leaned over, kissed my cheek. "Let us empty the wagons onto the patio. I promise to fetch you once that is accomplished."

Emma Rose chatted to and answered for the dolls she moved around the dollhouse. Teddy slept in my arms. Outside the window, I had a view of the orchard and the hills including a dramatic golden-brown outcropping of weather worn rock surrounded by green. It was a beautiful setting, one in which I hoped my children would be free to roam. Once the threat of danger passed.

Lopa came to take Teddy from my arms as his crib was now set up in the adjoining room. She nodded for me to join Carlo on the patio.

I was surprised at how large the collection of furnishings was. "Perhaps we got a little carried away. Is there actually room here for all this?" I asked Carlo.

He smiled, took me in his arms. "I want you to be happy and comfortable here."

"As long as I have you and the rest of our family here, I will be content."

I thoroughly enjoyed the next three days that it took to put the household in order. Won Toy approved of his new, well-equipped kitchen. Lopa was pleased to sleep in the room next to the nursery where she could keep watch over her children. Diego and Jorge supervised the building of a bunkhouse situated beyond the barn on a rise allowing a view of all approaches to the property.

Carlo and Diego were pleased with themselves having thought of every possible way in which to keep our family safe and the properties intact to be passed to the next generation. Unfortunately, they had not in fact thought of everything.

Chapter 97

We spent the next few weeks under guard.

We had fallen into a pleasant routine of planning, overseeing the planting of flower and vegetable gardens, playing with the children, enjoying Won Toy's cuisine, and card games with Uncle Diego in the evenings.

I had bristled at Carlo's edict that I was not to ride even with an escort. Finally, he brought me to understand that I would endanger not just my life, but also anyone sent with me.

But this morning, from the safety of our well-guarded garden, I watched Carlo, Diego, Jorge and Jose ride into the mountains. I noted that Jorge and Jose were the two trusted men who were privy to Diego and Carlo's secret lives. They were going to check on the stallions hidden in the box canyon.

I could have accompanied them. I stomped my foot. I was tempted to run to the stables, jump on my horse and ride after them. But I was still in my morning gown, hardly suitable for horseback.

I wandered to the nursery and joined Lopa in feeding and clothing Emma Rose and Teddy. I had coaxed the last bite of porridge into Teddy's mouth when I heard the sound of galloping horse hoofs at the front of the hacienda.

Lopa and I exchanged looks. "I'll go," I said before she could speak.

I hurried to the front patio. Two of Diego's men from the offices in the city pulled their horses to a stop.

"What is it?" I asked.

"Don Diego? Don Carlo?" one of the men asked.

"Not here. What has happened?"

He pulled a thick envelope from his vest. "Dónde está? Where are they?"

"Give it to me," I ordered.

He hesitated, looked to his companion who nodded in my direction. He leaned down and placed the thick package of what appeared to be official documents in my out-stretched hands.

I hurried to the library, sat at the desk and opened the envelope. The papers were court certified with elaborate stamps. The words were formal, official legalese, not understandable in everyday context. It seemed to me that some-one with a name I did not recognize had laid claim to Rancho del Mar. There was a court date. My heart raced. It was this day's date.

What to do? I couldn't send anyone after Carlo and Diego without exposing their secret and I had no idea who to trust.

I could go. I knew where the horses were hidden. But

could I really find that spot again? And what if they had decided to move them again? I might spend all day looking for them and by then the property would be lost.

Lopa with Teddy in her arms found me in the library. "I go with you," she said.

I did not question how she knew that I had just decided to ride back to the city, to the solicitor's offices and the courthouse.

"I need you to stay with the children." I avoided telling her that being accompanied by a native might not be the most political way to approach this problem. And I did need her with the children.

I thrust city clothing and the packet of documents into a saddlebag and threw on riding togs.

Lopa watched me from the doorway, still with Teddy in her arms.

"Who go?" she asked.

"Who would you suggest?"

She handed me Teddy and raced out of the room. I took Teddy to the nursery, kissed him and his sister goodbye.

Lopa returned with Won Toy. I shook my head. Taking a Chinaman would be an even worse choice.

"No, no." She shoved Won Toy into the rocking chair and grabbed my arm.

She pulled me to where one of the armed men saddled my horse.

Two men with guns in holsters and rifles in hand were already on horseback. They each held the reins of extra mounts.

"Go. No stop." Lopa said as soon as I was aboard.

"You tell Carlo to ride directly to the courthouse," I said.

"Si." Lopa nodded. "Go. No stop."

We broke into a hard gallop on the tree-lined road and stopped only once to change mounts for fresh horses. We left the tired horses by a shaded creek. Even moving as fast as we had, the sun was low in the sky by the time we arrived at the law offices.

I ran in, threw the papers at the lawyer who was supposed to be looking after our legal interests. I retired to the lady's lounge and changed into my city clothing.

"Do you see the problem?" I asked the lawyer when I as properly attired. He nodded, stood and took my arm.

We hurried from the law offices to the nearby courthouse.

Our entrance to the courtroom caused a stir of excitement, a buzz of whispers. The judge pounded his gavel and the room went silent.

Augustus Pennyworth and his usual companions sat at a table. The lawyer Atticus stood before the judge.

I recognized the judge from social occasions. He evidently recognized me.

"My ladyship." I did not correct his form of address that should have been formally "your ladyship," or informally "my lady."

I tried to recall his name, but decided "Your honor" and a bob of my head would do.

"I wondered if your husband, or his uncle, would appear before this matter was concluded."

"Please your honor, a postponement would be appropriate as I only this morning received the documents and neither Charles or his uncle have seen them."

"Where are they?"

"At Rancho del Mar," I lied. "Seeing to the herd."

It was possible. They could have moved the herd to del Mar. Of course, the implication was that they looked after cattle not a secret stash of black stallions. "I sent a message, but I doubt they will receive notification in time to arrive here today."

Lawyer Atticus cleared his throat. "Your honor, I object."

"To what do you object, sir?"

"This woman, I object to this woman addressing the court. She is not an officer of the court. Nor a claimant. Or a defendant in this case."

"Your honor, may I speak?" I asked.

"Please do your ladyship." The judge it seemed had caught on to the proper form of address being similar to his.

"The property in question did in fact belong to my father who bequeathed it to my brother and me. My brother, having responsibilities in England, as Earl of Redmond, assigned his share to the custodianship of my husband, Charles Anthony and our uncle Diego de la Vega to be held for our minor son Theodore. My brother, Lord William's affidavit to that effect has been previously presented to the court."

"Objection," Atticus yelled.

The judge answered his yell with an angry pounding of his gavel "I will not have voices raised in my courtroom, especially when there is a lady present."

"I object," Atticus murmured.

"Your ladyship," the judge began. "There is new information that has come to light regarding your father's claim to the property. The papers that were to be served several days ago," the judge took a moment to glare at first Lawyer Atticus and then at the men seated at the plaintiff's table, "outlined the problem."

"Your honor, would you please explain to me? I find the documents difficult to decipher."

"I object. It is not the duty of the court to explain the law to this . . . lady." Atticus turned to glower at me.

Our lawyer finally spoke up. "Your honor, having only received the documents minutes before we arrived in court, I have not had an opportunity to study them."

"Your ladyship, the simple explanation is that your father's wife, Maria Elena Guadalupe Valencia de Robles Wells, did not have clear title to the property when the title was transferred to your father. When the Mexican government took possession of California, all residents who were born in Spain were ordered to leave the state. She did not leave. Admittedly few of the Spanish born landowners left then. But her ownership was thus clouded."

"Thank you, your honor." I smiled my gratitude. "I have one more question, if I may?"

"Your ladyship?"

"Who said that the title of the property passed from doña Maria Elena to my father?"

Chapter 98

Pennyworth and every man at the plaintiff table stood in response to my question.

Atticus yelled once again, "Objection. I object your honor."

The gallery hummed with excitement.

The judge pounded his gavel so hard I thought it would break. Or crack the desk of his bench.

"This court is adjourned until nine a.m. tomorrow morning. I expect that by then you lawyers who are officers of the court will have familiarized yourselves with the facts, the true facts of this case. And Mister Atticus you will have learned to modulate your voice, as I will not allow even one more instance of yelling in my courtroom. Do I make myself clear?"

"Yes, your honor," both lawyers murmured.

The two men who had accompanied me on our race to the city stood flanking the doors to the courthouse. Our lawyer invited us all back to his offices for a conference.

My guardians declined to enter the offices and there again stood watch at the entry.

Once we were seated at his desk, our attorney offered me a cup of chocolate laced with brandy, which I gratefully accepted.

"Now my lady, please explain what you know about this transfer of title."

"The simplicity of the matter is that doña Maria Elena never held title to the property."

"Then how did title pass to your father?"

"Surely you are aware that under Mexican law, a woman cannot own real estate."

"Yes," he nodded.

"When doña Elena Maria was widowed, title to the property passed to her son Esteban who was born in California. You see, all of her other sons already had been granted substantial properties and had no need of additional lands." I stopped to take a sip of the brandied chocolate that was working to calm my racing nerves.

I continued. "But Esteban did not wish to stay in California. The life of a rancher did not appeal to him so he signed over the title to my father as part of his preparations to leave for Spain. Father provided the funds for Esteban's journey and stay abroad."

"But didn't your father die before Esteban left?"

"Sadly, yes."

"What happened to the title then?"

"Father's last will stipulated that all his property be divided between William and me."

"Leaving Maria Elena out in the cold?"

"Oh, no, definitely not. Father's will was written

before he re-married, but he knew that William and I would do right by his wife."

"So why doesn't she live on the rancho?"

It hurt to recall how Father's murder broke Maria Elena's heart. I understood why she had to leave, how impossible it would have been for her to stay there without Father.

"Doña Maria Elena wished to return to Spain with her son and daughter."

"They walked away from their property?"

"Once they arrived in Spain, my brother traveled from England to meet with them. Arrangements were made for an income for the three of them based on the production of, but not dependent on, the rancho. Regardless of the final disposition of the rancho, doña Maria Elena, our father's widow has been comfortably provided for. Don Diego has sold his much larger rancho in the south and used those funds to compensate doña Maria Elena and her family."

"And the affidavit of your brother's?"

"That arrived along with the explanation of the arrangements ten months after they left for Spain."

The lawyer nodded his understanding. "We must meet before court once I have studied this new document. Will your husband arrive in time for court tomorrow?"

"I hope so."

Chapter 99

The empty house at the edge of the city no longer felt like home. No one greeted our arrival. Every living person and animal had been safely moved to the rancho.

The men who had accompanied me refused to leave the entrance. "We stay. Don Carlo come."

I understood they would stand guard until Carlo arrived.

The furniture was covered with sheets. No fires blazed to take off the chill. No lanterns relieved the dark.

I was too exhausted from the stress and exertion of the day to do more than crawl into my lonely bed.

I awoke in the night to feel the warmth of another body next to mine. I snuggled against Carlo. "We have an appointment at the law offices at seven. Have to be in court at nine," I murmured.

The aroma of coffee enticed me from bed at dawn. I donned a heavy robe and stumbled toward the fragrance. Carlo and Diego sat at the kitchen table drinking coffee, eating bread rolls.

"Where did you find food?" I asked.

"Won Toy had a basket waiting for us when we returned to the rancho," Carlo explained.

I poured a cup and joined them at the table. It took me less than ten minutes to explain what had happened the day before.

Carlo leaned across the table to plant a kiss on my lips. "Thank you my darling."

"Carlo, thank you for marrying this lady." Diego patted my hand.

"Will you help me dress?" I asked Carlo.

"With pleasure."

We retired to my dressing room. Carlo pulled the ribbons of my corset overly tight.

"I can't breathe," I gasped.

"These damn contraptions must be the cause of much of the fainting and pneumonia among ladies." Carlo swore as he attempted to re-lace the corset. He soon adjusted the laces enough that I could breath and bend over to put on my own stockings and heeled boots.

We arrived respectably dressed at the law offices at seven.

Carlo read the official document. As he finished each page, he handed it to Diego.

I watched them read for a while. I thought I knew the gist of the papers, but I should have read them. Instead, I paced occasionally looking out the window to see who arrived at the courthouse.

"It is pretty clear that they do not have a case," Carlo announced, when he had read the last page.

"Agreed," said our lawyer, "They must have counted

on you not defending your claim." He scratched his beard. "Or perhaps Atticus failed to properly research. All of the documents showing the original grant and transfer of title are filed in Monterey. I sent word last night that we would compensate a clerk from there to present those documents in court today. Hopefully he will arrive in a timely manner."

Carlo pulled his watch from his vest pocket. "We should make our way to the courtroom."

The four of us took our seats at the defendant's table.

Pennyworth appeared disappointed to see Carlo arrive. All of the men at the plaintiff's table failed to return Carlo and Diego's greeting nods.

Everyone in the room stood as the judge made his way to the bench.

Once all had settled back in their seats, the judge surveyed the room.

"Well, your ladyship, I am pleased to see that you have located your husband." The judge smiled at me.

"Yes, your honor." I returned the smile.

"Now let us see if we can't straighten out any confusion there may be in this matter."

Our lawyer stood to address the court. "Your honor, if I may?"

"Yes, sir."

"A clerk from the capital, from Monterey is en route with documents that clearly show that the grants are in order and that the grantees have fulfilled the requirements of the Mexican colonization laws. We respectively request an adjournment until the documents arrive."

"Objection your honor," Attorney Atticus spoke in a carefully modulated tone of voice.

"On what basis, sir?"

"The provincial records of both the Spanish and Mexican governments have been acquired by American officials in order to investigate and confirm titles. Those records clearly state that don Esteban Antonio Guadalupe de Robles, the deceased husband of the widow doña Maria Elena Guadalupe de Robles, was the grantee."

This statement met with an even louder buzz. And Carlo, Diego and I smiled.

"As he and his widow were born in Spain and, like all Spanish born, had been ordered by the Mexican government to leave California, they did not fulfill the Mexican colonization laws."

Carlo leaned over to whisper to our attorney who quickly rose to his feet.

"Your honor, as many present here today can and will testify, Esteban Antonio Guadalupe de Robles is the son of doña Maria Elena. A son who was born in California, not in Spain."

The judge smiled. A few snickers were heard in the audience. The men at the plaintiff's table snarled at each other.

The judge addressed the Attorney Atticus. "If that is your objection, sir, I will order an adjournment—"

"Your honor, there is another matter."

"And that is?"

"The boundaries of Rancho del Mar are not clearly marked by survey."

"If I may respond your honor, that matter is also easily resolved."

The judge nodded at our lawyer.

"The boundaries are not in question. The west boundary is the Pacific Ocean."

This answer drew more laughs from the gallery.

"The southern is the city limit of Monterey. The eastern and northern sides border the rancho also owned by Charles Anthony and thus are not in dispute."

A titter of excitement ran through the audience. The men at Attorney Atticus' table glared at their attorney, their voices raised in anger.

The judge banged his gavel with enthusiasm. "This court is adjourned until tomorrow morning," he announced.

"I believe this calls for a celebration," Diego said. "Unless it has burned down while we have been away from the city, I suggest lunch at the St. Francis Hotel."

Outside the courthouse I took an arm of each of my gentlemen and we strolled to the hotel stopping to accept congratulations along the way.

Miraculously, the hotel had not burned while we were away from the city. We were seated at a table in the front window.

"Please, a bottle of your best champagne," Diego requested from the sommelier.

I realized how extraordinarily hungry I was having partaken of little but hot cocoa and coffee for the previous twenty-four hours. "Sir, please bring bread and cheese with the champagne," I asked of the waiter who also stood in attendance.

The waiter began a recitation of the day's menu.

"The squab sounds fine. Please add caviar to the lady's request," Diego ordered.

Diego raised his champagne glass. "To your ladyship, Lady Clarissa you have saved the day. This battle is all but won. Thank you."

Carlo and I touched our glasses to Diego's.

At the first sip, the bubbles went straight to my head. I was giddy with relief and the wine. I tore into the bread in a most unladylike manner.

We had barely been served the squab when a bellboy approached our table with an envelope. "This arrived for you, sir."

Carlo exchanged coins dugout of his pocket for the envelope. He placed the envelope on the table between us and continued to enjoy his meal.

"Carlo, it is marked urgent. Don't you think you should open it?" I asked. I wondered, what now?

"Yes, my darling." Carlo smiled at me. "As you wish my lady."

I returned his smile with a frown.

Carlo opened the envelope with his knife, pulled out a single sheet of paper. The smile disappeared from his face. He turned pale, then red with anger.

"What? I asked. "What is it?" My heart leapt to my throat. This was not good.

Carlo waved at the bellboy. "Who delivered this?" he demanded.

"I don't know, sir. The concierge gave it to me."

Carlo brushed past the bellboy to the concierge's desk. They exchanged words and Carlo returned to our table. He threw money on the table and said, "We need to leave." He pulled my chair away from the table, took my hand.

"Carlo. What is it?"

"Not here." He pulled me out the hotel door and headed towards Diego's offices.

Chapter 100

We entered Diego's private office. Carlo slammed the door in Diego's secretary's face.

Diego looked surprised at his nephew's uncharacteristic rudeness.

"It is a ransom note."

I grabbed the back of a chair for support. "The children?"

He shook his head, handed me the paper.

DO NOT APPEAR IN COURT TOMORROW
DO NOT PRESENT DOCUMENTS
SUSANNA WILL BE RELEASED WHEN YOU
RETURN TO YOUR RANCH

"What do we do?" I whispered. I fought back the panic that threatened to overwhelm me.

"First, we find out if Susanna is missing," Carlo said.

Diego stepped to the door, conversed with his secretary in Spanish.

"He will locate all of my men who are in the city to

watch our properties," he explained.

"Good, post two of them outside this door. Clarissa," Carlo addressed me, "Diego and I will go to the theater to see if Susanna is truly missing. You wait here."

"No. I am coming with you." I took his arm.

We used the landau that brought us to the courthouse to drive to the theater.

"Susanna received a message and went to meet someone at the St. Francis no more than an hour ago," explained the proprietor.

One of the women who shared living quarters above the theater with Susanna joined in the conversation. "She were excited the Countess's back in town. She run out without even her cloak."

It seemed unlikely that Susanna had gone to the hotel an hour ago. We were sitting in the front window. "We would have seen each other at the hotel if she had been there," I said.

Carlo agreed, "We should check on the Countess regardless."

"So, she is back?" I asked. Could the Countess be involved in this extortion?

"Not to my knowledge," Carlo answered, "but then I have been out of the city myself."

The Countess was not at the hotel, nor had she been for months. The landau driver sped back to Diego's offices where eight of his security force had gathered.

"Pennyworth must be behind this," I said.

"Agreed." Carlo looked at Diego. "Let's pay him a

visit."

Diego instructed his men. "Follow us and search his grounds, barn, stables, anywhere Miss Susanna could be hidden, while we speak with Pennyworth."

Diego opened his gun safe. He handed a double holster and two pistols to Carlo and strapped one on himself.

"Someone must stay here with Clarissa," Carlo said.

"No more of this Carlo. I am going with you."

Diego looked to Carlo who nodded. He handed me a small derringer that fit easily in my reticule.

Diego's men followed the carriage on horseback. Pennyworth's estate was on the edge of the bay. Workmen were busy building brick walls across the front of the property. More men were framing a large building in the center of the property. To the far side of that construction was a barn and stables. On the other side sat a two-story building with a long balcony above a porch that ran the length of the building.

Carlo spoke to our driver, "That is his office over there."

Our driver pulled the landau to a stop in front of the two-story building. The men who had followed us scattered in pairs through the property headed off to search the barn, the stables, and the grove of trees.

Carlo lifted me from the carriage over mud to the porch. Diego banged on the door. Once all three of us were on the porch, Diego flung open the door and we entered what appeared to be an office.

Augustus Pennyworth emerged from the adjoining

room. "Well, well, to what do I owe the honor of this visit by royalty?" He bowed, then stroked his mustache but that was his only sign of nervousness. His relaxed attitude signaled me that it was unlikely that Susanna was on this property.

Carlo brushed passed him, looked in the adjoining room, opened doors and cupboards.

"Keep an eye on him." Diego handed me one of his pistols before he headed up the staircase.

I trained the gun on Pennyworth. "Sit." I waved the gun at the chair in front of the desk.

"You wouldn't shoot me princess." But he sat in the chair.

"Just give me an excuse." I kept my finger on the trigger, but I wondered if I could shoot him. Maybe I could shoot him in the leg. Or if he went for the gun in his holster, I could shoot his hand.

Carlo returned to the office. "She is not here." He grabbed Pennyworth by the collar of his jacket, yanked him from his chair. "Where is she?"

"Where is she who?" Pennyworth was much too calm.

Diego returned from upstairs. "No sign of her up there." He went out to the porch where two of his men met him. Soon all eight of the men were in front of Pennyworth's office. They had not found Susanna.

Diego held out his hand for his pistol. I almost wished I had shot Pennyworth while I'd had the chance. Maybe, if I shot his foot and worked my way up to his manhood—. Maybe I could have scared him into telling us where he'd hidden her. But the truth was I wouldn't have been able to do it.

And I knew that Diego and Carlo wouldn't either. Zorro would have scared him with his sword, but Pennyworth was the last person the Spanish Fox would reveal himself to. And the Fox never operated in the city, too close to home.

Diego sent men to Atticus's offices, to the homes and offices of all of Pennyworth's associates. But I doubted they were stupid enough to keep her close to their homes. Pennyworth seemed to know that he was in no danger of incriminating himself.

My next thought scared the hell out of me. Maybe they had already killed her.

No, no. Hopefully they were smart enough to know that she was an ace in the hole for them. As long as she lived in the theater and appeared on stage, she would be difficult to protect. We would be vulnerable to their threats as long as she was alive.

Should we send men to our house? Have them check the stables, the bunkhouse? But that was not right either. We might stumble upon her there before tomorrow. Before the court opened.

The window behind Pennyworth's desk offered a view of his construction site. The sound of hammers nailing the framing had not stopped. Diego's men had not distracted the workmen.

I motioned to Carlo to join me outside. "Do you have anything under construction at the moment?"

The look he gave me said you want to make conversation about my work now. "No," he said.

"Is the chocolate factory finished?"

"The building itself is. Ghirardelli is finishing the interiors with his own crew." Carlo was still looking at me as though he had no idea where I was going with this.

"I think I have a pretty good idea where she might be. The construction on your warehouse, it's done?" I whispered.

Carlo nodded. "You think she is hidden in our warehouse? But we have watchmen there."

"Are your men there now?"

"Good point. We pulled them off to search." Carlo hugged me. He yelled to Diego. "Vámonos. Let us go. But leave a couple men with Pennyworth to make sure he does not leave, or contact any of his associates."

Carlo leaned close to our driver, said something to him that no one else could hear. Diego and I climbed into the landau. Carlo took a horse from one of the men left behind.

We raced across the city.

Carlo and the men on horseback were able to travel faster than the carriage.

When we arrived, I saw Carlo kick a broken lock aside and pull open double doors.

I jumped from the carriage. Diego grabbed my arm. "If she is in there, armed men could be with her."

Carlo stood to one side of the doors, peered into the dark interior.

I shook off Diego and rushed to Carlo's side.

318

"Stay back." Carlo pushed me away from the doors.

I heard grunts and a clanging. "She's in there."

Diego used both arms to hold me back from the opening.

Carlo had his pistol in his hand. He swung around the door, leapt into the shadows and looked for trouble inside the warehouse.

The clanging grew faster, louder.

I tried to breath. My heart pounded.

Please God let them both be safe.

Chapter 101

"She is alone," Carlo yelled from inside the warehouse.

Diego released me.

I ran into the warehouse.

Carlo was in the back corner removing a gag from Susanna's mouth.

Her hands and feet were hogtied but she still had managed to kick the pile of cast iron stoves hard enough to lead Carlo to where she was hidden in the dark depths of the warehouse.

I kissed her tear-stained face while Carlo cut away the ropes that tied her hands to her feet.

By the time she could sit upright and I could hold her close, we both had tears running off our chins. "I was so afraid we had lost you." My voice shook as much as my hands as tremors ran through my body.

I took a deep breath and rubbed circulation back into her limbs. She moaned.

"Did they hurt you?" Carlo asked.

Susanna shook her head. "They was in a hurry. One

grabbed my privates," she sobbed. "Promised ta be back soon." Susanna shuddered.

We sobbed in each other's arms while Carlo searched the warehouse for whiskey. He returned with a bottle and had us both take sips.

Then he and Diego each drank giant chugs.

Diego sent the men back to their usual posts and returned to where we sat on the floor of the warehouse. He pulled up a crate and looked at Susanna.

"Do you have any blankets in here?" Uncle Diego asked Carlo.

Carlo found a box of blankets, wrapped one around Susanna's shoulders and laid several on the cold ground for us to sit on.

"Are you up to telling us what happened?" Carlo asked Susanna.

She sniffled, wiped her face with her skirt, and nodded.

"A note arrived on hotel stationery." She took a long breath. "Asked me ta come ta the hotel right 'way. Said the Countess wanted to see me 'fore she had ta sail."

She shook away a chill. Carlo handed her the whiskey bottle.

Susanna took a long drink, choked it down.

"I ran out ta go an' someone threw a black sumthin' over me."

"Could you see who it was?"

She shook her head. "Na, I din't see 'em. They was behind me."

"And then?"

"Pict me up, toss'd me into a wagon, drove off fast. Wagon stopp'd, tied me up, put me here."

"Could you recognize their voices?"

She shook her head. "I were too scared."

"If you heard them again?"

She shook her head. "I dunno."

Carlo helped her to stand and half carried her to the carriage. "Let us get you into a warm bath." He covered her with blankets and I climbed in beside her, wrapped my arms around her.

"Uncle Diego, please speak with your men." Carlo said, "I want to double the number of watchmen at the house tonight. And someone should stay here in case these guys come back. I will take first watch here, if you will please escort the ladies to the house."

Diego nodded his agreement.

"And let us keep it quiet that we found her. In fact, I think we should be real low key about staying in town." Carlo turned to Susanna and me. "I know this has been a trying experience, and it is not over yet. I want to keep the house dark tonight, if the bastards think we haven't found her, we might be able to catch them."

Chapter 102

Diego and three of his men took Susanna and me to the house. Two of Diego's men and the two men who had accompanied me from the rancho were to guard the house and us.

Diego walked us into the house, bowed and flourished his hat. "Ladies, I take my leave. You will be safe here. I will gather my men from Pennyworth's and then join Carlo at the warehouse." Diego explained while his men took the carriage and the horses to the stables. "I will be careful to tell the men that we are returning to the rancho in earshot of Pennyworth."

He kissed our cheeks. "Remember what Carlo said, no lights after dark." He said as he closed the front door.

I filled the kettle, made tea. While Susanna sipped her tea, I heated water and filled the bathtub. I helped her undress and into the tub.

I was relieved to see the only wounds she had were on her wrists and ankles. Lopa's ointment would soothe those wounds, but I worried that the experience might revive the trauma she had experienced as a young girl when her family was killed and she and her sister were kidnapped.

While she soaked, I broached the subject of her future. "I'm afraid it won't be safe for you to be on your own here in the city. After court tomorrow, would it be acceptable to you to come down to the ranch for a few days?"

She nodded.

"How is living above the theater working out otherwise?" I asked.

"Ya know, I were really excited about the Countess being back as I need advice ya know, about my future career. I hoped she would let me travel with her. I'd sure like ta perform in Europe."

"Huhmm, we'll have to see what we can do about that." I had an idea, but I wanted to discuss it with Carlo before I told Susanna.

Chapter 103

Carlo and Diego returned late into the night.

I was relieved to have Carlo home. Even though I was exhausted from the drama of the last two days, I had been too anxious to sleep.

"We left guards at the warehouse, but no one came near the place while we were there." Carlo voice was heavy with disappointment. "We have no proof that Pennyworth had anything to do with kidnapping Susanna.

"I'm sorry darling. Please come to bed. We may still be able to get a few hours of sleep before we must appear in court in the morning."

When he climbed into bed, I hugged him to me. "The important thing is that we found her, that she is safe."

Carlo pulled me tighter against his body, nestled his face against my neck. "You feel so good. We do not need to sleep, do we?" His hand traveled down from my breast, across my belly to between my legs. "Why are you still awake?"

"I was too worried about you to sleep."

"I can help you relax."

"I'm fine now that you are here. We should sleep."

"You do not want me to relax you?" He teased with his voice and his fingers.

The tingling sensations racing from his fingers through my body demanded satisfaction.

I moaned.

"You do want me?" Carlo nibbled at the back of my neck.

I groaned with want.

"I think you do," he whispered. His finger rhythmically stroked me inside, then out. His other hand reached down to rub one place while his fingers slipped in and out.

The sensations built to a crescendo of little explosions followed by a deep want.

"Do you still want to sleep?" Carlo whispered.

"Hush and get in here." I spread my legs in welcome.

Carlo turned me over onto my knees; his fingers still rubbing while his manhood slowly entered me.

I whimpered.

He slammed faster, harder.

The worries and drama of the day disappeared as my world centered on this man, this act.

Chapter 104

We timed our dramatic entrance into the courtroom to the last minute. I was on Carlo's arm, Susanna on Diego's.

We had not yet taken our seats when the bailiff asked that we stand for the judge to enter.

I took pleasure in the shock on Pennyworth's face. And the look on Attorney Atticus's face clearly said that he had not expected us to appear either.

Our attorney handed the documents to the bailiff who examined them before offering them to the judge.

The judge looked them over. "These seem to be in order. And clearly state that Esteban de Robles transferred title to Edward Wells. Now, for the record, we will need a witness to testify as to Esteban's place of birth." He looked around the room.

Diego stood. "I could do that your honor. I was at the Rancho del Mar on the day of his birth and present at his christening at the Mission San Juan Bautista."

"Please be sworn in and take the witness stand, sir."

Diego did as asked and under oath recalled the day of Esteban's birth.

"And the christening?" our lawyer asked him.

"Took place at La Mision del Glorioso Precursor de Jesucristo, Nuestro Senor San Juan Bautista."

"In English?"

"The Mission of the Glorious Precursor of Jesus Christ Our Lord, Saint John the Baptist."

"Thank you, sir." Our lawyer nodded to Diego.

"That takes care of the record." The judge lifted his gavel but before he could bang it, Attorney Atticus stood to object. "Your honor, am I to be allowed to cross examine this man's testimony?"

The judge nodded his assent.

Atticus addressed Diego. "Sir, actually I believe, correctly you would be addressed as don Diego? Is that so?"

"By Spaniards, yes."

"What does that form of address signify?"

Our lawyer stood. "I object your honor, what does this line of questioning have to do with the testimony?"

"Your honor, I will make it clear if you will allow me."

Carlo tugged at the sleeve of our lawyer. "Let it be."

Our lawyer sat down.

"Continue," said the judge. "Repeat your question."

"What does the title 'don' signify?"

"It is an honorific, usually given to older men."

"Is it not true it is generally given to important Spanish men?"

Diego raised an eyebrow at Atticus. "By Mexican custom, it is a title used to show respect," he answered.

"But in Spanish usage it is a title for men of nobility, especially those of royal blood. Which would qualify you to be called don Diego de la Vega even in Spain, correct?"

"Sí, yes." I knew Diego was flustered by the line of questioning when he slipped into speaking Spanish.

"You are of Spanish royal blood?"

"Yes."

"Where were you born?"

"In California, on my father's rancho near the Mission San Juan Capistrano."

"A property that you recently sold, correct?"

"Yes."

"And you have relocated your staff and cattle to Rancho del Mar, also correct?"

"Yes."

"Where are you going with this, Sir?" the judge interrupted.

"Your honor, it is clear that this man has reason to lie to protect his own interests in the Rancho del Mar."

The judge glared at Atticus. "I am not following your reasoning for this wild goose chase."

"Being of Spanish royal blood, this man would not qualify under the Mexican colonization laws thus he could not protect his right of ownership to the rancho near San Juan Capistrano."

"That's enough," the Judge growled. "He is not here regarding that property." He turned to don Diego. "Sir, please explain your interest in Ranch del Mar."

"I sold my property in the south because it is far from

my family. My nephew and his wife and children live here in the city and on my nephew's property just south of Mission San Jose. I plan to operate and care for Rancho del Mar as custodian for my great nephew."

The judge studied Diego's face. "Is it true, this stuff about not meeting the qualifications under Mexican colonial law?"

"It is not true. My mother was a native Californian, a Kumial princess in fact, and I have been advised that my relationship to her met the qualifications."

"Attorney Atticus, sit down. You will not waste any more of the court's time with this nonsense." The judge turned back to Diego. "I will resolve this matter myself. Hold on here, sir, er . . . don Diego, would the mission have record of the christening?" the judge asked.

"I would assume so. But if not, as the missions have had some disruptions since many of the priests returned to Spain, the Roman Catholic Diocese of Monterey would have the record."

"We will adjourn until this record is delivered, this being Thursday, we will reconvene next Monday." The judge addressed our lawyer, "Can you get the record by then?"

"I believe so your honor."

"See to it." The judge banged his gavel.

We stood while the judge left the courtroom. "Now what Charles?" I asked.

Chapter 105

"We high tail it back to the rancho. I want to get everyone to safety." Carlo lifted Susanna and me into the landau. "We will stop at the theater for Susanna's things. I am sorry to say my dear girl, that you are not safe there until this matter is fully resolved."

Susanna nodded in understanding.

If Carlo had been concerned that she would protest, he need not. Thanks to the influence of the Countess and her stories, Susanna was thinking beyond the provincial little theater.

It was well into the night when we arrived at the ranch. Everyone was hungry and tired. We foraged for food in the kitchen and managed to wake Won Toy with our banging into racks of pots and pans. He ordered us out of his domain and made omelets and biscuits.

With our hunger satisfied, the four of us sipped hot cocoa laced with brandy.

"I have an idea for Susanna's future I would like to propose," I said.

"Is this something better discussed in the morning

when we are all well rested?" Carlo asked.

"No, I think you will all be pleased with this solution, although one aspect of my plan makes me sad."

Susanna's eyes lit up expectantly

"I suggest we send Susanna to William."

Susanna's face fell. "I'da rather be stuck here on the ranch with ya and the kiddies than in some farm in the middle of no where with strangers."

"I'm thinking that William can provide you with a chaperone to accompany you to Paris. He maintains a small residence there. You could study music there much like the Countess did," I explained.

Susanna clapped her hands. "Oh, da ya think I could?"

Carlo looked at first Susanna, then at me. "And the sad part?"

"I'll, we will all of us miss her, but she will be able to safely pursue her music career."

"We need to get word to William." Carlo rubbed his chin. "Maybe this new messenger service, Central Over-land California Express Company, will speed up that process."

Susanna's eyes reflected her sadness, her mouth formed a pout. "Oh, it'll be a long time ta arrange, huh?" she asked.

"No, my dear, just a couple months, maybe three. The world is growing smaller with all these new-fangled services." Carlo smiled at Susanna attempting to cheer her up. "And I read about a new invention that might soon be able to send messages across hundreds of miles instantly.

Incredible as that might seem. Going to call it tellygraff, or cablegram, or something like that."

Chapter 106

Carlo and Diego returned to the city on Sunday evening carrying a letter from the Monterey Diocese certifying Esteban's christening at the Mission of Saint John the Baptist, locally known as Mission San Juan Bautista.

I spent Monday with Susanna and the children. Susanna appeared to be fine, her attention on the prospect of traveling abroad, studying music in Paris. In the three days since we returned to the ranch, she had not mentioned anything to do with having been snatched off the street.

Carlo and I had been concerned that having been kidnapped and trussed up like a farm animal might have been particularly disturbing for Susanna given her history. Being kidnapped again must have been very frightening for her. While she lay tied up in the warehouse, didn't she perhaps think she was about to be sold into white slavery?

I signaled Lopa to take the children off for their naps so that I could speak with Susanna. "Susanna, sweetheart, please talk to me about what happened last week."

She shrugged. "Wat's ta say? Ya saw."

"Were you terribly frightened?"

"Sure."

"Do you want to talk about it?"

"Nah."

"If you should decide you want to talk to someone about it, I would be pleased to listen."

She nodded. "Do ya think the clothes I 'ave will be good for Paris? Do I need to get more?"

I smiled. It was good to know her thoughts were on the future. "Let's go to your room and look at the condition of your wardrobe." I took her arm, hugged her to me as we walked.

Susanna pulled the clothing we had made for her, out of the bags we had hastily stuffed as we rushed to leave the city.

Surveying the pile, I said. "We'll have everything cleaned and mended but I doubt there is much reason to have dresses made here."

"William will happily arrange for you to have new things made in Paris as our styles are no doubt hopelessly out of style with the fashions of Paris. And these garments will be acceptable for London."

"I'm really gonna visit a Lord?" Her eyes shone with excitement.

How fortunate I had come up with this plan for her. "I am certain that William will be pleased to have your company. And he will enjoy taking you to Paris." And playing Pygmalion to Aphrodite. Yes, I thought, this plan will work out well.

"I think, as soon as Carlo agrees to us visiting the city, we will have a warmer hooded cape made for you to wear in London."

Susanna jumped with joy, clapped her hands. "Oh yay."

She hummed, then sang, *"Oh, Susanna, don't you cry for me,"* as we folded and hung her clothes in the wardrobe.

Chapter 107

"Won Toy, I hope you remembered how to make that sangria and paella we discussed yesterday, because we have much to celebrate," Carlo shouted as he and Diego entered the patio court. He strode to the kitchen and brought glasses and a pitcher of sangria to the parlor.

"It went well?" I asked.

"Oh yes, it did." Carlo grinned, that grin, the one that makes sensations in the lower part of my body. "The judge took one look at the letter from the Monterey Diocese and said, this is a clear-cut case. He said there was no reason to continue to tie up the court's time and attention with anymore nonsense regarding Rancho del Mar."

Carlo poured the sangria into six glasses, called to Lopa, Won Toy, and Susanna to join us.

While we waited for them to appear, Carlo described the day in court. "He chastised Atticus for bothering the court with such nonsense, said the court would issue official confirmation of Clarissa and Charles Anthony holding title to Rancho del Mar, in custody for their children."

When all the adults gathered around the table, Carlo raised his glass, "To Rancho del Mar, and all who have come before us to establish its magnificence, and to all who come after us to maintain it." We clinked our glasses together and drank to Rancho del Mar.

Won Toy had definitely learned to make delicious and potent sangria. He may have substituted whiskey for the usual brandy mixed with red wine, because after the first glass we were all rather gay. When Diego insisted on a second round, I promised myself I would only drink the first sip to his toast. But it was so delicious.

Won Toy's paella was also delicious, but with the strange disconnect between my hand and my mouth, it was too much trouble to eat it. So, I drank another sangria.

Wined and dined, finally relaxed after the tension of the last several days, the group broke up early and headed off to sleep.

I was so relaxed that my husband carried me to our bedchamber.

"Liked that sangria, my darling?" Carlo grinned as he deposited me on to our bed.

Oh, what that grin does to me. I sat up long enough to get out of my skirt and blouse. I lay back into the pillows, but the room began to tilt.

"Oh dear," I whimpered. "I over did the sangria. The room is doing strange things."

"I can help with that." Carlo hurried out of his clothes, crawled across the bed and caressed my neck. His mouth found mine. His tongue teased mine sending a thrill from my mouth to between my legs.

His tongue followed the path of the thrill, down my neck, stopping briefly at each breast, then my stomach, and finally licking between my legs. He flicked his tongue and then buried it in me. My world became centered on the sensations, and the want.

I pulled him up to my face, tasted myself in his mouth. My hand reached down his body finding and stroking his manhood until he was groaning with desire. I opened my legs and guided him into me.

My body immediately convulsed with quivers of pleasure.

Carlo slammed into me and the sensations began to build again until we both cried out with satisfaction.

As we lay entangled in each other's limbs, I realized we had been rather loud. Would I be embarrassed in the morning?

Chapter 108

We enjoyed several quiet, pleasant months with our children and the remaining members of our unusual family.

Diego arrived each Saturday in time for dinner, went to mass with us on Sunday mornings and ate Sunday dinners with us before returning to Rancho del Mar.

Won Toy and Lopa traded recipes and worked together harmoniously in the kitchen. They both refused to attend Mass with us, instead prepared feasts for our enjoyment. Each Sunday afternoon we sat together sharing food, stories and laughs.

Teddy began to take his first steps walking from the arms of one of us, a few steps, to the safety of another set of arms.

Susanna taught Emma Rose to sing and to play her ukulele. Lopa taught Emma Rose native California languages. Carlo and I both helped her with her letters. Evenings were spent reading aloud to both children.

One of those evenings, after we had tucked our children into their beds, Carlo seemed preoccupied by his thoughts.

"What is it? Is something wrong?" I asked.

"All the men in our family traveled to Europe to complete their educations," Carlo said. "I would rather our children did not have to leave the state to be educated."

"I would prefer to keep them close to home," I said.

Carlo smiled and nodded his agreement. "There is a fellow named Durant, Henry Durant I believe, who started an academy for boys, across the bay, in Oakland. I should speak with him. We will need a college, an university here in California."

"I would have loved to have studied at university." I remembered how envious I was of William when he went off to university.

Carlo rubbed his chin. "And Emma Rose should be allowed to attend university too. She is so smart, look how quickly she learned her letters."

He sat quietly thinking for a few minutes. "We must begin the planning for that. Perhaps it is safe for us to return to the city, do a little socializing and start the citizens thinking about the future."

"We will open up the city house and give a party. Invite the respectable, leading citizens. Ralstons, Fremont, Stewarts, Hamiltons, Rankins, Gearys, the whole lot of them."

"Sounds wonderful fun. I'll start the guest list, writing the invitations. Let's set the date for next month." I jumped up, hurried to my writing table for a tablet. "Such a good idea. And I want to take Susanna to our seamstress to have a cloak made for her to wear in London. And I could use a few new dresses myself."

"Juan and I will take two of the housemaids to the city, have them open the house for our return."

Chapter 109

The afternoon of the party at our city house, we received a response from William. He said he would love an excuse to spend time in Paris. He looked forward to setting Susanna up in his pied-a-terre, and he had a grumpy housekeeper in the London house that would scare away any ill-intended men. The London house had become too much for the aging housekeeper, but she could run a smaller household in Paris easily.

Susanna was beside herself with excitement. London! Paris! Music school! She spent the rest of the afternoon twirling around the house, running over to the dressmaker to check on the progress of her winter cape, and packing her belongings into her new trunk.

Carlo had more good news. "Henry Durant, the man who started the academy for boys in Oakland, has agreed to attend our gathering tonight."

Juan, Jorge and Jose waited outside our garden gate to help our guests alight from their carriages and then drove each carriage to outside the barn. They could be counted on to reconnect each party with their correct vehicle.

The house was filled with fragrant flowers, glowing candles, piano music, and tables laden with delicious food and drink. Carlo and I waited at the entrance to welcome our guests.

When the schoolmaster, Mr. Durant arrived, Carlo shook his hand, introduced us and invited Mr. Durant into the library for a short discussion. I knew he intended to offer Mr. Durant either land or cash for a university.

I enjoyed seeing friends after the isolation of the rancho, but exhausted by the end of the evening, I was content to sit and compare notes with the rest of the family.

Carlo's satisfied look when he and Mr. Durant emerged from the library conveyed that the meeting had been successful. "Yes, the conversation went well. He was grateful for the encouragement and for the generosity."

Carlo sipped his brandy, winked at me. "Turns out I'm not the only one who has approached him about the need for an university. He intends to start with a college at his current location in Oakland, but he has his eye on a piece of land nearby that would be large enough for a university. I offered to anonymously assist with funding for that property provided the university accepted female students."

"And how did he respond?" I asked.

"He agreed," Carlo said. "In fact, he promised that not only would women be accepted, they would be encouraged to attend."

"Wonderful news," I exclaimed. "Emma Rose will be able to attend a university."

Diego smiled at me. "And you could also my dear."

"And you Susanna, how was your evening?" Carlo asked.

"Got lots of advice about travelin' abroad," she said. "Especially 'bout how ta handle advances of foreign men." She laughed. "I wonder if any of 'em have noticed how many foreign men hang 'round the theaters in this here city."

"Speaking of your travels, I need to check on my properties in New Orleans. I'm thinking now might be an opportune time to sell them."

"Why now?" Diego asked.

"Several reasons. From the rumors, I think that part of the country is in for some rough times. Possibly even a civil war as outlandish as that seems." Carlo frowned, shook his head. "But primarily because we are building our life as a family here in California and I want to stay close to home. And a little more cash might be useful, for things like universities and other expenses that come with a wife and children."

Diego smiled, nodded his satisfaction with Carlo's answer.

"I bring this up now because I plan to escort Susanna to New Orleans and see her safely onto a ship headed to England," Carlo said.

"I'd like to do that," I said.

"Really?" Carlo looked at me with surprise. "But the children?"

"With the new inter-oceanic railroad across Panama, I hear the trip across there only takes one day," I said. "And that was the difficult part of the travel. Could we not bring the children?"

"I think that is a bad idea," Carlo said. "I am going to be busy with getting the hotel spruced up and sold. This isn't to be a vacation."

But I pestered him, insisted on going along and taking the children.

PART FIVE

New Orleans
February 1853

Chapter 110

Emma Rose loved sailing to Panama City. And Carlo's sweet hacienda there was a beautiful and romantic as I remembered it. It seemed that all of our party enjoyed the stay there. In fact, we changed our train reservations in order to spend more days, as the children and Susanna loved playing on the sunny beach and in the warmer ocean waters.

The one-day trip by railroad was uneventful in comparison to our earlier trip across the isthmus. But Emma Rose and Susanna were thrilled to ride the train. Even Lopa, holding tight onto Teddy the whole way, seemed, in the end, to enjoy the experience.

When we boarded the Crescent City steamship, I found myself missing my former traveling companion, my brother. "I almost wish we were going to England," I said to Carlo. "I do miss William."

"Perhaps in a few years when both the children are older, we will visit William and also Susanna."

The children did not enjoy being confined to our stateroom, even though it was much larger than the one

William and I had shared. By the time we arrived in New Orleans, we were all travel weary. And as welcoming and lovely as Carlo's hotel seemed when William and I arrived there years earlier, it now appeared shabby.

Carlo immediately hired workmen to spruce the place up. He was busy supervising that activity and locating new furnishings from the moment we arrived. When I complained that he spent little time with his family, he reminded me that he had not wanted us to come along on the trip. "The children are still too young. And New Orleans is not a city I would choose for my family."

Emma Rose and Teddy played in the fountain courtyard of the hotel, but their squeals, as they tried to catch the koi fish, were not appreciated by guests there to rest. Susanna and Lopa did their best to find ways to keep them entertained, but New Orleans French Quarter was not child friendly; especially not for children who were used to running free over many acres, as they had done at our rancho.

It fell to me to book Susanna's passage to England. She would have to wait for three weeks for the next ship. I was secretly grateful to have her with us for as long as possible, but she was impatient.

The third day after our arrival in this exotic city, Carlo announced he had rented a house in a nearby neighborhood. There was only a small garden but the children could be noisy and there were broad porches oriented to catch the breezes. We were more comfortable once we had settled into the shotgun house, but it was not perfect.

Lopa did not like New Orleans. Keeping the children inside the mosquito netting at night was challenging. The shopkeepers were slow to wait on her. The strange accents meant she could not understand what anyone was saying. She missed Won Toy. But what she disliked the most was the humidity. A native Californian, she had never experienced the damp air that increased the intensity of both the heat and the cold.

Once we had rested from our travels, Susanna and I were restless. We pestered Carlo to take us with him on his purchasing outings. He finally agreed. To give Lopa a break, we brought the children with us in the rented open carriage.

"Where are we going Papa?" Emma Rose was excited to be out of the house.

Carlo gave me a look that conveyed his doubts that this was a good outing for children, but he lovingly answered his daughter. "We are going to the docks to find rugs to buy."

"Why the docks Papa?"

"Ships from the Orient arrive there, and they bring beautiful rugs that I want to use in our hotel."

I held Teddy who sat quietly sucking his fingers. Emma Rose squirmed on Susanna's lap, stretching to see the exotic sights of the markets we passed through on the way to the docks.

"Mama, look at all those birds." Emma Rose pointed out a market stall that was filled with colorful parrots and other exotic birds. "Papa, please can we look at the birds?"

"If you promise not to touch them, we'll stop nearby." Carlo directed the driver to pull close to the parrot vendor's stall.

"Oh, so be-a-utiful!" Emma Rose said. "But Papa, why are they in cages? And some are tied to the sticks they sit on. Why Papa?"

"They are for sale. This man is selling them to people to take home."

"When the people take them home, do they fly away?"

"No, they are kept in cages, or inside on those perches." He pointed to the birds that sat on the sticks to which they were tied.

I was afraid she was going to beg her father for a bird, and I doubted he would refuse her anything. But instead, she cried. Her eyes filled with tears. One tear ran down her cheek.

"What is the matter sweetheart?" Carlo asked her.

"I feel bad for the birds. Birds like to fly. Our birds at home fly everywhere. To the river, to the ocean." She sniffled. "I wouldn't want to be in a cage if I were a bird."

Carlo looked at me in hopes I would know what to say to her. I didn't. I could almost hear him say, "I knew this was a bad idea."

Susanna knew what to do. "Look Emma Rose, look at the beautiful silk scarves. Look at all the colors." She pointed to the stall opposite the bird vendor's.

I tried to wipe Emma Rose's nose with my handkerchief, but she pulled away.

"Would you like a scarf Emma Rose?" Carlo asked.

"Yes, please Papa. And I think that Lopa would like that gold and brown one. She is sad you know."

We left the scarf seller's stall with a large package of scarves; one for Won Toy, one for Uncle Diego, and for Juan, Jorge and Jose, and even one to send to Uncle William.

Past the market stalls were the docks with goods being unloaded from the ships and informally spread on the wood planks. When rolled up for transport, the colors were muted. As each rug was unrolled, we exclaimed at the bright, beautiful colors of the dyes and the hand knotted intricate patterns.

After the first few rugs were shown, Emma Rose lost interest in rugs and began to look around the docks. "Papa, look over there!" She pointed. "Those people are naked."

My stomach jumped, my heart raced. Oh, dear God, this was a very bad idea. I put my hand over Teddy's eyes, then, turned him so that he looked at me.

"Why are they naked Papa?"

Carlo scowled at me. Remembering the birds, how the hell was he to explain a slave trader to his four-year-old daughter?

"Look Papa, look Mama, that naked man has chains on him."

"Driver, take us home." Carlo's eyes spit fire in my direction.

Chapter 111

After the incident on the docks, the only outings we enjoyed were walks to a nearby park. We took bread to feed to the ducks in the pond.

No attempt was made by any of the adults to explain what she had seen on the docks, but I overheard Emma Rose trying to explain what she had seen to Lopa.

"What do you think Lopa?" she asked.

Lopa shrugged.

"Why was that man naked?

Lopa shook her head.

"Why was there a chain on his legs?"

Lopa shook her head again.

"Why was Papa angry?"

Lopa put her hands on Emma Rose's arms. "Man bad."

"The man in chains? Was he bad?"

Then Lopa spoke the longest consecutive speech I had ever heard her say.

"Lopa no see man. Bad place, man do bad here. No good for you. No like. Go home."

I was ready to go home too. As exotic and exciting as

New Orleans once seemed, I missed the fresh dry air of California, and the open spaces of our gardens. I was tired of the smell of mold and decay that pervaded every space even outdoors.

But until Susanna sailed, and the hotel was sold, we would have to wait here.

Carlo had not forgiven me for exposing his daughter to the sight of a slave auction. He continued to be absent most of the time. I seldom saw him, but when I did, he said, "I knew it was a mistake to bring you and the children here." He was packing a bag. "I will do my best to complete the work on the hotel as soon as possible."

That night he moved back to the hotel.

Chapter 112

The day before Susanna was to sail, we decided to have a going away party for her. Carlo had stopped by the house to see the children and I thought he would stop to speak with me before he left. He didn't.

"Did you tell him about the party for Susanna tonight?" I asked Lopa.

She shook her head.

I hurried after him to remind him that Susanna was sailing the next day. I was sure he would want to tell her good-bye. And the truth was that I was sad that she was leaving us. It would have been nice to have him present for some emotional support.

He was correct that it would have been better if we had said our good-byes in California. I would still have been sad, but here, in this strange place, the sad loneliness was magnified.

As I rushed down the narrow brick street, I saw Carlo ahead of me. He cut through a small pocket park square. I hurried after him.

Intent on keeping him in sight, I did not immediately

realize that this was not the direction of the hotel. I saw him duck into a building that did not look like a furnishings or building materials establishment. I could see scantily clad women on balconies above the entrance. This did not appear to be a place where I would be welcome.

I peeked over a wall into the adjoining garden. A small dark-haired boy played with a toy. A pretty mulatto woman watched him. Carlo entered the garden. The boy rushed to his arms. The woman stood, walked to Carlo and the boy. She caressed Carlo's face with her hand. He kissed her cheek. He swung the boy to his shoulders as he spoke with the woman.

My heart raced. Panicked, I ran back through the tiny park and down a few more streets until I realized I had no idea where I was. I waved down what I thought was a carriage for hire. The vehicle passed by without hesitation even though it carried no passengers. Perplexed, I twirled around looking for another carriage.

A man approached me. "Hey, girlie, kinda early for you to be on the streets, huh?" He reached for my arm.

I brushed him off.

The next man was more persistent. He pulled me to him. I pulled away, but he hung on.

"Unhand me, sir," I demanded.

He released me suddenly. I sprawled on the ground.

I had rushed out of the house without taking a reticule, or a hat and gloves. I was dressed in a lightweight muslin that I usually wore only at home.

I stood, took a deep breath, and suppressed my panic. I

could not think about what I had just seen. I must find my way back to my children.

I looked around at my surroundings searching for something familiar. I needed to get out of this neighborhood of ill repute. Nothing looked familiar.

I walked in what I hoped was the direction of our house. This area would have to end at some point I reasoned. Several blocks later I found a row of shops that looked respectable. I entered a milliner's.

"I am embarrassed to say I have lost my way," I said to the clerk in my most aristocratic manner. "I ran out of the house chasing . . . our dog. And I got turned around. Now I cannot find my way back." I told him the name of our street.

The milliner's delivery boy guided me back to the house. I had him wait while I fetched a few coins.

I rushed to my room, splashed water on my face, and changed into a clean gown.

Emma Rose poked her head around the doorway. "Mama, where did you go?" She did not wait for me to answer. "Come see the decorations we made for Susanna's going party."

They had looped sweet pink jasmine vines through the chandelier over the dining table and around the wall sconces. Several glass jars held a variety of flowers from the garden.

Lopa handed me Teddy. "I go. Late." Her frown scolded me for disappearing just as she was to leave to pick up party refreshments.

I hugged my son to my chest so tight that he squirmed to be let down. I let him escape long enough to call Emma Rose to my side and then I pulled both my children into my arms. I held fast while I finally allowed myself to consider what I had just seen.

Carlo had been acting strange since we had arrived in New Orleans. I had put his distracted air down to his concern for selling the hotel in a timely fashion. He had been absent even when he was with us. And he was seldom with us.

Was he with that woman? And the boy? Was the boy his son? The child's wavy black hair resembled Carlo's dark hair. Torrents of thoughts raced through my mind, each one tumbling over the last.

The boy looked to be older than Emma Rose. He was taller. If he was older, then he was conceived before Emma Rose. Before I fell in love with Carlo. Was he conceived when we were last in New Orleans? Was Carlo in love with his mother? Had Carlo been coming to be with them each time he disappeared from our life together? Were there other children? How many families did Carlo have?

Why was he selling the hotel? Were we to take the other family home with us? Who was he married to? A native chief had married us. Were we in fact married?

Susanna skipped into the room forcing me to stop my frantic thoughts. She was sailing the next day. I would think about all this once I put her aboard the ship. I did not want to air this dirty laundry right before she left. She would worry William.

I forced a smile. "Come join us in a family hug. It will have to last us for a while."

She wrapped her arms around the three of us and we held each other for several minutes.

I wondered if it was too late to book passage on her ship.

No. I had to at least attempt to sort this out once she was gone.

Teddy wiggled free and we released each other.

Again, I made myself smile.

"The decorations are lovely," I said as I surreptitiously wiped a tear from my face.

"See Susanna. For your going party." Emma Rose took Susanna's hand and led her to look at each vine, each bouquet.

Then Emma Rose turned to me. "Don't be sad Mama. We'll see Susanna soon. Papa promised."

"Yes, my darling," I answered. "Now what shall we wear for our party?"

"My clothes are all packed except what I will wear tomorrow," Susanna said.

"Let's look in my wardrobe." We hurried to my bedchamber and pulled out jewelry, hats, shawls, and scarves. We littered the bed with our treasures and wrapped ourselves with the shawls and scarves clowning in the mirror. I pinned a brooch to hold a scarf on Teddy. He looked at his image and giggled.

I looked up from my son to see Carlo watching us from the doorway.

"Papa, come get partied," Emma Rose said to her father.

He allowed his daughter to wrap a multi-colored shawl around his shoulders. He kissed her cheek and picked her up.

"Did you see the decorations, Papa?"

"Yes, my sweet. Lovely."

"They are beautiful, Papa."

"Of course, beautiful."

He carried both of his children to the dining room to admire Emma Rose's handiwork.

Susanna wrapped her arm around my waist and we walked together to follow Carlo.

Lopa was setting platters of cookies, cakes, fruit and croissants filled with ham and cheese on the table. A pitcher of lemonade sat next to bottles of champagne.

Carlo put Emma Rose down and she scrambled onto the tall stool she used as a chair. He secured Teddy into his highchair.

He popped the cork of the champagne, poured four glasses and handed us each one. "Here is to Susanna." He held his glass aloft. "May she have an enjoyable voyage, and sail through music school to become a prima diva, the toast of Europe and America."

We touched our glasses with a musical clink and drank to Susanna.

"I want to drink to Susanna," Emma Rose whined.

Lopa poured lemonade into a champagne glass and Emma Rose proposed a toast of her own. "To my Susanna, the best big sister ever, except for me of course, and the best singer ever."

After everyone except Teddy had proposed a toast, we dug into the food while Carlo explained the schedule for the next day. "We'll leave for the dock at noon. You must all say your goodbyes and then I will escort you Susanna."

"But Papa, I want to see Susanna sail. Mama says we can wave to her from the dock."

Carlo gave me a quick scowl before he smiled at his daughter. I knew he was thinking of the last trip to the dock. "Your Mama has sailed from New York city. It is a much nicer pier. I'm not sure if . . ."

"Papa! Please?"

"Alright we will all go to the dock, but I will see Susanna aboard. You will all stay in the carriage and wave goodbye from there. Understood?"

Emma Rose jumped from her chair, hugged her father. "Yes Papa."

Carlo stayed to tuck the children into their beds. "Close your eyes and I will tell you a story about the puppy and the kitty."

Susanna and I sat on the porch. "Any last questions?" I asked.

"I think I have it all. I call William my lord if anyone else is around, but I don' have ta call him sir or anything but William when we are alone. And I ask William who I curtsy at."

"To whom you curtsy."

"To whom I curtsy." Susanna frowned. "Oh dear, I

don' want ta embarrass William, but I don' know if I ken do right."

I looked at Susanna and saw that she had grown into a beautiful, petite young woman. "You know Susanna, you need not worry about any of the language, or the customs."

I took her hand. "I noticed each time we visited our grandparents in England, the British look down on Americans no matter who we are. Being William's ward, they will be polite to you. Your beauty will enchant them and once they get to know you, they will be charmed."

"Oh, I hope you're right."

I waited on the porch after Susanna went to her bedroom.

Carlo walked by with a perfunctory good night.

"Wait." I called to him as he walked to the front gate. "We need to talk."

"Not tonight."

"No, not tonight. But after Susanna . . ."

Tomorrow I would find out the truth.

Chapter 113

I didn't bother to hold back my tears the next morning. I knew the others would assume I was crying because Susanna was leaving. And truth be known, I wasn't sure what made me cry.

I was sad that I had been a failure as a wife. I had foolishly believed that my husband loved me faithfully. Sad that my children may grow up with only one parent as I had. That we may never return to my beloved California. That I had insisted that we accompany Carlo to New Orleans.

As the time for Carlo to arrive neared, I splashed cool water on my face, rubbed rouge on my cheeks and lips. I put on my brave face. Today I would find out the truth. But did I want to know?

Carlo arrived just before noon. We tied bonnets on the children, then piled into the carriage.

Susanna looked smart dressed in her traveling attire. I had booked a cabin appropriate for the ward of an English nobleman.

Carlo spoke with the steward, handed him a gratuity

while I went with Susanna to her cabin.

"This is too much," she cried. The room was compact but with all the accouterments needed to provide a comfortable passage; a snug bed built with side rails against the wall, a vanity, a desk, and a small sitting area.

"Get used to it. This is your life now." I hugged her one last time. "I hope you know how very much you are loved," I whispered holding back tears.

She had all the trappings needed to start a new life. I hoped she was going far enough, geographically and socially, that she could leave the pain of her past behind.

Carlo took my arm as we left the ship. Neither of us spoke until we reached the carriage.

Susanna made her way to the deck and waved to Lopa and the children. We sat in the open carriage waving and throwing kisses for far too long for the children's amusement. Teddy fell asleep in Lopa's arms. Emma Rose looked around for other subjects of interest.

Carlo had the driver raise the bonnet over the carriage forestalling the possibility of Emma Rose once again viewing anything inappropriate for a child and we rode back to our temporary home.

Carlo helped us from the carriage and carried Emma Rose into the house. Lopa put Teddy in his crib and hurried to the kitchen. We ate the cold meal she had prepared in silence.

"Papa, when shall we sail home?" Emma Rose asked.

Carlo glanced at me, then turned to his daughter. "Well pumpkin, the hotel has required more reconstruction than I had foreseen. Once that is done, we must sell the property and there is no way of knowing how long that will take."

"When do we go home Papa?" Emma Rose wanted a more quantitative answer, as did I.

Lopa, Emma Rose and I all looked at Carlo awaiting a more specific answer.

"My best guess, two more months."

Emma Rose rolled her eyes upward while she calculated what that amount of time meant. "But Papa, that's much longer than the time we've been here," she complained.

He nodded, smiled with pride. "Yes, my sweet it is." He stood, thanked Lopa for the meal. "The sooner I get back to work, the sooner we can get out of here." He bent to kiss Emma Rose's cheek. When he came over to me, I ducked his kiss, and stood to follow him out the door.

"Carlo, we were to talk today."

"I know my dear, but this outing has taken far too long and now I am late for an appointment." He continued walking toward the front gate.

"Are you avoiding me?"

He turned, looked at me with surprise. "I have explained the amount of work."

"But you used to let me work with you. You used to want me by your side."

"This is a much different city. It has degenerated far beyond expectations in a matter of a few years. Not a place fit for a lady."

"When did I become too much of a lady?"

"Perhaps when you became the mother of my children." He smiled, returned to my side. "My darling, I am sorry to have been neglecting you." He wrapped his arms around my waist, bussed my neck, my cheek.

I pulled away and he let me. He strode toward the gate.

"What about the other mothers of your children?" I called to him. "Are they ladies?"

He ignored my jab, acted as though he had not heard me speak, opened the gate, climbed into the carriage and waved with a smile as the driver pulled away.

I ran straight to my room afraid that I would burst into tears again, but that relief was no longer available. Anger would not let me rest.

I poked my head into the nursery. "Lopa, I'm going out."

She shushed me as Emma Rose was going down for her nap and Teddy was already asleep.

I picked up my reticule, gloves and hat. I did not want to be mistaken for anything other than a lady.

I thought I could find the walled garden where I had seen the woman and boy. If Carlo would not tell me who they were, I would find out for myself.

Chapter 114

Finding the walled garden did not prove to be all that difficult. The boy was playing at building cities in the dirt.

I leaned against the brick wall and called to him. "Hello."

He turned to look at me and my heart lurched. Carlo's green eyes were big in his dark face.

"Bonjour, good day, Madame." He smiled and I saw the dimpled grin that always pulled at my heartstrings.

"Where is your mother?" I asked.

He shook his head.

"Ta mère?" I said.

Again, he shook his head. He returned to his play in the dirt.

"What is your name?"

He did not answer.

"What are you called?" I tried in French.

"I am not supposed to speak to strangers," he answered in French.

"Please, tell me your names."

"Charlee Antoine."

"Merci," I whispered as I moved away from the wall and attempted to walk on shaking legs. I made it as far as the park square where I collapsed on a bench. Dear God, what do I do?

Chapter 115

I sat on the bench frozen with grief and indecision oblivious to the increasing activity around me. As the sun lowered, the number of people in the square and on the adjoining streets grew. More than once, men sat beside me on the bench and tried to start a conversation. I gave them my haughtiest look and they moved on.

But once the sun went down, the look failed to deter attention. When a man smelling of a mix of body odors reached for my breast, I stood, swung my reticule at him and walked away.

I asked a gentleman for directions to the railroad station and he kindly escorted me there. He waited while I did my business and saw me into a cab.

I ignored Lopa's scowl of disapproval as I entered the nursery. I pulled the children to me. "I have a surprise. We are going to visit our cousins in Virginia."

Teddy flapped his arms and shook his feet to show his excitement. But Emma Rose said, "I would rather go home Mama."

"You will like it at your cousin's home. I loved going

there when I was your age. They have horses and dogs and lots of room to run around."

"Is it like home Mama?"

"Well, not as big as the rancho, but there are big lawns to play on, fields to ride across. I think you will like it. And I would like to introduce you to my family." I pulled her into my arms and kissed my daughter. "And we get to ride on a train again. This time one with berths and private compartments."

I looked at Lopa. "Will you help me pack?"

"Far?" she asked.

"I'm not sure," I admitted. "I believe it is little more than one long day's ride but there will be berths for the children to nap."

"When?" Lopa asked.

"Tomorrow."

PART SIX
Barrington Oaks Plantation, Virginia
April 1853

Chapter 116

The train ride kept the children entertained for the first hour. I tried to point out interesting sights along the way, but they were soon restless. We took them into the dining car but the conductor was not pleased to see dark skinned Lopa in the first class diner.

"She must help me with the children," I explained.

"She is your nanny?" he asked.

"Yes."

He looked at her again, noted her regal manner, and then the pile of crumbs below Teddy's chair. He sniffed. "She could do a better job of it."

After that we ate from the basket of food Lopa had packed before we left.

I read the same three children's books over and over again amazed that they never seemed to tire of them even when Emma Rose could recite the words on each page from memory. Finally, they slept.

The train lurched to a stop. The conductor came by to explain that the journey had been delayed due to a problem with the tracks ahead and he sent a porter to open our berths.

"When will we arrive in Richmond?" I asked him.

He shrugged. "Maybe late afternoon?"

We transferred the children to a berth and Lopa lay down next to them. I tried to sleep, but the inactivity made it impossible to ignore the pain and panic. I had done a good job of pretending all was well. As long as I stayed occupied, I nearly fooled myself. Now that there was no need to pretend, and I thought of what I had seen, and what I had done, my heart raced. It felt as though it would burst from my chest. I slid from my bunk, wrapped a shawl around me and left the compartment. I had no destination in mind, only to escape the panic. I stood in the corridor watching lights flash by as the train began moving again.

The fear subsided replaced by overwhelming loneliness. As I watched houses glowing with warm lights go by, I envied the families living in them. I imagined that the people who lived in those simple houses lived simple lives uncomplicated by betrayal, or by inherited responsibilities. Or the need to keep up appearances, to be a good example of a noble family.

We arrived in the late afternoon. I arranged for a carriage and driver to take us to the Barrington plantation. The dispatcher advised an early start as we still had a long journey ahead of us. I wondered if I should send a messenger ahead and wait here at the hotel for a response from my cousins. What would they think were we to arrive unannounced?

But the hotel near the train station was not suitable for

children. One night would be possible only because they were tired. The several nights I assumed it would take for a messenger to go and return were unimaginable. I decided to send a messenger ahead to let them know we would arrive shortly.

I left Lopa and the children in the hotel room and returned to the lobby. "How would I send a message to a plantation?" I asked the concierge.

"I can arrange that," he replied. "Which plantation would that be?"

"Barrington Oaks."

He smiled. "Would that be Mr. William Barrington's plantation?"

"Yes."

"I am holding packages for Mr. Barrington that arrived on this morning's train from New York. I expect them to be picked up tomorrow."

That would not be suitable. We should not arrive together with their shipment. Confused, I stood there wishing I were not so tired that I could not think clearly.

"My point ma'am, is that some member of the Barrington household must be here in town tonight in order to be here early tomorrow. Perhaps we should send a messenger to their townhouse?"

"Oh." I nodded. "Please do."

I knew so little about my cousins. It had been ten years since I had last visited their plantation, and that was the only one of their properties I knew anything about. What had I been thinking? I needed sleep.

"Would you care to write a note?" The concierge handed me a quill, ink, and hotel stationery.

"Dear Cousin,
My children and I are in Richmond and thought to pay a visit. Best regards, Clarissa Barrington Wells Anthony."

"I will have this delivered immediately ma'am."

I was looking forward to a good night's sleep, but at the door to our room I heard squeals of giggles. My children were wrestling on the bed. Teddy was not yet speaking more than a few words, but the one word he could say clearly was "Emma". From his first months, his eyes followed his sister, and now that he crawled he pounced on her at every opportunity.

Lopa sat in a chair watching them use up restless energy. I collapsed into the other chair. Tired as I was, I smiled at their antics. We were still sitting there when we heard a knock at the door. I assumed the children were too noisy for other occupants, but it was a bellboy with a note for me.

"Dear Cousin Clarissa,
We are so pleased to receive your note. May mother and I call on you at your earliest convenience? Warm Regards, Will Barrington"

"Who brought this?" I asked.
"Mr. Barrington."

"Please ask him to wait a moment." I smoothed my hair back into a bun, straightened my wrinkled dress. "Lopa, I will be right back," I said as I hurried out the door and then down the stairs.

A tall, broad shouldered blonde, Cousin Will, was standing at the concierge desk. A grin lit his chiseled face when he saw me. "My oh my, Cousin Clari, ya did grow into a fine lookin' woman." He reached for my hand.

"You're not so bad yourself, Cuz." I clasped his hand, smiled into his bright blue eyes. I had forgotten how much Cousin Will looked like my brother William. A moment of longing for my brother brought tears to my eyes.

"There, there Cuz, are ya alright?" He looked at me with concern.

"Just tired, it has been an exhausting trip. It was an impulse to come here without an invitation. I'm afraid I have been terribly rude and—"

"Clari, you by no means need an invitation to visit your family. Mother is very anxious to see ya'all, to meet your children, and to catch up." He looked up the stairs. "Now where are those children?"

"Do you and Auntie Mary want to call on us in the morning?" I asked.

"Are they asleep?"

"Oh, not hardly, jumping from bed to bed more like it."

"Well, then let's collect them and take ya'all home to Mother."

I led Will up the stairs and to our room. "Lopa, this is

my cousin Will. Will, this is my dear friend and traveling companion, Lopa."

Lopa and Will exchanged nods. Clearly neither of them knew quite what to make of the other.

"Emma Rose, this is your Cousin Will."

Emma Rose flew at Will. He grabbed her and flung her into his arms. "What a pretty li'l thing ya are."

"Please excuse my children they have been cooped up first in the train compartment and then in this room, and they are a little wound up." I pointed at Teddy who slid off the bed, but sat on the floor watching Will. "This one is Teddy."

Will held out his hand to shake Teddy's. Teddy stared at Will without moving, then put his fingers in his mouth signaling his uncertainty about Will.

"Lopa, please help me clean these children up a bit. We are going to visit Auntie Mary this evening."

"Cousin Clari, that is not necessary. Mother understands ya have been travelin' and the children can get ready to sleep at home. Let's just collect ya'all's things and get out of here."

Will had brought a carriage and a wagon presuming we would be traveling with trunks. He was noticeably surprised to see the carpetbags we had brought.

We drove through the town that was far more civilized than anything my children or Lopa had ever seen. Emma Rose quieted. Her blue eyes widened. I took advantage of her quiet to prepare her for meeting the rest of her cousins. Flinging herself at Auntie Mary would never do.

"When we meet Auntie Mary, please curtsy as you and Susanna practiced."

"Yes mama. Do I call her milady? Or your highness?"

I smiled to realize that Emma Rose had absorbed Susanna's lessons better than Susanna.

I kissed my daughter's cheek. "Ma'am will do, my sweet."

The carriage pulled into a circular drive in front of a tall portico. Emma Rose turned to me, her eyes even wider at the grandeur of our destination. "Our cousins live here?"

"Yes. This is their townhouse."

She raised her face to look at the height of the front façade. "It is way bigger than our house in the city." She turned to look at me. "Is their rancho much bigger than ours too, mama?"

"They call their rancho a plantation. As I recall the house is quite large and there are several buildings on the property." Including the slave quarters. I thought there was no need to mention those. "But our property has more land."

Two black men lifted each of us to the ground. Will took Emma's hand and Lopa carried Teddy. Another black man opened the massive door and greeted us. "Missus Mary is in the library, Master Will." He led the way down a wide central hall to a room overlooking a formal orna-mental flower garden, a smaller version of Versailles South Parterre.

Auntie Mary stood as we entered. "Clarissa, my dear, give your old auntie a kiss."

I hurried to her arms, kissed her cheek.

"Auntie Mary, this is my dear friend Lopa."

The two women exchanged nods and I finally realized that taking Lopa to my southern relatives might have been asking for awkwardness.

"And this young lady?" Auntie Mary smiled at Emma Rose.

"This is my daughter Emma Rose."

Emma stepped forward and executed a perfect curtsy. "Ma'am."

Auntie Mary clasped her hands with delight. "Oh, what a beautiful child you are."

Lopa allowed Teddy to wiggle from her arms. He stood leaning against her legs sucking on two fingers.

I picked him up recognizing his unease. "This is Ted."

"Please sit." Auntie Mary waved at the empty chairs. "And your husband?"

"He is dealing with business matters in New Orleans."

"That loathsome place. But you traveled here unescorted?"

"A simple train ride," I assured her.

She shook her head. "Well my dear, you were smart to get the children away from that city. Once summer arrives, it will be a most unhealthy place. Supper will be served shortly. Have the children eaten?"

I remembered then that at my cousin's plantation the children were not fed in the dining room until they were much older than Emma and Teddy. There will be a lot for my family to get used to here I thought.

Auntie Mary nodded at Lopa. "Your girl can take them to be fed."

Oh, dear. How will I deal with this?

Chapter 117

"Auntie Mary, California is, uh . . . that is we live in a world very different from this one. Lopa, although she often acts like it, is not my slave, or even my servant."

"She is not your servant? What is she?" Auntie Mary let her manners slip at my shocking statement and scowled at me.

"She is my best friend, and as a favor, acts a governess to the children."

Auntie Mary studied Lopa's dark handsome face, her straight black hair pulled back into a bun, her simple clothing. "Is she not an Indian?"

"She is a native Californian."

"And she is best friend to the sister of an Earl? Well, bless your little heart!" Auntie Mary did nothing to conceal her shock at my choice of friend.

"In her tribe, in her society, her rank is far higher than mine."

"Like an Indian Princess," Cousin Will interrupted. "We have two noble women and the young heir to an earldom as houseguests."

Auntie Mary sighed, apparently resigned to the unconventional arrangement of my household.

I had never thought about Teddy being brother William's current heir. But anything that eased our inter-action with Auntie Mary, and no doubt her snob friends, would be acceptable to me.

"Auntie Mary, I had made arrangements to be driven to Barrington Oaks tomorrow. I thought I would find you there."

"Oh my dear, with hired drivers." She turned to Will. "You must cancel that arrangement."

"Already taken care of, Mother."

"We have one more social occasion tomorrow evening for which you must join us." Auntie Mary looked at Lopa as though wondering what to do with her.

"Me stay with children," Lopa answered her ques-tioning look.

"I doubt I have appropriate attire with me," I added. "Honestly, I thought only to take the children to see the rest of their family and to enjoy your plantation home as much as I did as a child. When do you plan to return to Barrington Oaks?"

"In a few days. As to attire, Will's wife, Savannah has a city wardrobe here that will fit you nicely."

"I have not met Savannah. Are you sure she won't mind a stranger wearing her clothes?"

"One, you are family, not a stranger, and Savannah is heavy with child and thus stayed at Oaks. Her dresses will be out of style by the time she returns to society, you may as well put them to use. Now, let's get these children fed. Will, please show your cousin around the house and tell Jennings to arrange their rooms in the east wing." Auntie Mary's usual friendly expression had returned to her face. "Clarissa, my dear, please excuse an old lady. I have been on my feet too long today. We had a full day of shopping and fittings."

Will showed us the house and gardens. Both were so formal I was certain that my children would do significant damage in a few days. Carefully trimmed topiary, gilt and velvet covered furniture, pale colored silk carpets; oh dear, even carefully arranged loose stone walkways.

"We must keep the children corralled somehow," I said to Lopa.

"Cousin Clarissa, not to worry. We won't be back here for months. Plenty of time for Jennings to put everything back in order. It'll give him and his staff something to do."

"Jennings is the butler?" I asked thinking Jennings an unusual name for a black man.

"Jennings is the name all of our butlers have been called here in the city. At Barrington Oaks they are called Jackson. Name goes with the position."

We left Lopa and the children in our rooms. "Jennings will have trays brought up for supper as surely you are tired after your travels," Will said.

"But Cousin Clarissa, I must show you Savannah's city wardrobe." He led me to the opposite wing of the house, into a large mirror lined dressing room and opened one of many cupboard doors. "I believe any of these will be appropriate for tomorrow evening's ball."

Ball? Oh, my lord.

I looked at the row of gowns and realized they were all intended to fit over hoop underskirts. I would need to spend the next day practicing sitting and maneuvering in one of those contraptions.

Chapter 118

Cousin Savannah's ball gowns fit only after Lopa helped Savannah's maidservant to assist with the corset and hoops. The dance slippers were only a little tight and since I did not plan to dance, that should not have been a problem. I selected a pale blue silk gown with a flounced skirt.

Savannah's maid curled my hair in ringlets she then piled on top of my head. She also schooled me on how to sit in the hoopskirt because if ladies were not careful to lift and stack the wood circles behind their rear ends as they sat, the skirt would fly up leaving pantaloons in full view up to the waist.

My first effort to sit on the hoops entertained Emma Rose and Teddy. When I sat, the bottom of my skirt flipped up hiding my face, but not my pantaloons. Even Lopa giggled. The children rolled on the floor with laughter.

After a full afternoon and evening of preparations, Auntie Mary finally pronounced my appearance acceptable to accompany her and Cousin Will to the ball. Looking in the mirrors of the dressing room, I understood why women were willing to withstand the miserable discomfort of sitting on the wood hoops. Between the corset and the bell shape of the hooped skirt, my waist looked tiny.

Climbing into the carriage in that skirt was a further challenge. My skirt filled an entire bench seat as did Auntie Mary's leaving Will no choice but to ride with the driver.

Auntie Mary enjoyed the pleasure of introducing her niece as her Ladyship laying it on a bit over the top encouraging her friends and acquaintances to curtsy. Initially, I blushed with embarrassment, but when I saw how much fun she was having, I went along with her scheme.

Cousin Will and I enjoyed one twirl around the dance floor before a line of young men formed asking for my dance card. Being a married woman, I did not have a dance card, but that did not discourage those who I believe merely wanted to brag that they had danced with an English noblewoman.

The tight slippers soon became torture. I wished I had refused the first dance, but now that I had accepted one dance partner, I could not politely avoid the others. The night became a blur of sore feet and nervous young men.

Finally, Cousin Will rescued me, offering his arm to escort me to midnight supper in the adjoining dining hall. He showed Auntie Mary and me to seats at a candlelit table. Waiters poured champagne in our glasses, while Cousin Will directed other black men to heap plates with shellfish, meat-filled pastries, and all manner of delicacies.

"Are you enjoying yourself my dear?" Auntie Mary

asked.

I smiled. "Yes, thank you," I said as politeness demanded. Truth was I was relieved to sit and force the slippers off my feet. Thirsty, I drank champagne a little too fast. To relieve feeling as though I was still spinning on the dance floor, I looked around the banqueting hall.

A figure of a man standing in a far corner caught my eye, and alarm coursed through my body. He was sandy haired and shorter than the men near him. It couldn't be Pennyworth.

"Are you alright my dear?" Auntie Mary asked. "You suddenly went pale."

"I, uh . . . I suppose I am a bit tired."

"Oh yes, of course, after your travels, this was perhaps too much without more rest. How thoughtless of me to insist you come with us." Her eyes twinkled. "But I did enjoy introducing you to my friends." She turned to Will. "We should take Cousin Clarissa home."

"Please don't leave on my account."

"Oh, my dear, I never stay at these things past supper. The young people will dance until dawn and then enjoy a breakfast. I am much too old for all that."

I struggled to gracefully get my feet back into the dancing slippers without lifting my skirt. In the end, I shuffled along with only my toes in the slippers, and like Cinderella, lost a slipper on the steps before entering the coach. Unlike Cinderella, my lost slipper would not bring me a prince.

Chapter 119

On the drive home, Auntie Mary announced that she had decided it was time to return to the plantation. Will was obviously glad to be going home, back to his wife and family. And I was relieved to get my children out of the formal town house. I hoped the plantation had remained informal enough to be child friendly.

"Tomorrow will be spent packing and organizing the household. We will leave early the next morning. So Clarissa my dear, if you have any shopping you wish to do, Jennings will arrange a driver for you."

"Thank you. And thank you for a lovely evening." Tomorrow I would have to buy another pair of slippers for Savannah for I had lost one and damaged the other.

Lopa kept the children quietly occupied as late as possible the next morning. I dressed, drank a quick coffee, and the four of us hurried down to the front entrance. Jennings had a driver awaiting our shopping trip. Jennings was noticeably relieved to get us out from underfoot in the busy day ahead.

Our driver, Timmy, knew exactly where to go to find

replacement dance slippers.

"Mama, look how be-a-u-utiful these hats are!" Emma Rose exclaimed.

"Do you have child sized sun bonnets?" I asked the clerk.

"Of course, madam. Please come this way." She ushered us into an adjoining room filled with children's clothing. Emma Rose loved trying on dresses and bonnets. We bought tiny riding outfits, sundresses and bonnets, and cotton trousers for Teddy. I started to wonder if I had brought enough funds to see us through until . . . until what I didn't know. I guessed we could return to our house in New York, but my heart ached thinking of our life in California.

"Where should we take the children for lunch?" I asked the driver. He nodded and drove us to a café with an outdoor dining area. We fed the children without lingering and returned to the carriage.

"Is there a bank nearby?" I asked Timmy. He nodded. We traveled a few short blocks and pulled in front of an imposing edifice.

I handed Lopa coins and pointed to a candy shop. "Let them buy treats, but save all but one for later." Timmy helped us climb out of the carriage.

I walked into the bank building feeling more than a little uncomfortable. How could I be so ignorant? I knew that there were funds in a New York bank and that my name, as well as my brother's, was on the account, but I had no idea how one accessed the money.

A familiar looking man stood saying good day to another man near the entrance.

"Lady Barrington, I believe?" He nodded a quick bow and offered his hand.

"Please call me Clarissa. And excuse my bad manners, but I met so many people, so quickly last night."

"Of course, my lady. John Townsend, at your service."

"I, uh, have a question. I'm afraid I know very little about banking, please excuse my ignorance." I paused, "You see, I know that my brother and I have funds on account at a bank in New York, but I do not know what bank. How does one find out? And how would one access the funds?"

He smiled. "Of course, your ladyship would not concern herself with such matters. But I can make inquiries and arrange to have funds transferred here if you desire. How much would your ladyship require?"

"Oh dear, I don't know, maybe one thousand."

Mr. Townsend's eyes widened in surprise. "Dollars?"

"Is that too much?" I asked.

"It is a large amount," he said. "But then ladies do have expenses. I will have papers prepared. Would your ladyship care to return tomorrow to sign them?"

"Hmm, I don't believe that is possible as we leave for Barrington Oaks early tomorrow. Perhaps I can give you a letter of authorization. Does that work?"

He took me to a writing table, gave me notepaper and pen and ink. I wrote my full name, Clarissa Alexandra Theodora Barrington Wells Anthony and a note authorizing

Mr. Townsend to transfer one thousand dollars to the Richmond Branch of the Bank of Virginia.

"I believe this should suffice my lady. If not, I will send a messenger to Barrington Oaks." He hesitated. "Should your ladyship require immediate funds, I would be happy to advance —"

"Definitely not necessary."

I thanked Mr. Townsend. I failed to realize at the time that I had just drawn a road map for anyone attempting to locate us.

Chapter 120

We kept the children away from the house as long as we could find means to entertain them including allowing them to run around in a public square. Our driver, Timmy was uncomfortable with the four of us hanging around a public park, but the children had energy that needed burning off.

Jennings greeted us at the entrance. "Milady, a gentleman called and left a package for you." He handed me a small package wrapped in brown paper. I knew from feeling the outside it was the slipper I had left on the steps. I had hoped no one had noticed, but obviously someone had seen me leave it behind. Auntie Mary would be unhappy if I embarrassed her. Perhaps in the commotion of preparations for tomorrow's departure, my package went unnoticed.

When we reached our rooms, I opened the package. A note card was inside the now well-worn slipper.

"Your ladyship, I believe this is yours." It read.

It was unsigned.

Chapter 121

The trip to Barrington Oaks was long and trying with restless children. I was grateful we had not attempted the travel with a hired driver and coach. And travel via the river was much faster. Still, it was late at night by the time we arrived. Fortunately, the children slept the last several hours.

Lopa and I carried dozing children up the grand curved staircase and slept with them on the sleeping porch I remembered from my childhood.

Teddy awoke with the sun the next morning. "Ma, Ma." He pounded on my head.

"Mama, can't you make him be quiet," Emma Rose moaned from the cot next to ours. Seconds later she bound from her cot and ran to the screens that enclosed the porch. "Mama, look outside. Everything is green."

The main house sat on a knoll far above the river. A deep green lawn ran three hundred feet from the house to the water's edge. A dense row of willow trees blocked the view of the wharf farther down river.

I held Teddy with Emma Rose at my side and pointed

out the things I loved as a child when I spent weeks of the summer with my Barrington cousins. "Over there," I pointed to the right, "are the stables where the ponies were kept."

"Are there ponies there now, Mama?"

"After breakfast, we will go see." I stroked my daughter's hair with my hand and then pointed. "Over there, behind the house are the kitchen garden and the cutting flower garden."

"Can we cut flowers? I love flowers."

"We'll have to ask Auntie Mary. You'll see when we go downstairs, floral arrangements in this house are serious business. But there are lots of fun things to do here. One day perhaps, I will take you to the creek where we caught tadpoles and frogs."

"Oh yes, please."

Lopa stood by with Teddy's clothing in hand.

"But first we must dress and have some breakfast."

Jackson greeted us at the bottom of the stairs. I was disappointed that he was not the same Jackson as the butler with the same name had been when I was a child.

"I'm confused. Where is the older Jackson who was here when we arrived last night?"

"My father, called Uncle Jackson around here, came to the house jus' to greet you. I have taken his job."

We followed him to the children's dining room in the basement. Lopa and I ate with the children although my presence seemed to fluster the kitchen servants. Even so the four of us eating there seemed the best solution.

And soon we heard the sound of children's voice headed our way. Two boys with blonde hair, and a girl with light brown ringlets bounced into the room. Two older black women followed them. All looked startled to see me in the children's room.

"My lady." The girl, who looked about five years old, curtsied. She looked at Emma Rose. "My name is Jeanne. Welcome to Barrington Oaks."

The boys, who I knew were seven and four, stood perfectly still until I addressed them.

"And you are?"

"I'm Willie," said the taller one. He pointed his thumb at his companion. "He's Johnny."

I introduced Lopa, Emma Rose and Teddy.

"What are your plans for the day?" I asked.

"Usually we spend mornings in the schoolroom, but our tutor left to see his sick ma. So, we are kinda on vacation." Jeanne explained.

"Would you like to join us on a tour? Perhaps you could show us around?"

"Yes, my lady," Jeanne said.

"And please call me Cousin Clarissa."

Jeanne studied me with soft brown eyes. "I don' think I'm allowed . . . my lady."

"Alright we'll discuss that with the grownups. Now everyone finish up your mush. I'm excited to see the stables. Do you still have ponies?"

"Oh yes, my lady." Jeanne smiled.

*   *   *

Emma Rose was thrilled to see the dozen ponies. The groom asked, "Is she good rider?"

"She has a pony at home," I answered.

"But Mama, look at that thing they use for a saddle. How does one sit on that?"

"I don't suppose you have a western style saddle?"

"Whas that?" The groom scowled with confusion.

"Never mind. I think until she gets the hang of this style of saddle, a very gentle mild-mannered pony is best."

The groom looked at me, puzzled by our talk of saddles.

"Do you understand?" I asked.

"Yes'm."

Teddy cried when we left him with Lopa. As we left the stables, I spotted the pony cart we had used when I was a child. It looked to still be in usable condition so Lopa and Teddy drove around in it while Emma Rose and I rode following the three children.

"This is so fun Mama. Can we stay here for a long time?"

I was glad to hear that Emma Rose was happy here, but my heart sank at the thought of being apart from Carlo for a long time. Should I send a message letting him know where we were?

Chapter 122

We had spent four idyllic weeks on the plantation.

Running wild with the other children, Emma Rose enjoyed a freedom she had never experienced before. My children had been cooped up traveling, and then in the small house with no grounds in New Orleans. Even in California, they were constantly watched and guarded. I empathized with their pleasure recalling the difference between my New York City home and the plantation.

The only other place my brother and I had run free was on the English estate of our grandparents. I began to consider taking the children to William rather than to New York. I was doing my best to put aside my emotions, to ignore the pain of missing Carlo and to think only of the children's welfare.

Emma Rose tore at my heart each time she asked for her father. I continued to explain that Papa was busy with his hotel business. "And isn't Barrington Oaks much more fun for you and Teddy than New Orleans?"

"Yes Mama, but I miss Papa."

I put off making any decision hoping that once the

emotional pain subsided, it would be easier to think clearly. But it had been weeks since I had discovered Carlo's betrayal and the pain had in no way lessened. In fact, it seemed that once the activity of travel and settling the children in a new place was over, numbness began to wear off and I was an emotional mess.

Lopa tried to talk to me about my plans. I had let her believe that we had left New Orleans in order to find a more appropriate place for the children while Carlo finished the hotel project. I had not told her what I had discovered.

Lopa wanted to return to California. She asked when we would begin the journey back.

I realized that I could not selfishly expect her to travel to England with me. Once, when we were in New Orleans, she had explained to me that she was afraid of being out of California. After a very long session of me asking questions I finally understood that she feared dying away from her native land, that her soul would wander endlessly trying to find her way back.

Nevertheless, I asked her, "What would you think of going with us to see William in England?"

Lopa stared at me.

"We are closer now than we will ever be in California. Perhaps now would be a good time to go?"

Lopa shook her head. "What bad?" she asked.

I knew she meant, "What is the matter with you?"

I answered by bursting into tears. She carefully placed an arm around my shoulders. Her sympathy brought sobs as

I choked out my story.

She nodded her understanding.

When I finished explaining about the boy and then learning his name and then Carlo refusing to talk to me about it, she said, "That all?"

She wasn't making less of my upset. She wanted to know if there was anything else I hadn't told her.

"That's all," I said.

"No go England."

"I wouldn't expect you to go."

"You no go."

"I don't know what to do."

"Talk."

"I'm not going back to New Orleans."

She nodded her head. "We wait."

I guessed we were waiting for me to come to my senses.

I couldn't think anymore. I hurried to the stables and asked the groom for my favorite horse. I had reacquainted myself with riding sidesaddle. It was nowhere near as exhilarating as riding with legs straddling the animal, but Auntie Mary would be horrified should I don breeches.

I rode through the willows, did my best to ignore the slave quarters, the tobacco fields, and the men loading barges from the wharf. I urged my horse up the hill into the forest. Tree stumps evidenced the logging that had provided materials for the plantation buildings. Here and there fallen logs had been left behind. My horse easily cleared the logs as we raced up the hillside. At the top of the hill I enjoyed the view of the tobacco fields, the green pastures, even greener lawns, and the curve of the river.

A breeze, seldom felt on the plantation below, cooled my mount and myself. I missed the cool, dry air of California. I was nostalgic for even the fog of San Francisco. I really did not want to go to England. I wanted to go home.

I wanted my husband back and I wanted my family back together. But how could I ever forgive him? And would he ask for forgiveness? Did he want us back together?

We ambled back down the hill, tore across pastures, and trotted into the stables. I was sweating and dirty. I would have to get into clean clothes before Auntie Mary caught sight of my disheveled appearance including my tear stained face.

I hurried around the corner of the house hoping to get to my rooms before I saw anyone. I heard voices from the porch and was about to turn around to find an alternate route when I heard a familiar voice.

"There you are my darling." Carlo sat on the porch swing, sipping lemonade. "Ready to head for home?"

ACKNOWLEDGEMENTS

The Gold Rush brought people from all over the world to California creating a diversity of cultures that mixed with the beauty of the land to make California a very special place. I am grateful to my parents, grandparents, and great grandparents for making me a native Californian.

Thanks to my team of editors, Alison Farr, Elisabeth James Rhee and Michael James. I am also grateful for the efforts of Kate James and David Oh for the fabulous cover. I am grateful to them all for their patience and understanding.

Thanks to all the brave adventurers who made their way to this golden state providing a never-ending supply of stories and characters.